DEAD TALES

SHORT STORIES TO DIE FOR

Anthony Giangregorio

DEAD TALES: Short Stories to Die For

Softcover   ISBN 13: 978-1-935458-02-9
             ISBN 10: 1-935458-02-7

This is a work of fiction. Names, characters, places and incidents either are the product of the author's imagination or are used fictitiously, and any resemblance to any actual persons, living or dead, events, or locales is entirely coincidental.

This book was printed in the United States of America.

For more info on obtaining additional copies of this book, contact:
www.livingdeadpress.com

Acknowledgments

Always to my loving wife, Jody

AUTHOR'S NOTE

This book was self-edited, and though I tried my absolute best to correct all grammar mistakes; there may be a few here and there.
Please accept my sincerest apology for any errors you may find.

This is the second edition of this book.

Visit my web site at undeadpress.com

OTHER BOOKS BY ANTHONY GIANGREGORIO

THE DEAD WATER SERIES

DEADWATER
DEADWATER: Expanded Edition
DEADRAIN
DEADCITY
DEADWAVE
DEAD HARVEST
DEAD UNION

ALSO BY THE AUTHOR

DEAD RECKONING: DAWNING OF THE DEAD
THE MONSTER UNDER THE BED
DEADEND: A ZOMBIE NOVEL
DEAD TALES: SHORT STORIES TO DIE FOR
DEAD MOURNING: A ZOMBIE HORROR STORY
ROAD KILL: A ZOMBIE TALE
DEADFREEZE
DEADFALL
DEADRAGE
SOUL-EATER
THE DARK
RISE OF THE DEAD

Table of Contents

Foreword

When I started writing more than a year ago, I went to one of my closest friends and asked him if he would want to read my first book when it was finished.

His answer was: "I'd love to, but I just don't have the time."

How many other people are out there that feel the same way?

Thinking about my friend's time constraints in his hectic life, I realized while he could read the book if he really, really, wanted to, some people just feel like once they start a book, they must finish it in a timely manner, not read a few chapters and then put the book down for a week or two when life's demands take control once more and it pulls you in three different ways at once.

So after some thought, I realized if my friend wouldn't commit to reading a regular sized book, then I'd write a short story, maybe ten pages or so.

When I finished it, I gave it to him and told him, "I understand if you don't have time to read it, but give it a try, okay? Put it in the bathroom. Everybody usually has at least a few minutes a day in there when all you have to do is stare at the wall while you conduct nature's business."

The next week, I ran into my friend and I couldn't help asking if he'd read my story.

Surprise, surprise, he had!

As the months went by, I had many other ideas for short stories.

Stories that didn't need three hundred pages to tell, but could be told in ten, twenty or thirty pages; so I put them into print. One at a time I gave them to my friend, who when I would see him again, had always read them.

Thankfully, he said he liked them, (shameless promoting, place here).

What I learned from my friend is that there are a large number of people out there in the big wide world that enjoy reading, but treat a book like a project, one that needs to be finished in a timely manner.

But short stories, on the other hand, can of course be finished in one sitting or sometimes two; if the story is a little long.

And that's what this book you hold in your hands is for.

For all the people out there who have the attention span of a modern day adult, I hope you enjoy these stories and hopefully, one day, you'll realize that a book can be picked up and put down any time, and that the worlds and characters inside its covers are on your time table, not the other way around.

As for the rest of you that love reading in any form, I hope you enjoy these stories and the thousands of others out there just like mine.

To you others I say: "Don't be afraid to start reading something longer than ten pages, because the reward you'll get will be ever-lasting."

Anthony Giangregorio
August 2007

A Ghost of A Memory

Robert Weaver stared into his cup of coffee, wondering how everything could go so wrong, so fast. He had just returned home from burying his wife, the bitter taste of watching her casket drop into the ground still fresh in his mind.

In the pit of his stomach was a vast loneliness so profound it couldn't be put into words.

He looked across the kitchen table to the countertop, his wife's purse exactly where she'd left it three days ago.

He'd touched nothing since he'd received that phone call no one in their right mind would ever want to receive.

Steam from the coffee swirled up into his face, fogging his glasses. He plucked them from his face, wiping them on his shirt.

He almost felt the urge to weep yet again, but he forced it back down. He had cried enough. Oh, he knew there would be more tears, but for just a few moments he wanted to sit in his home, in the kitchen, and try to imagine his wife was still alive.

Three days ago, it had been a night just like any other. His wife, Susan was going out on the town with her girlfriends. Robert had been watching a football game, barely listening to her. She had told him her entire agenda, but he had only nodded, more interested if the Patriots would get the first down than what his wife would be doing that night.

When she had been ready to leave, she had tried to kiss him goodbye, leaving her purse at home rather than risk it becoming lost or stolen. He had pecked her on the cheek, but he'd then been distracted when his team fumbled the ball.

Shaking her head, with a sly smile across her lips, Susan had left him to his vices.

Now, as he watched the black liquid cooling in his cup, he wished with all of his heart he could somehow go back in time and redo that moment. If he'd known that would have been the last time he would ever see her again, he would have shut off the goddamn game and hugged her and kissed her and told her that he loved her.

But it was all too late. Truth was; he had taken her for granted, expecting her to always be there for him.

Well surprise, surprise, she wasn't.

She was gone...forever.

The phone rang, pulling him from his fugue and he answered it, a slight cringe affecting his face as he saw the number displayed on the caller ID.

It was his mother, and though he had a relatively good relationship with her, he wasn't up for her cheerful spirits this morning. Since Susan's death she had done her best to be positive and supportive, but all it did was drive Robert mad.

His wife was dead! He was supposed to feel bad about it.

She figured she could help him work through his grief, because more than five years ago she had lost her husband, Robert's father.

But she was wrong. However she had handled his dad's death was between her and God. Robert would find his own way to deal with his loss.

Bringing the phone to his ear he said: "Hello, Mother, what do you want?"

"Hi, dear, I was just wondering how you're holding up. Once again, I'm so sorry for you. Susan was a wonderful woman. She'll be sorely missed."

Robert sighed, not wanting to act the grieving widower. "Look, Mom, I'm really not in the mood to talk about this right now, okay? How 'bout tomorrow?" Or ten years from now, he thought.

"Look, honey I know you're sad, but moping around the house isn't going to help you. Time heals all wounds, you'll see."

Robert wished he could reach through the phone lines and strangle her. "Time? What a load of crap. Time heals shit. It's more like we as a human race have a short attention span, and as time moves on, we just forget. We just forget! Nothing is ever healed, nothing!"

The line went silent for a few seconds and Robert was about to ask if she was still there when she answered him.

"Okay, honey, maybe you're right, and we should talk later. Just remember, I'm here if you need me."

"Yeah, sure whatever," he said in a soulless voice.

"Bye, honey, I love you, my prayers are with you," she said and hung up the phone.

Robert placed the phone down and stared at the wall. Why did everyone always think they needed to console someone when there's a death? Did anyone ever think that you might just want to be alone with your thoughts?

But no, when someone dies you have to go through this friggin ritual. Wake, funeral, reception after the funeral, where you feed and thank everyone for coming to something almost every single one of them would have preferred not to come to.

But, hey, if you don't go to theirs, then when you drop dead they won't go to yours, right?

With a lack of control, he let his anger get the better of him and he knocked the coffee mug off the table to clatter to the floor. He regretted his outburst as soon as he'd done it. There would be no one else to clean that up but him.

With a heavy sigh, he stood up and grabbed a dish towel from the rack near the stove, wiping the spill up before it could spread to the small carpet near the sink.

Before he could stop it, the tears started again and he placed his head in the spill and wept.

The question was; was he sobbing for his dead wife, who no longer felt pain? Or was he crying for himself, who now had to go on living alone.

Susan and he had never had any children. She had wanted to wait a few more years, concentrating on her career as a legal analyst. He had a more mundane job as a truck driver for a local milk company.

Though he had to get up at two in the morning almost every-day, he relished the freedom of not being in an office, but instead was out on the road, in the city, where he met different people everyday.

Getting his weeping under control, he finished cleaning up the spill and decided to take a nap for awhile. Yes he was depressed, but no more than he should be in his situation. But sleep would be a good way to just shut out the world and pretend everything was still fine; that his wife was still alive and would be home late that day.

Standing up, he walked over to the phone and disconnected it. His mother's call was enough for one day and he didn't want to have to field anymore calls from consolers.

Taking a second to disconnect the doorbell to the front door, as well, he trudged up the stairs to his bedroom, firmly prepared to sleep forever, or to the time when he wouldn't feel so alone.

That night, after hours of slumber, no thanks to the five sleeping pills he'd taken over the course of the day, she came to him in his dreams.

Or at least he thought it was a dream.

He had been in a field of yellow daisies and Susan had been there, too. She looked as good as the day he'd met her, not at all like the battered and bruised corpse he'd been forced to identify at the coroners office.

The coroner had been very understanding and had told him it had been a drunk driver. The man's car had jumped the medium, killing himself and everyone in Susan's car, as well.

No one had survived.

But now, in the dream, she was whole again, her light blonde hair blowing in the gentle breeze.

He held her close and cried.

"Don't cry, baby, it's all right. I'm in a good place now. I just had to see you one more time, to say goodbye. Someday you'll be with me, too, I promise," she said in a lilting, singsong voice.

"But I want to be with you now," Robert pleaded. "It's not fair. You shouldn't have been taken away from me, not yet. We were just starting our life together."

She caressed his face, wiping his tears away. "I know baby, but life is like that sometimes, it's just fate. We can't stop it; no matter how hard we try."

He stared at her speechless. They hugged each other for how long, Robert couldn't imagine, time in dreams being unknown.

But then the clear blue sky started to darken and Susan's face went ash-grey.

"What's wrong, why are you shaking?" He asked her, feeling her body trembling.

"I have to go," she stammered. The wind had become a maelstrom and Susan continually looked behind her, searching for something.

"Why, what's wrong, tell me!" He yelled, shaking her in his concern.

"I can't, Robert, I just can't. Listen to me, whatever you do, you have to let me go. Please, just let me go!"

The wind was howling now, leaves and twigs flowing around them like they had a life of their own. Some of the daisies snapped from their stems to fly about them, some catching in Robert's clothing.

"I can't, I love you, I need you, please don't go!" He screamed over the wind.

Susan started walking backward, her eyes never leaving his.

She kept looking over her shoulder, as if she was worried something was trying to sneak up on her.

Robert held out his arms for her, but she slowly moved into the distance, until she was on the slight slope looking down on him.

"I can't, Robert, I'm sorry, I have to go. I've already stayed too long," she called to him, the worry evident on her face.

Just before she vanished, he saw something dark overshadowing her. He caught her flash of fear and then like a light switch being turned off, everything was gone.

The field, his wife, everything.

The sound of a rumbling truck outside his bedroom window pulled him from his slumber, the real world slamming back into place like an iron lid.

Sitting up in bed, he rubbed his face, staring at the clock on the nightstand that read four-fifteen. The sheets were wrapped around him tight, evidence he had been squirming while he slept. His body was covered in sweat, the sheets moist.

Sliding to the edge of the bed, he was going to go to the bathroom when he felt something slide off his lap and brush his bare leg as it fell to the floor.

Bending over in the darkness, he reached around, his hand finding the object.

Clicking on the lamp on the nightstand, his blood went cold when he saw what was in his hand.

It was a yellow daisy, looking as if it was just picked; the stem where it had been broken off still damp.

Dropping the flower onto his lap, he placed both hands to his head, shaking it back and forth.

This can't be happening, it can't be true, he thought

But if it wasn't true, then why was there a fresh yellow daisy lying in his lap?

He couldn't sleep for the rest of the night and so he got up, prowling the house like a wild animal.

He walked through the rooms, all the different items scattered everywhere only reminding him of his wife more than ever. He stopped in the living room, picking up a paperweight from the mantle. It was in the shape of a train. It was a souvenir from Storyland, an amusement park in Storybrook, Maine. It had been Susan's idea to go there, as a lark, she'd said.

Despite the fact it had been just the two of them, they'd had a wonderful time and afterwards, Susan had even started talking about having children of their own.

A smile crossed his lips and he set the paperweight back down on the mantle.

Letting out a deep sigh, he looked around the room, never realizing how truly lonely a house of only one is.

Walking over to the couch, he plopped down, turning the television on and doing every insomniacs pastime: flicking channels.

Sometime around six in the morning he drifted off to sleep again, the television still droning on about the most wonderful food processor in the world.

He awoke to the sound of a semi truck driving by his house, the back of the cargo container rattling on the potholes in the street, sounding like a clap of thunder had occurred directly overhead.

Stumbling to his feet, he turned off the TV and moved through the house.

He wasn't relishing his first true day without his wife in his life, but he knew he had no choice in the matter.

With a stumbling motion, he went to the bathroom to start his day; however it would end would be anyone's guess.

The entire day was nothing but a blur. Robert had left the house around eight, far too restless to stay indoors anymore. He had gone for a walk, followed by a trip to the market to grab a few items.

Once he'd purchased them, however, he had realized that almost everything he'd bought were things Susan liked, some of the items he didn't even care for.

He had been on automatic, buying the things he knew his wife would enjoy.

Walking to his car, his face had been one of stone, no emotion showing.

He had calmly opened the car door and slipped inside it, dropping the bundles next to him.

Then he had sat there and cried. God, how he missed her. If it was supposed to get better in time, then when exactly would that be? A month, two months, a year? When exactly was he supposed to get over her leaving him?

After driving home, he spent the rest of the day in front of the television, his mind wandering, not even seeing the flickering screen.

Darkness fell and still he sat, only getting up to use the bathroom and to feed his hunger. Though his stomach screamed for food, he didn't want to eat, so he cracked open a can of Franco, eating the spaghetti and meatballs out of the can.

Normally it would have been one of his favorite things to eat. Right out of the can, no dish required, room temperature was perfect, but today it was tasteless, today it was only fuel for the machine that was his body.

After shoveling another spoonful from the can into his mouth, he thought of his wife. Susan had always yelled at him for eating out of the can, telling him to put it in a bowl and warm it up. But why, this way it's one less dish to wash, he'd tell her.

She would usually make an exasperated noise and then throw her hands into the air. Men, she'd say and walk away, leaving him to his canned bit of heaven.

Now the food had no taste and he shoved spoonful after spoonful until the can was empty.

He had consumed the entire can in less than a minute, setting it on the counter. With the spoon still sticking out of the top; he wandered back to the couch in the living room.

When his eyes became droopy and he knew he would fall asleep, he dragged himself to his bedroom. Not wanting to risk waking in the middle of the night, he popped three sleeping pills, one more than the required dose and dropped into his bed, clothes and all.

His hand reached out in the darkness, for just a moment expecting to feel Susan's warm body next to him. He would usually snuggle up close to her, wrapping his arm round her body. She would usually moan in her sleep and roll over, lost in her own slumber.

He would then squeeze her breast playfully, just a few times. She would grunt in her sleep and snuggle closer, then the two would drift off together, two people becoming one.

But now his hand came back empty, her side of the bed never to be filled again with her flawless skin and soft curves. He pulled her pillow to him and breathed deep, her scent still there.

He wondered how long it would take for her scent to diminish, until all he would have to remember her by were memories and ghosts of memories.

Burying his head under the pillow, he felt like sobbing again, but held it back.

Enough, already, how much can you weep for the same person. How many tears are enough?

The sleeping pills started to kick in and without realizing it, he fell into a deep pit that he wondered if he'd ever climb out of again.

* * *

He found himself in the same field again, yellow daisies dancing in the wind.

His heart skipped a beat, remembering the place from his past dream.

Was Susan here? Would she be coming?

He started walking through the dream world, over gentle slopes and flowing valleys.

He was about to give up hope that he would find her again, when he felt a soft caress on his cheek.

Turning abruptly, his face lit up when he saw Susan standing there. She was wearing a yellow sun dress that showed off her legs and hips and her hair was tied back into a ponytail.

She looked beautiful.

"Susan, oh my God, I've found you, again. What happened last time, where did you go? What was that dark cloud I saw?"

She shook her head from side to side. "It doesn't matter, nothing does, just hold me," she pleaded, sliding into his arms.

He held her tight, not wanting to ever let go. "I want to be with you, Susan, just tell me how. I'll kill myself if I have to, then we can be together forever. I don't want to live without you."

"No, Robert, you can't. You need to go on and continue living a full life. Someday we'll be together again, I promise, but..."

She stopped mid-sentence, looking around her, her face grew worry lines as she looked back and forth in the surrounding field.

"What's wrong, you look worried, can I help? Susan, what the hell's going on? Where did you go last time?" He yelled.

She broke from his grip. "No, you don't understand, I'm not supposed to see you anymore. Once I died I'm not supposed to return, but I can't stop myself. I just wanted to see you one more time, and then another. Oh, Robert, I'm so sorry I went out that night. If I'd stayed home and watched your stupid game with you, we'd still be together."

"Don't you think I know that? Don't you think I've thought about nothing else since you died, but it doesn't matter, none of it does. We're here now, together, and we can stay together forever."

The wind had started to pick up, blowing the daisies sideways. Susan's hair flew around her head like a halo, her ponytail coming undone.

"No, Robert, we can't. I'm so sorry; I should never have tried to reach you. The dead have no right talking to the living and I've broken rules by doing so. There'll be consequences.

"Consequences? What the hell are you talking about?"

The wind was picking up, making it difficult to stand in one place without being blown over. They now had to yell to be heard, the howling wind ripping their voices from their mouths.

"I can't tell you, Robert, there are rules that even the dead must obey and if not, there are punishments, as well.

"What, but…I don't understand," he stammered.

A crackling, booming sound filled the plain and Susan pulled free of his hands. "I have to go, they've found me again; he's found me again."

Who's found you again? Jesus, Susan, what are you talking about, it's crazy. I'm dreaming all of this because I miss you so much!"

She nodded. "Yes, Robert, that's right. Believe that and go on with your life, just remember I love you and always will." Then she began to pull away from him.

Robert wasn't letting her go that easily.

Reaching out to her, he caught a piece of her flapping dress and he held on with all his might.

"No! I have to leave, don't stop me!" She yelled, tugging on her dress.

"I won't let you go, Susan, I can't!" He screamed, the maelstrom once again engulfing the plain and the valley around it.

"No!" She shrieked and pulled so hard her dress ripped. She ran then, running over the plain like she was almost floating.

Robert watched her, prepared to go after her when an ominous dark cloud began to appear around Susan.

She stopped running and fell to her knees, looking up into the obsidian cloud.

"No, I'm sorry, I couldn't help it, please don't punish me, I won't do it again!" She pleaded to what Robert couldn't discern.

"Susan, no!" He called to her.

Her head snapped in his direction and he could see the terror on her face. She held her right hand in front of her, palm out. "No, Robert, don't, stay back, you can't go where I'm going!"

He was about to throw caution to the wind and charge after her when the black cloud descended over her, absorbing all light in its vicinity.

Susan let out one high pitched scream and then she was gone, swallowed whole.

"Susan, no!" He shrieked, the shock of seeing her swallowed by the creature overwhelming his senses. He charged after her, heedless of the danger he might be placing himself in, only thoughts of his wife flooding through his head.

The black cloud reared up and for just a heartbeat, Robert saw hundreds of teeth and red glowing eyes.

Then a loud shrieking siren filled his head and as the black cloud descended on him, he was pulled from the dream and found himself back in his own bed once again.

Pillows were knocked onto the floor and he was wrapped so tight in the sheets it was as if he was about to be entombed like a mummy.

Reaching to the nightstand, he turned off the alarm. He had forgotten to turn the damn thing off and now he was awake.

Wisps of his dream and Susan swam in his head, like ghosts.

Rubbing his face with his hands, dry washing away his sleep, he felt something on his cheek and he pulled his hand away.

There in his palm, a piece of thread wrapped around his ring finger, was a piece of yellow material, like from a sundress. The same dress Susan had worn in his dream.

His world fell away and he stood up on wavering legs.

Walking over to the bureau in the corner of the room, he picked up the daisy from the night before. Though a little dryer than the previous night, the daisy was still real.

Holding both items, one in each hand, he stared at them.

If they were real, then that means Susan is real, that she still exists somewhere.

But she was in trouble, that black shape wanted to hurt her, to punish her.

Throwing on whatever he could find, he ran down the stairs.

If she was still out there, perhaps in his dreams on another plane, then he would find her again, and this time one of them was staying with the other.

*   *   *

The library opened at nine in the morning and Robert was the first one through the doors. The only one, actually. He could probably count on one hand how many times he had stepped foot into a library over the course of his life and now he looked around himself in awe.

So many books, there must be thousands of them, hell, maybe a million. Or so it felt as he stepped into the gloomy building.

The lights weren't on yet, but as soon as he moved up to the empty desk, the overhead fluorescents snapped on, humming softly while they warmed up, one or two flickering, reminding him of an old man trying to get out of bed in the morning, the will strong, but the flesh weak.

Behind the wide open desk situated in the center of the room was a small doorway, leading to the rear of the building.

Out of this room came a prudish looking woman with grey hair and thin glasses perched on the edge of her nose, and a beaded chain attached to the end, of course, so she could hang them from her neck when not using them. If she was an inch over five feet it was because of her shoes.

She looked down her nose at him, as if he was intruding on her privacy.

In her hand was a book, her finger holding her place so she could continue reading once she had returned to her desk, but those plans were now dashed, thanks to Robert.

She reminded him of his first grade teacher, Mrs. Thomas. That woman had had a way of glaring at you that would make you feel guilty, even when you were completely innocent of all crimes.

She continued looking at him, waiting for Robert to speak first.

"May I help you, young man?" The words, young man seeming to taste like bile in her mouth, or so it seemed.

"Uhm, yeah, hi, I was hoping I could do some research on a few subjects?" He asked her nicely.

Her eyebrows went up with curiosity. "Oh, really? Then why don't you surf the web like the rest of you young folk. I'm sorry to tell you we do not have the internet here. The city council was planning to install it, but then changed their minds. Budget restraints and all that."

Robert scratched his head. "Oh, well, uhm, that's okay. I'm not much of a computer user anyway. Just never really got into them. I kind of like the hands on approach, you know, holding the books in your hand, and stuff. I'm not even connected on line at home. My wife used to go online at work, but she never bothered having it installed at home. Funny, huh."

"Why do you use the past tense to refer to your wife, young man? Don't you know proper grammar?"

Robert's head dropped so he was looking at the floor. "Oh, well, uhm, my wife just died. It was only a few days ago. Drunk driver," he said softly, the pain and loss welling up inside him again.

The librarian's face softened almost immediately and Robert saw a different person in front of him now. She stood up from behind the desk and walked over to him.

"Oh, dear, I'm so sorry for you, and so young."

She led him over to a large round table at the opposite end of the room.

"Here, you sit here. Now tell me what you're looking for and I'll see what I can do." She seemed to hesitate for a moment, seeming to be weighing something in her mind. Then she spoke again.

"My husband of almost forty years just recently passed away. I know how you feel. Cancer, it was." She leaned over him, after he had sat down, and smiled, her dentures gleaming in the fluorescent light.

"Now, what are you looking for, dear?"

"Well, I'm not sure really. I've been having these dreams, about stuff." He left it at that, not wanting to sound deranged. "And I was wondering what you might have on death, you know the grim reaper, stuff like that. Maybe something on what's between this world and the next."

She pursed her lips, contemplating his words, then she nodded. "You stay here. I'll be back in a few minutes." Then she was off, waddling away on her tiny legs, her shoes echoing in the labyrinthine aisles.

Robert sat quietly, listening to the humming lights. A car backfired outside and he jumped, not realizing how on edge he was.

He started to have second thoughts. Perhaps instead of researching dreams, he should be researching a good psychiatrist, because he was obviously losing it.

The minutes passed and he was starting to get restless when he heard footsteps along with the sounds of a squeaking cart.

A few seconds later, the librarian came from around a corner aisle, pushing a metal cart piled high with old books, some of them looking a hundred years old if they were a day.

Stopping by his chair, she leaned on the cart.

"Sorry it took so long, but these were on a top shelf in the back. Some of these books haven't been opened for more than fifty years, maybe longer."

"And these should have what I'm looking for?" Robert asked.

She nodded slightly. "Perhaps, dear, perhaps. All you can do is try. If not, there's always the internet." She actually smiled then, and Robert saw a much different person than the one he had first met when he had walked in a short time ago.

Now she looked at him as a kindred spirit, both having suffered the same loss; the loss of a mate.

He returned her smile with one of his own, reaching out for the book she was handing him. "Thank you so much; I really appreciate your helping me."

She scoffed, waving her hand in front of her, casually. "Oh, that's all right, that's what I'm here for. Now why don't you get to work and I'll leave you be. If you need anything else, you know where to find me."

"Okay, thanks again," he said and turned to the book sitting on the table in front of him.

He flipped through it, not knowing exactly what it was he was looking for. When he had reached the last page, he sighed, and then picked up the next book in line.

Three hours later he had a large pile of books in front of him, only leaving enough room to fit the next book he was perusing.

He was almost to the end of the last book on the cart, already preparing to just give up and go home, when he found something that looked promising.

The second to last chapter of the book, titled: **DEATH AND THE HEREAFTER** had a picture, hand drawn, of an entity that looked a lot like the one he'd seen in his dream.

The picture showed a black cloud-like form with bits of red and slits across its anatomy. The cloud seemed to hover over the land and below it was a drawing of men and women, all cowering in fear.

There was a subtext below the picture that read: The Guardian ushers souls from this world to the next, preventing those same souls from wandering from their appointed destination.

"This is it, it's got to be," he said, closing the book, and rising from his chair with the book in his hand.

The librarian looked up as he walked over to her and for the first time, Robert saw the name plate in front of her.

Ms. Periwinkle, it read in neat print.

She looked up at his approach, the faintest hint of a smile on her lips.

"So, did you have any luck, dear?" She asked, sweetly.

He nodded. "Maybe, I'm not sure exactly. Look, is it possible for me to take this book home with me?"

She nodded. "Do you have a library card with us?"

He shook his head no.

"Okay, how about a driver's license?" She asked.

He answered her by pulling his wallet out and pulling it from its slot. She took it and nodded.

"Okay that fine, just give me a few minutes and I'll make you a card."

Robert did, biding his time by looking at the ornate wood carvings scattered across the ceiling and corners of the library.

The book felt hot in his hands, feeling like a live thing, and he had to stop himself from simply running out the front doors of the library with the book in hand like a common thief.

All he wanted to do was get home and study the book in more depth, without the worry of prying eyes.

Minutes passed and Ms. Periwinkle returned, handing him a green, laminated, card. The card was still warm as he placed it in his pocket. Ms. Periwinkle then took the book from him and checked it out.

He almost resisted when he had to hand it to her, not wanting to let it go.

Something deep down inside him told him this was his one chance to find his wife again, and he'd be dammed if he was going to let it go now.

After a few quick stamps on the index card inside the book cover, she handed it back.

"Did you see the date on the card? The last time this book was taken out it was 1959. That was two years after this library opened."

"Interesting, but I really need to go, thanks again for all your help," he said with a smile.

"My pleasure, dear. Good luck on your research."

Waving farewell, Robert took the book from her hands, and quickly left the library, taking the front steps two at a time.

It was almost one o' clock. He had spent more than half the day in the library, but now, with the book in his hand it was all worthwhile.

Jumping into his car, he had to control himself, wanting nothing more than to floor the pedal to race home as fast as he could.

Eventually he made it, the library being only fifteen minutes from his home.

Jumping out of the car, he ran to the front door, throwing the door open and almost running to the living room.

He noticed the phone on the wall had three messages flashing for attention.

Checking them quickly, he realized two were from his mother, the other from Zack, a close friend from work. Watching the messages flash for attention he regretted plugging the phone back in. Same for the doorbell, he should have left them disconnected.

He ignored them all, now having a purpose, not just another victim who had to deal with the loss of a loved one, helpless to do anything about it but mourn their passing.

Tossing his keys onto the kitchen table, he walked to the living room, dropping down into the side chair and immediately opening the book to the second to last chapter. Susan's sweatshirt was draped over a nearby chair, looking like she would be by any minute to pick it up and go for a jog.

He ignored it.

Hopefully, there would be some clue as to what he could do the next time he was with Susan, some way to protect her from the creature.

As he started reading, taking in every word like his life depended on it, his eyes seemed to almost glow with hope.

He would find a way to save her, because the alternative was too much to bear.

When he had finished the last page of the book and snapped it shut, his eyes were staring across the room, seeming to be looking through the wall and out into the void beyond. The book had been vague on some of the items he had hoped to learn, but in others it had explained things clearly.

As he sat all alone in his home, he tried to put all the pieces together, to make them coherent.

Apparently this Guardian was some form of gatekeeper to the afterlife. Its purpose was to keep the souls of the dead where they belonged, in limbo, as they waited for judgment.

But sometimes a soul would slip free and it would be the Guardian's responsibility to find and return the wandering soul back to the ether.

That's what had happened to Susan. She had loved him so much that she couldn't just leave and go on to the next plane of existence without telling him goodbye. So she had come to him in his dreams.

She had only wanted to say goodbye to him, but each time she managed to escape, the Guardian would find her and pull her back to the void.

Somehow, he needed to find a way to stop the Guardian and by doing this, perhaps save Susan from limbo.

Standing up and placing the book on the coffee table, he found his sense of loss had lessened.

Though he still ached to have her with him again, he found that now, with a sense of purpose, he felt slightly better.

He also found he had an appetite now.

Going into the kitchen to make himself a sandwich, he hummed a tune both he and Susan had sung together.

It was still hours before dark, but once the darkness had descended on his home, he would sleep, this time making sure there would be no disruptions.

And he would find his wife and save her.

A little past seven in the evening the doorbell rang.

Robert raised himself from the couch, where he had been perusing the television channels, waiting for night to come, and stumbled to the door, having no idea who it could be.

Reaching the door, he looked through the peephole, frowning when he saw who it was.

It was Zack.

He was just debating if he was going to pretend he wasn't home when Zack pounded on the door again.

"Come on, man, I know you're home, I saw your shadow cross the peephole." Zack said.

With a heavy sigh, Robert opened the door and, without even a hello, walked back into the living room, taking his place back on the couch.

Zack opened the screen door and stepped in, not the least bit insulted.

"Hey, dude, I just came to check up on you, and seems you don't want to answer my calls..." He held his arms out to his sides, spread wide. "Well, here I am."

Robert frowned, staring at the television. Jerry Springer was on, some woman arguing about who was the father of her three kids. He wasn't actually paying attention to it, but it was a mild distraction whenever the fights broke out.

Zack grunted and disappeared down the small hallway to the kitchen. Robert heard the refrigerator door open and a few seconds later, Zack walked into the living room with a cold beer in his hands.

Robert saw this and glared at him. "Help yourself, why don't you," he said, sarcastically.

Zack plopped down on the matching chair in the corner. "Thanks, I will," he said, cracking the beer and drinking deeply.

For a few minutes Zack remained silent, seeming to be lost in the world of trailer park men and women, then he spoke up.

"You know they say all that stuffs just fake, that it's all choreographed from the beginning of the show," he said, gesturing to the television.

Robert crossed his arms over his chest and only grunted in response.

Zack took another sip of his beer and then leaned forward. "Look, Rob, I'm really sorry about Susan, is there anything I can do?"

Robert shifted in his seat so he could see Zack easier. "Yeah, you could leave," he stated brusquely.

Zack sighed. "Come on, Robert, I know it's rough, but don't be that way. I loved Susan, too."

Robert's eyes flashed angrily. "Don't you dare compare how I feel for Susan to you. You barely knew her!" He snarled, threateningly.

Zack held his hands up in a sign of defense. "Whoa, easy there, buddy, that's not what I meant and you know it." He finished his beer and set it on the side table situated next to the chair. When he stood up, he let out a loud burp, then he walked to the entrance to the living room.

"Look, I'll give it to you straight. Your mom called me and asked me to check up on you. She's worried about you, so am I. If you want me to leave, I will."

Robert looked up at Zack from across the room. His countenance was one of anger, but after a few moments it softened and he relaxed. Even his body seemed to relax, his muscles loosening.

"Look, Zack, I'm fine, okay? I'm just working through Susan's death in my own way. Tell my mom I'm doing fine, will ya, and that I'll talk to her in a few days after I've worked a few things out."

That seemed to satisfy Zack and he nodded. "All right, but if you need anything, you'll call, right?"

Robert nodded. "Yeah, man, I'll call. I just need another day or two to take care of a few things. Then I have a feeling everything will be fine, one way or another."

Zack was about to leave when he hesitated, taking in Robert's words. Then he shrugged, deciding he was putting more into the words than was needed.

"Okay, bro, you be good, we're all here for you. I'll see you in a few days when you get back to work."

Robert waved to him and then focused his attention on the television. One of the men wasn't taking the news that he was the father of the children very well, and he was throwing things around the studio, the crowd cheering his efforts.

Zack opened the screen door and left. Less than three minutes later, Robert heard a car start, then the vehicle drove away.

He stood up and closed the door, making sure to lock it. Then he disconnected the doorbell and pulled the phone jack from its socket.

After making sure his cell phone was off, as well, he went upstairs to take a shower and shave.

He was feeling sleepy and he wanted to stay awake until it was at least, dark outside. Then he would put his plan into action and pull his wife from the jaws of death.

When ten o' clock finally rolled around, he decided it was time.

Dressing in a pair of pajamas, just in case he didn't wake up— no one wants to be found dead in their birthday suit, he figured— he popped ten sleeping pills and washed them down with a full glass of water.

He wasn't trying to kill himself, but just making sure he was so doped up, there would be no way he could be pulled from his slumber.

Unplugging the alarm clock, he climbed into bed, taking the book with him.

With the night lamp on, he read over some of the pages that stood out, hoping he knew enough to save Susan.

Without realizing it, he passed out, falling into a pool of blackness.

At first there was nothing, only an obsidian wall, but soon the wall disappeared and he found himself back in the field of daisies.

After a few moments to get his bearings, he cupped his hands to his mouth and called his wife.

"Susan, are you here! It's me, Robert!"

He stood there in the gently flowing daisies, praying his wife would come to him, but as time passed and she didn't appear, he started to lose hope.

Walking over the hills and valleys, not knowing how much distance he traversed, he slowed at the sight of a small figure in the distance.

Running toward it, he jumped and climbed over logs and boulders spread out across the valley. Soon the figure came into focus and his heart leaped at the sight of the yellow dress the figure wore.

When he was finally able to discern her face, he almost screamed with happiness.

It was her. He had found her again!

"Susan, oh my God, I've found you!" He screamed as she jumped into his arms.

She kissed him hard on the lips, followed by more kisses on his face and neck; then back to his lips again.

"Robert, no, this is wrong. You can't be here. I can't be here."

"I don't care. I won't let that thing take you from me. If I have to, I'll follow you to the hereafter and protect you."

She shook her head from side to side. "Oh, Robert, I wished it worked that way, but it doesn't."

"Why? Why can't it? I want to be with you and I don't care how."

She hugged him then, the two of them squeezing each other so tight neither wanted to let go.

And then it happened, as he knew it would.

The tempest started.

The trees on the horizon started to shake and sway. The daisies were blown almost horizontal to the earth. The leaves and twigs and other wooded debris became airborne, swirling around them.

The maelstrom continued and Susan started to pull away from him.

"That's him, he's coming for me. I have to leave now, Robert!" She screamed over the howling wind.

"No, not this time, Susan. This time I'll fight for you. I'll face them, him; anything that keeps you from me!"

"You can't, they're too powerful. He's too powerful!"

Above their heads blackness so dark all light was absorbed coalesced, tendrils reaching out to surround Susan.

Robert charged at her, picking her up and holding her close while the tendrils swarmed around her, and Robert.

His hair blew about his head, and her long tresses struck his face while the swirling tunnel crashed around them.

"Let me go, before you die, too!" She screamed.

"Never. If you go, then I go, too!" He hollered back, he was committed, despite the aching he felt in his arms struggling to keep her close to him.

He gritted his teeth, closed his eyes so as not to see the horror before him and held on to her for both his life and hers.

The funnel of wind blew so loud it sounded like a creature from prehistoric times, but still, Robert held on to Susan.

Her feet left the earth, as the Guardian tried to pull her away from him, but he roared with his own rage and pulled her back to him.

Suddenly, like a thunderclap, the wind, and blackness were gone and the field of daisies was back.

After the roaring and noise of the wind echoing in his ears, Robert was dumbstruck by the cessation of violence.

Opening his eyes, his jaw dropped at what stood before him.

A man in a yellow suit, looking like it would burn to the touch, stood before him. He had a thin mustache and his black hair was slicked back like a refugee from a 50's movie.

He had the air of an aristocrat and the most off-putting was the wide smile he flashed to both Susan and Robert.

He pulled a cigarette from his breast pocket and lit it with the tip of his finger.

After several puffs, he stepped two more feet closer to Robert.

"Mr. Weaver, would you mind telling me what you think you're doing here?"

His voice was deep, intelligent, and articulate. Not what he would have expected. Though, if he had to really guess, he would have answered he wouldn't have known what to expect...certainly not this.

The yellow-suited man looked to Susan.

"Susan, my dear, you may step away from him. You'll be staying here until we can get this all sorted out. Now, I can't have my souls just doing anything they please, can I?" He glanced back to Robert. "Mr. Weaver, what part about dead don't you understand?"

Robert closed his mouth and swallowed hard. "Who the hell are you?" He said in a whisper.

"Why, I'm the Guardian, who else would I be?"

"What happened to the black cloud?" He asked and glanced up into the sky, expecting it to reappear at any moment.

Yellow-Suit waved his hand in a casual gesture. "Oh, that's for the tourists. I think we're past that, don't you?"

He stepped closer to Robert and Robert smelled lilacs and cloves.

"Mr. Weaver. If you haven't realized it, your wife is very dead. And she can't keep sneaking out of limbo, it makes me look bad. How can we settle this so that all parties are pleased, hmmm?"

"Send her back to me so we can spend our lives together," Robert stated simply in a steady voice.

The Guardian started to laugh. "Oh, Mr. Weaver, you do want a lot, don't you. I'm sorry, but that just won't be possible." He placed his arm around Robert's shoulder and moved in close, like he was going to tell him a secret.

"How about this. I'll keep Susan with me in limbo for as long as you live, mind you, that means a full and happy life, no suicide or any such nonsense, and when you pass on, she'll be waiting for you, here. Then you two can wait for judgment together."

"No deal," Robert said. "I want to be with her now."

The Guardian seemed to grow in stature so it felt like he was blocking out all light on the plain of daisies.

"You misunderstand me, Mr. Weaver. You either take my offer or your wife will spend the rest of her stay in limbo in Hell. And you can take her place with me as your guide."

Susan hugged Robert tightly, her body shivering. "He's right, Robert. You can't win here. At least this way I'll be waiting for you when you finally come here. That's good; take it, please, for me."

He looked up at the face of the Guardian and then back to his wife's.

Sighing, he realized he really had nothing to bargain with. He was powerless to stop this entity and by some form of a miracle, he had managed to wrangle some kind of deal from it.

"Why are you doing this? Why not just take her and be done with it?" Robert asked, looking a gift horse in the mouth.

The Guardian shrugged. "Let's just say I have a soft spot for love. Now you need to decide, and quickly, Mr. Weaver. Your time grows short. What will it be, yes or no."

He looked back to Susan and she nodded. "This is the best deal you can make, believe me. No one has ever done this before, at least not that I know of," she said.

"All right, fine, you win, but so help me, if she's not here when I get back," Robert threatened.

The Guardian chuckled. "Oh, spare me, will you. Listen, my friend. While you may live a lifetime, it is but a blink of an eye for your wife. When you arrive here in fifty years or more it will seem like you just left her, I promise."

Robert pulled Susan close to him and hugged her tight.

"I'll let you go, but only because I know I'll be getting you back," he said, kissing her cheek.

"And I'll be waiting for you. Now go back and live a full life. Hell, you can even remarry after a few years. How about Carol, she always had a thing for you?"

"Carol, are you kidding? Really? I had no idea."

She shrugged. "We girls talk about everything. It's okay if you want to, I won't mind. Just don't forget me."

He kissed her gently on the lips. "Never, you know that. I crossed planes of existence to find you again; a few years on earth won't change that."

The Guardian tapped his watch, a Rolex if Robert was correct. "Tick tock, Mr. Weaver, times up. Have a good life and stay out of my domain. I won't be as forgiving the next time."

"But wait, I'm not ready yet," Robert pleaded.

Susan smiled and blew him a kiss. "Yes you are, my love, go, I'll be here waiting for you. I love you."

"I love you, too, Susan." Then everything went white and he found himself looking up into the bright light of a small flashlight.

He tried to sit up, but realized his hands were tied down.

"What...what's going on, where am I?" he asked, his voice croaking with the effort.

"You're in Saint Judas hospital, Mr. Weaver. Your mother found you earlier this morning unconscious in bed. She called an ambulance and when you arrived, we found out you had taken a little more than the prescribed dosage of sleeping pills. Your stomach's been pumped and you'll be fine. How are you feeling?"

The penlight disappeared and Robert saw a middle-aged man in green hospital scrubs.

"I feel fine. In fact, I can't remember feeling this good since my wife died."

Really? No feelings of suicide?"

He shook his head, no. "Nope, should I be having them?"

"Hopefully not. Are you so distraught over the loss of your wife that you would take your own life, Mr. Weaver?" The doctor asked.

Robert scoffed. "Never. Yeah, I took some extra sleeping pills, but it wasn't to kill myself. I just wanted to make sure I stayed asleep. You see in my dreams..."

He was about to say his wife would come to him in his dreams, but stopped. If he was on some kind of suicide watch, he doubted if it would be in his best interest to say he saw his wife in his dreams.

"You were saying, Mr. Weaver?"

"Oh, uhm, I was saying that I just wanted a few good dreams. After everything that's happened to my wife and all, I just wanted to get a good night sleep." He lowered his face, trying to look bashful and embarrassed. "I guess I over did it, huh?"

The doctor smiled; a genuine smile and patted his shoulder. "Yeah, I think you did. Listen, the hospital psychiatrist will have to see you, but if your attitude stays the same, you should be out of here in two more days. Just in case it was an attempted suicide the hospital is required to keep you for three days to make sure you're healthy."

Robert grinned. "That's okay, Doc, I could use the break. Hey, listen, I'm starving, how about something to eat."

The doctor nodded. Sure, Mr. Weaver, I'll see what I can do." With a curt wave he left the room.

Stepping outside, Robert's mother was waiting for him.

"So, Doctor, how's my son? Is he going to be all right?"

The Doctor smiled happily. "Yes, Mrs. Weaver, I'm glad to say he'll be fine. Whether he took those sleeping pills on purpose or by accident, he seems fine now. He's even hungry. A healthy appetite is a good sign. Whatever demons your son had on his back seem to be gone now. He should be out of here in two more days; barring anything unusual."

Shaking hands with the Doctor, Robert's mother told him thank you and then stepped into the room. Robert was staring out the window, the sky a deep blue, reminding him of Susan.

He turned his head and smiled when his mother walked in.

"Hi, Mom, sorry about all this, but I promise you, I'm okay now." He glanced out the window again and then looked back to her. "Oh, and I'm sorry for being such a jerk to you. I know you meant well."

His mother leaned over and kissed his cheek. "Oh, honey, it's so nice to hear you say that. I was so worried when I found you in your bed. I kept trying to wake you but nothing worked. You're all I have left with your father gone." A few tears appeared in her eyes and Robert frowned.

"Come on, Mom, not the waterworks, please. Say, how did you get into my house, anyway?"

She looked like the bank robber caught in the act of robbing a bank. "I had a key from back when you and Susan went to Florida on vacation. Remember, she wanted me to water her flowers and feed that parakeet she had."

Robert's eyes lit up with recognition. "Oh, yeah, Mr. Tweety. God, how I hated that damn bird. Well, I'm glad you kept it."

She backed away from him, letting go of his hand. "I was about to go get a cup of coffee, do you want anything?"

He nodded, "Yeah, how about a sandwich, my stomachs empty. Literally," he chuckled, referring his pumped stomach.

"Sure, honey, no problem, I'll be back in a few minutes."

Before she left though, Robert stopped her. "Wait, Mom, I want to ask you something."

She stopped at the doorway. "What, honey. What is it?"

Robert gestured with his chin, his hands still tied to the bedrails. He was pointing to the vase of flowers on a table set against the far wall. On the table sat a vase filled with fresh daisies. In the middle of the bouquet was a yellow card.

"Will you see who those flowers are from? You don't know do you?"

She shook her head. "No, honey, I never saw them before and I'm the only one who's been here, though Zack said he'd come by later after work."

"Yeah, can't wait," he joked.

She walked across the room and pulled the card from the flowers, then walked back to Robert.

"There's no name. It just says: Get well and live long. Do you know what that might mean, dear?"

Robert leaned back into his pillow and smiled, a warmness growing where there had been nothing but a deep loneliness.

"Yeah, Mom, I think I might know what it means, thanks. Now how 'bout that sandwich?"

She set the card down, waved a finger that she'd return promptly, and then she was gone.

Finally alone, Robert gazed at the daisies in the vase. Was it his imagination or did they seem to be swaying slightly in the wind, despite the fact the window was closed?

Closing his eyes, he smiled to himself.

He would be all right, and somehow, he knew, Susan was all right, too, and she was out there somewhere in the void, waiting for him.

And someday he would find her again.

All Things Must End

Michael Ellis sat in his living room and stared out the boarded window that looked out on what was once a quiet street on the outskirts of Boston.

Now the street resembled a battlefield more than a thoroughfare for automobiles.

The street was littered with the bodies of his neighbors as the walking dead wandered the streets in the light of the full moon.

Soon they would come for him.

But that was all right. In the time since his wife and children had died, he had slowly made peace with his own mortality.

After everything he had witnessed in the last few weeks, death didn't seem so scary anymore.

In fact, Michael was almost looking forward to it.

He turned in his chair to look through his house to the backyard.

Through the windows of his den, which overlooked his small yard, he could see the markers he had placed over the ground where he had buried his family two days ago.

There were two small graves no more than three feet long and one more about five and a half feet long.

The tears starting flowing again and as his vision became blurry, he had to turn away.

Better to look out front. Better to see people who he didn't really care about.

While the tears continued to flow down his cheeks, he thought back to only two weeks ago.

*   *   *

He had come home early to celebrate his promotion from work. He had hoped Janie, the sixteen year old girl who lived next door, would be able to baby sit their two kids so he could take his wife out for dinner that night.

When he told Beth, she'd agreed whole-heartedly and immediately called Janie to check if she was free.

But the phone had been out. Curious, but not yet worried, she had gone over and knocked on their door.

Two minutes later, she ran back into the house and called for him and told him to put on the news; that something horrible had happened.

Michael immediately did as she'd requested, and as the two of them sat together on the couch with their arms around each other and listened to the news reports, his whole life fell out from under him.

While his two children played video games upstairs in their rooms, Michael and Beth listened as an anchorman explained how terrorists had set up a series of events that had enabled them to release a biological agent into the air over the middle of the United States.

Direct contact with the agent had already killed millions. But they didn't stay dead.

Instead of killing millions of people in America, the biological agent had mutated and was now bringing the dead to life.

Already, contact with the Midwest was shaky as the infrastructure began falling apart.

And if that wasn't bad enough, anyone who was killed by these bloodthirsty demons would be reanimated into one of them. And like a domino effect it would continue indefinitely until every human was either killed or transformed into the walking dead.

Nothing could be done, the anchorman said. The toxic cloud was even now spreading across the United States and within a week the entire country would be exposed.

The military was cautioning people to stay calm, but Mike knew what that really meant.

They were all screwed.

The worst thing, the anchorman said, was how the biological agent affected the very old and the very young. If exposed to the gas, these two exclusive groups would quickly become sick, and within a matter of hours would die and reanimate as the walking dead.

Thinking of his children, he held back a scream. He had to be strong.

Beth buried her head into his chest and cried. He wanted to join her but held back.

Have to remain strong, he thought. Be the rock the others could hold on to.

Within fifteen minutes the street in front of his house was in chaos as some of his neighbors tried to escape.

To where? There was no place to go.

His two children, Lisa and John, came running down the stairs after hearing the commotion outside.

He held out his arms and they jumped onto the couch with him and his wife.

Then the four of them sat together, while outside their windows the end of the world continued.

A week later was when it all started going to hell for Michael. About seven days ago he went upstairs to check on his kids for breakfast when he saw they were infected.

Both of them lay on their beds, the sheets around them soaked in sweat. Their faces were as white as the sheets they lay on and when he touched their skin it was as cold as ice.

A few minutes later, Beth came up, and when he told her what was wrong, she'd burst into tears and then flung herself onto bed with her children.

Michael didn't know what to say as the tears fell down his cheeks to splash on his shoes, so he went downstairs to give her some peace.

The television was just static and had been for the past half day as America slowly died.

He sat in his chair and listened to his wife crying upstairs as he watched the snow on the television.

From outside he heard gunshots, but they sounded far away. In the past few days it had been getting worse and he had already decided he was going to have to board up his windows to keep any trespassers out.

He looked down on the coffee table where his .38 sat peacefully.

Now he was glad he had ignored Massachusetts gun laws and had bought the gun when he had been given the chance.

He walked over to the front window of his house and looked out on the street, seeing smoke coming from a block over.

Now that he thought about it, he could smell it, too; that woody/charcoal smell that only a burning house can give off.

But Michael knew there would be no alarms as fire trucks screamed through the streets to save the burning building, no paramedics to rush to the scene to help anyone who was hurt.

No, those days were gone... along with hope of a future.

Suddenly, he heard his wife scream from upstairs. Taking the steps two at a time, he bolted up the stairs and charged into his kid's room to see his two loving children attacking his wife.

His daughter had sunk her small teeth into his wife's right arm while his son had gone for her throat. Luckily, he had missed and instead had sunk his teeth into her shoulder blade instead.

Running to her side, he pulled one, and then the other child off his wife and tossed them back to the bed.

Beth was bleeding, but it didn't seem to be too serious. Then his children were jumping back up and trying to bite him!

He pushed them away. Pushing his wife out the door, he then followed and slammed the door shut behind them.

Locking the door, he then helped his wife to the bathroom where the two of them managed to bandage her wounds; her face hung slack as shock started to set in. Then he helped her to the bed to lie down, where she promptly turned her face into the pillows and started to cry.

He then went back to his children's bedroom door and stood there. He could hear them crawling around on the other side of the door and as the tears started again, he just stood there, paralyzed.

What the hell was he supposed to do now?

They were his children, for God's sake.

Then he heard the sound of breaking glass and the scuffle of tiny feet.

Unlocking the door and entering the room, he saw the bedroom's only window was shattered. There was no sign of his children.

Going to the window and looking down to his driveway, he let out a howl of pain and then collapsed to the floor crying.

His children had jumped out the window to escape, but alive or dead, their frail bones couldn't take the impact of the two-story drop.

In the driveway below, his two children were dragging their shattered bodies down the driveway, trying to escape... what exactly?

Him perhaps?

After a few minutes of sobbing, he regained enough of his composure to get up and go outside and retrieve them.

Making sure to detour through the living room to collect his gun, he walked outside into the morning rays of the sun.

His children were at the end of the driveway when he reached them. His son's legs were shattered and he watched his daughter's head flop back and forth while she tried to move herself across the warm cement.

He fell to his knees and howled his pain as his children turned and started for him, their mouths salivating with hunger for his flesh.

When they were only inches away, he almost let himself just lie down next to them and let their small teeth take his life. At least then he wouldn't feel the pain he felt now.

But at the last moment his survival instinct kicked in and he rolled a few feet away from them.

Still they crawled toward him.

God help him, he knew what he had to do.

With his vision so blurry from tears he almost couldn't see, he pulled the .38 from his pocket and walked over to his son, placing it to the back of his small head.

"I love you, son. I'm so sorry," he said. Then he pulled the trigger and gave his son peace.

"I'm so sorry, honey. It wasn't supposed to be this way." He sputtered around the crying fit he was having. He almost couldn't stop shaking, the spasms were so bad.

Then he put the gun to her temple, closed his eyes and pulled the trigger.

He fell to the warm cement of the driveway and cried. He cried for over ten minutes until he heard footsteps coming up the sidewalk.

Wiping his eyes, he turned to see his neighbor from down the block. But Chuck didn't look the same as the last time Michael had seen him.

Now Chuck had half his neck missing and as he stumbled toward him he made a gurgling sound that seemed to come from his neck rather than his mouth.

Michael stood up and wiped the tears from his eyes. With Chuck walking toward him, something told Michael to keep his distance.

That hole in his neck maybe?

Then Chuck lunged at Michael and with teeth bared, tried to bite him.

Michael pushed him away and backpedaled some more; his children forgotten for the moment while he fought to stay alive.

Chuck came at him again and this time Michael punched him in the face.

Chuck's head turned with the blow, but otherwise was unaffected. Although now Michael could see the impression of his knuckles on his neighbor's face. It reminded him of Silly Putty, the way the skin was holding its shape.

When Chuck came at him again, Michael decided he had no choice and raised his .38. When Chuck was no more than three-feet away, Michael shot him point blank in the chest.

A fist sized hole blew out the back of Chuck's body and he stumbled backward, thrust off balance by the impact of the bullet. But he quickly regained his footing and came at Michael again.

Muttering imprecations under his breath, Michael raised his gun again. This time he aimed for right between his dead neighbor's eyes.

When Chuck was only inches away and about to lunge at him again, he squeezed the trigger.

Chuck's head snapped back and the top of his skull blew off from the impact of the .38 slug. As his brain's leaked out onto the driveway, Michael tried to control the shaking that had come over him.

Five minutes later, he thought he was better and got to work with the miserable task of burying his children.

After getting a shovel from his shed, he dug two small holes and then he retrieved their bodies, gently placing each one into a hole.

With the tears flowing again, he covered the holes with the extra dirt and placed some stones he had laying around the yard for markers.

Finished, he tossed the shovel to the ground and walked back inside the house to check on his wife.

He left Chuck where he'd fallen.

Beth wasn't doing very well.

She was delirious and feverish and when he walked into their bedroom, she called to him.

"Mike, is that you? How are the children, are they feeling better?"

He felt another crying fit coming on and forced it back down.

"Yes, honey, they're fine. They're sleeping now," he said, sitting down on the edge of the bed. "You just rest."

"I heard gunshots outside. Is everything all right?"

Michael fought to keep his voice level and he squeezed his hands so tightly his nails dug into his palms.

"Everything's fine, honey, you just sleep. When you wake up everything will be back to normal."

She nodded her head and turned her face to the side. The pillow was covered in sweat. She lay there staring at the wall, her breath coming in short gasps, but finally she closed her eyes and nodded off to sleep.

Michael went back downstairs and noticed the television was off. Walking into the living room, he tried the light switch and frowned when the light also stayed off.

Well, he knew it would probably have happened sooner or later.

He'd just hoped it would be later.

The house was silent with the power off. The gentle hum of the refrigerator now sorely missed as he walked around his dead kitchen.

From out of nowhere he felt a new wave of grief rising up from inside him and though he tried to keep it down, this time it would not be denied.

Leaning against the wall, he slid down to the cold tile of the kitchen floor and cried.

He cried for his two children now dead in the ground in his backyard.

He cried for his wife now dying upstairs in the bed they had made love in countless times.

And most of all, he cried for himself as he slowly watched everything he had ever loved disappear and blow away, like new fallen leaves on an October morning.

After a few minutes had passed, the waves of grief subsided and he stood and wiped the tears from his face.

He made himself a cup of cold instant coffee and then went and sat down in the living room and looked out the window.

There were more of those...zombies outside. He couldn't believe he had just thought that.

Zombies.

One had stumbled onto his front lawn and Michael went to the window and watched it. Did it have something in its hand?

Studying the creature through his window, he paused. On closer inspection he could see it was carrying what looked to be a piece of liver.

Human liver?

As he watched it put the red and pink morsel to its mouth and started chewing.

Michael could feel the bile rising in his throat so he closed his eyes and turned away.

Then decided he should board up the windows before those things got any ideas.

Going into his basement, he retrieved as much wood as he could find and then, after grabbing a hammer and nails, went back to the first floor to board up the windows and doors.

To keep those creatures out or keep him in; did it really matter?

Dropping the wood onto the floor, he got to work. In less than an hour he'd managed to cover most of the windows on the first floor and had put an extra heavy piece across the front door.

Then he sat back down in his chair. Through the cracks in the wood, he quietly watched the shuffling creatures wander around the street.

An hour after he had sat down, he found himself nodding off, the stress and grief of the morning catching up to him.

He drifted off into a restless sleep, dreaming of the time only a month or so ago when he and his family had gone to the beach for the day.

He smiled to himself remembering how the kids played in the water and waved to him and Beth as they splashed each other.

He had turned to Beth and in the glare of the sun her skin had glistened. He had leaned over and kissed her then and had told her he loved her.

Then he had jumped up and ran to the water and had played with his kids until it had been time to go home.

After that, his dream became jumbled. Images of his children crawling on the driveway; their little bodies broken and shattered came into his head.

He tried to turn the images off, but they just came back stronger.

He was jolted awake by the sound of his wife's voice floating down the stairs from their bedroom.

Jumping up, he ran up the stairs on weak legs to check on his wife.

She didn't look well.

Her eyes had sunk back into her head and her skin had turned a pale white color.

Checking her wounds, he frowned when he saw they were infected. The smell of rotting meat assailed his nose when he'd redressed her wounds. When he was finished, he tucked her back into bed.

She moaned softly in her sleep while he stood in the hallway and watched her.

If she was like his children then it wouldn't be long now.

He went to the bathroom and turned on the faucet, relieved to see the water still flowed.

Washing his face, he then dried himself off.

Then he went downstairs to retrieve his .38 from the kitchen table where he'd left it after burying the children; then he returned to his wife's side.

Within a matter of hours he was going to need it again, he thought, staring at his wife's body as she squirmed on the bed in her final death throes.

It had happened about eighty minutes later.

He had been sitting on the floor with his back against the bedroom door when his wife had died and then come back.

His head had been on his knees, hanging low, while he waited for what he knew was inevitable.

He looked up when he heard the bed creak and watched in horror as the woman he loved slowly sat up.

The bedcovers slipped off her chest, crumpling in her lap; and then she opened her eyes.

But instead of seeing the woman who had birthed his children in those eyes, he saw nothing but a hollowness that went beyond the boundaries of what his mind could grasp.

At first she looked around the room, her eyes just staring, vacuous. Then her head turned to look at him and he saw nothing but malice in those eyes.

Her mouth opened and a hollow rasping sound escaped her lips.

Before she'd even moved an inch off the bed, Michael stood up and walked to the foot of the bed, raising the .38.

The tears were back now and he tried to keep his arm steady; his body shaking with grief.

"I'm sorry, honey, I love you." He whispered; more for himself than for her.

Then he squeezed the trigger.

Her head snapped back and hit the back wall and then, as if she was going to sleep, her body fell back to her pillow and remained still.

Michael collapsed on top of her legs and cried again.

He looked up at the ceiling and asked God how he could be so cruel.

In one fell swoop he had lost everything he had ever cared about.

He lay there for hours and finally, with the sun setting outside, he managed enough courage to drag himself up and carry his wife downstairs.

He carried her through the shadows of the house until he was at the back door. Pulling it open, he walked out into the cool night air and set his wife's body down on the ground next to the two small graves of his children.

An hour later he was standing over the fresh mound of dirt where his wife had been laid to rest. A rustle of leaves caused him to turn around and he wasn't surprised to see three zombies wandering into his back yard.

Rage filled him as they shambled forward and prepared to attack him.

"You bastards!" He yelled. "It's your fault. Why can't you just leave me alone?"

He grabbed the shovel lying at his feet and ran at them.

He swung the shovel like a bat and knocked the first zombie to the earth, the ghoul falling over one of his children's graves. Swinging the shovel around, he used the wooden shaft of the shovel to push the second one away.

The third one held a familiar countenance. What was once Mrs. Murphy tried to rake talon- like hands at his face; her eighty year old hands swiping at his face like she was a caged animal.

He pushed her aside and then went at the one he had just hit with the shaft of the shovel.

Pulling the shovel back like he was hammering in railroad spikes, he let the shovel fly over his head where it then connected with the top of the zombie's skull.

The force of the blow sent the zombie to its knees and Michael quickly kicked it away. The zombie's head was crushed and it was definitely not a threat anymore.

Mrs. Murphy came in for the kill again, so he kicked her away. She hit the ground with a broken hip and while she struggled to rise from the grass, he whacked her on the side of the head with the shovel.

The shovel clanged as the metal hit bone and Mrs. Murphy fell to the ground with her brains falling out of her cracked skull.

Heaving with exertion and covered in blood, he looked up as more zombies entered his yard.

He knew he couldn't fight them all, so he did a hasty retreat back into his house.

The zombies shuffled to his back door where they started to bang on the painted wood.

Michael backed away and watched as the door shuddered with their weight, but continued to hold.

For now he was safe.

Walking to the bathroom in a daze, he went through the motions of cleaning himself up.

Halfway through washing up the water cut off, whatever powered the tap finally giving out.

Not even caring he walked back downstairs and sat in his chair and looked out onto what was once a quiet little street.

He set his .38 next to him on a side table and that's where he'd been ever since.

Over the past few days, more zombies had arrived at his back door and now there had to be at least fifty banging on his front door, as well.

They would be breaking in soon; it was just a matter of time.

The tears came again as he thought of his dead family buried in the yard behind his house.

Then he heard a shattering of wood, the back door finally collapsing under the onslaught of bodies.

Moments later he began hearing the first creaks from the wood of his front door, the weight of the zombies continually pounding on it.

He chuckled actually. It was nice to be so wanted by so many.

He heard groans and grunts when the first of the walking corpses stumbled into what was once his house, but was now nothing more than a morgue of regrets.

The first zombie walked around the corner of the room and stepped into the living room.

There were so many more behind it, as well.

Michael smiled and looked up into the dead face of the living corpse and sighed.

"I've been expecting you," he said calmly.

Then he picked up his gun, placed it under his chin, and closed his eyes, thinking of his family one last time.

Then he squeezed the trigger.

Camping Trip

An eagle soars over the sprawling landscape of the New Hampshire, White Mountains; its wings catching the subtle changes in air drafts. The majestic bird rises and falls as it glides, looking for its next meal.

Below its soaring form, the landscape is full of trees and boulders. Off to the eagle's left can be seen a small stream meandering through the forest. Small animals forage for food during this crisp autumn day.

The leaves have just started to change, the golden oranges, reds and yellows making the landscape look as if God, Himself had reached down from the heavens with a paintbrush and had decided to add some color to the world.

The eagle continues to soar overhead, barely acknowledging the brilliance of color, all it knows is that it's hungry, and if it doesn't find food soon, its belly will stay empty for the night; until the sun rises again the next morning and the battle to survive begins again.

Then the eagle catches movement in the peripheral vision of its left eye. Darting towards the earth, it swoops low and spies a field mouse sitting next to a black pool of water.

The eagle circles, preparing to attack.

On the ground, near the blackened pool, the mouse struggles for its life, while tiny black tendrils pull it towards the pool. In its tiny brain it regrets going near the black pool that had just appeared only days before.

The black sludge-like substance had boiled up from the ground. Slowly at first, but over the past few days, the substance had continued growing until now the spreading edges measured at over thirty-feet from end to end; the impression in the land keeping the pool hidden from prying eyes until a creature was directly on top of it.

The mouse had been curious, wondering if this was a new source of water for itself and its family; hidden in the rocks another twenty-feet away. But now, it found itself fighting for its life, the tendrils pulling it closer to the obsidian pool.

The eagle watched the struggle on the ground, circling the area, deciding the time to attack was now.

Darting in like a dive bomber, it dropped from the sky with talons extended, preparing to scoop the juicy morsel off the ground and then continue into the air to find someplace safe to feed.

With its eyes on the prize, the eagle was only inches from its prey when another black tendril shot from the smooth surface of the pool and wrapped itself around the shocked bird.

Its wings stopped in mid-flight, the bird dropping into the pool, sending tiny ripples across its smooth surface.

The majestic bird fought to stay above the viscous fluid, but soon felt itself being pulled down beneath the surface. Fighting for air, it started to choke, the tar-like substance suffusing its lungs and body, making itself one with the eagle.

In the blackness of the pool, the eagle stopped fighting and became motionless.

But it wasn't dead, not quite anyway. The black sludge changed the eagle, combining its essence with the feathered creature and becoming one entity.

This continued for some time, while from the air, the surface of the pool appeared calm.

The mouse was gone, as well, sucked into the black void to be transformed with the eagle.

Hours went by and the pool remained still, until a giant bear wandered into the pool area. The animal was one of the few left in the massive mountains, others of its kind dying off. Its curiosity peaked, it moved closer to the pool, nose sniffing the air for any signs of danger.

Just when the bear decided the pool was harmless, a black tentacle shot out of the smooth surface and wrapped itself around the bear's leg. While the animal fought and attempted to escape, other tentacles erupted from the surface to cover the bear with appendages. The bear screamed in pain and fear, sensing that what was happening to it was unnatural.

With the exceptions of rogue hunters, the bear was the dominant animal in these woods.

Slowly, inch by inch, the animal was pulled into the black depths, until only its head remained above the surface of the rippling pool.

Then that, too, disappeared. In moments, the surface became smooth again, the violence that had just occurred already forgotten in the dense forest.

Hours later, a deer wandered into the pool area and with tentacles securing it, the deer was pulled into the black depths to become one with the essence.

The sun moved across the sky and the shadows grew long in the forest.

Suddenly, the smooth surface was shattered, the animals disgorged back onto dry land. Their fur and feathers were covered in a thin black translucent film, and they stumbled out of the pool on wobbly legs.

Normally, these animals would have been mortal enemies, one killing the other for sustenance, but instead, they all moved as one; the essence of the pool instructing them what to do.

Find humans and bring them here. Only then could the essence of the pool become whole. Then it would take its teachings across the earth until every soul had been harvested.

From whatever black depths of Hell the pool came from, it was here now, and it wanted to flourish, to spread its seed to all; whether the world liked it or not.

*   *   *

A winding road cut through the White Mountains, like a scar in the land. A small Toyota Corolla followed the yellow line, like a toy car on a child's board game.

Inside the car were the Murphy brothers; Steve and Billy. Also in the car, sitting next to each man, were their prospective girlfriends.

Steve had Carla on his arm, the two of them cuddled up for warmth in the back seat. Steve's hand was conspicuously hidden from view and as Billy watched in the rearview mirror, Carla would giggle, leaving an idea where that hand might be.

Next to Billy was his own girlfriend, Kelly. He had been seeing her for a little over two weeks and only brought her along camping with his brother and girlfriend so he wouldn't be a third wheel.

He sneaked a glimpse in the rearview mirror at Carla, the focus of his attention oblivious. Carla was really the one person he wanted to be with.

Ever since he had met her six months ago, when his brother had brought her home to meet the family, he'd been in love.

He had never believed in love at first sight, but you better believe he did now.

He watched her covertly, sneaking glimpses whenever possible. Her eyes lit up as she giggled from Steve's machinations under her jacket and he felt a slight giddiness, wishing it was him in the backseat with her instead of his brother. It broke his heart to see them together, but he loved his brother and would never do anything to jeopardize his relationship with him. He could only pray that the relationship between him and Carla would fall apart by itself and then he would have his shot.

Until then, he would suffer in silence, going through the motions with a girl on his own arm so as not to be discovered.

He was knocked out of his reverie when his big brother slapped him on the back of the head playfully.

"Hey, Billy, how much longer to the campsite? I feel like a sardine back here."

Steve said, referring to the small backseat. Billy felt bad, but not everyone in the family could be a big-shot, writing software for a major company and bringing in over a hundred-thousand a year. Billy had to settle for being a line cook at a local diner. It wasn't big money, but it paid the bills; hence his crappy car.

"We'll be there in another hour. I told you already, it's really up there. When I said there's no other people around, I meant it," he said over his shoulder.

Carla curled up even tighter against Steve and purred with contentment.

"Just think, a whole weekend but nothing to do but hike and fool around in our tent," Carla said in a low voice.

Steve smiled. "Hell yeah, it's gonna be great, right, little brother?"

Billy cringed inside. He hated being called that. He was only a year younger than his brother, but the older sibling loved to remind him of it at every opportunity.

"Uh, yeah, great," Billy mumbled. "How you doin' over there?" Billy asked Kelly, the foot and a half of space separating them feeling like the Grand Canyon.

She gave him a quick smile that didn't seem to reach her eyes.

"I'm fine; I'm just not much of a camper, that's all. Can't say I get a charge out of sleeping on the ground and going to the bathroom in the woods; not my style."

"Then why'd you come? You could've said no," Billy told her.

The car had come to a steep hill and he stepped on the gas a little more to keep the vehicle at speed.

Kelly shrugged. "Dunno, just figured, what the hell, you know, that's all."

Billy watched her for another second and then focused on the road again.

Deep in his subconscious, he wondered if this camping trip was such a good idea. The only reason he'd been able to survive Carla with his brother was because he kept his distance. But his brother had been adamant about them doing something together, and Billy had finally given in to his coercion.

So here they all were, driving down a lonely road in the White Mountains, with nothing for him to do for two and a half days but watch the woman he loved make woopie with his brother.

Yeah! Good times for all.

A green road sign with the left side shaped like a face, to resemble the Old Man of the Mountain, told him his destination was a half mile away.

With Carla and Steve in the back playing footsie and Kelly staring out at the trees flying by her window, Billy sighed: it was going to be a long weekend.

* * *

The Toyota pulled into the small dirt patch on the side of the road, small dust clouds swirling around the tires. There was an opening in the trees that showed a small trail that led deeper into the forest, with a sign marking the trail for any potential hikers.

Turning off the engine, the Toyota knocked a few times before going silent.

Damn cheap unleaded gas, Billy thought, climbing out of the driver's seat into the brisk autumn air.

The others followed, and after a round of stretching to loosen tired limbs, they all prepared for the hike.

Billy went to the trunk and unlocked it. The trunk sprang open like a jack in the box, the four backpacks inside finally getting their freedom.

Billy still wondered how he'd managed to fit them all inside the small compartment and close the trunk, as well.

Steve pushed in next to him and retrieved his backpack. With a playful slap on Billy's back, he stepped away to check it.

Carla was next. When she reached into the trunk to retrieve her pack, her body brushed against Billy's. He felt a tingle from the contact and stood perfectly still while she reached lower into the trunk. Then she had what she needed and pulled away, to walk over and stand with Steve.

Billy tried to ignore the sensation of touching the woman he secretly loved and reached into the trunk for his own pack, as well as Kelly's.

He'd had to pack hers himself, as she'd made it quite clear she had no idea what to bring.

Slamming the trunk closed, he walked over to the others.

"Aren't you going to set the alarm?" Steve inquired about the Toyota.

Billy forced a smile. His brother knew damn well that the Corolla didn't have an alarm, but he just wanted to rub it in.

"Ha, ha, very funny. Come on, let's go, it's at least a three hour hike to where we're gonna make camp. The sooner we get there, the sooner we can relax." Billy said, starting towards the trail.

The others followed and with Billy in the lead, they headed up the trail.

The moment the four hikers entered the trail, the gloom of the forest surrounded them. The canopy of trees did an excellent job of deflecting the sunlight, turning the day into dusk.

For the first hour, each of them remained quiet, lost in his or her thoughts, while they enjoyed the scenery. But soon boredom set in and the talking started. Carla and Steve were talking about some movie they'd seen the other night while Kelly and himself talked about how tough the job market was in Boston and the surrounding states.

Steve called up to the front of the line. "Hey, little brother; how 'bout we take a break? My legs are killing me."

Billy noticed a set of boulders just off the trail and started towards them, the others following.

Soon they were all lying or sitting on the rocks, talking and enjoying their surroundings.

"Wow, I can't believe how large this forest is, it goes on for miles and miles huh?" Kelly asked Billy.

He nodded. "Uh-huh, that's why we need to be careful out here. Cell phones don't work and if one of us got seriously hurt, we'd be screwed as there's no one around for miles."

"You think there's a serial killer running around out here just looking for some tender young hikers to carve up like Halloween pumpkins?" Steve asked, grabbing Carla quickly to startle her.

"Knock it off, ya big jerk, that's not funny," Carla said, but she scooted closer to her boyfriend on the boulder, anyway.

"Sorry, I'm just having fun. You know I don't mean it," Steve said, kissing her on the cheek.

Billy watched all this with a knot in his stomach. That should be him holding her and joking with her.

Kelly moved closer to him and touched his shoulder. "You okay? You seem upset."

Billy made himself smile and he turned to look at Kelly. "I'm fine, probably just tired, I'm not used to this hiking stuff, either." Then he hopped off the boulder and picked up his pack.

"Come on, breaks over, let's keep moving. We should be there in another hour or so."

The others were shrugging into their packs when a howl sounded through the forest, catching them all off guard. Carla stepped closer to Steve and he put his arm around her protectively. Kelly did the same to Billy and he hugged her, as well.

The howl or scream seemed to last for an eternity, then, like a light switch being flipped, it stopped. For a few minutes no sound could be heard in the forest, it was utterly silent. Then slowly, the sounds of the forest returned. Birds chirped in the trees and crickets could be heard.

"What the fuck was that?" Steve said, looking around himself; trying to see everywhere at once.

"Don't know, a bear maybe, caught in a trap?" Billy suggested.

"Shit, if that was a bear in a trap, I don't want to know what kind of trap," Steve said.

"Steve, I don't think I like camping anymore, I want to leave now." Carla said, with her head buried into his shoulder.

After the minutes ticked away and the sound didn't occur again, they all started to calm down; Steve getting his bravado back.

"Whatever it is, it sounds like it's gone. I'm sure we're fine now. Let's keep going. I didn't come all the way out here to leave because some animal was stupid enough to get caught in a trap."

Then he started walking, continuing up the trail.

The others looked at each other and Billy shrugged.

"He's probably right, you know. I mean, this is real life, not some cheesy horror movie. It was probably just an animal. We are in the woods, after all." Billy smiled at the two women.

Carla seemed to relax a little. "Yeah, you're probably right, still, it's creepy, you know?"

Kelly nodded in agreement. "No shit, but Steve's right, it's nothing. Let's go."

As if on cue, Steve's voice floated down the path from up ahead.

"Come on, you babies, let's go!"

Billy and the women smiled at each other and started up the path after Steve, pushing the dark thoughts from every horror movie they'd ever seen away to the backs of their minds.

An hour later they'd made it to their campsite. Really it was just an open expanse of land surrounded on all sides by a copse of trees and shrubs.

If they hadn't liked it, there were a dozen other places to make camp in the same area, but Steve said he liked the way this site felt.

They hadn't seen another person on their way up the mountain, which wasn't that unusual for this time of the month. Most people were getting ready for the holidays and had already made their treks up the mountain weeks before.

Billy didn't mind, though. The solitude always gave him the feeling he was one of the only people left on earth.

The group busied themselves with setting up tents and starting a campfire.

Billy took responsibility for the fire personally.

After gathering some dry sticks and larger branches, he pulled his survival knife from his belt. He started shaving one of the sticks, sending the thin pieces into the pile of kindling. Once he had a sufficient amount of wood shaved, he pulled his lighter from his jacket pocket and after a few failures, managed to start the fire.

The flames crackled and some of the green wood he had mistaken for dry, popped and sent smoke into the evening air, the sap oozing from under the bark. Within another hour the sun would set, leaving the forest in utter darkness.

Once tents were finished everyone gathered around the campfire to warm up. The group was relaxed, enjoying each others company when another shriek echoed across the forest. The four stopped what they were doing and listened. The night was already starting to close in, giving every tree and branch an ominous look.

Carla moved closer to Steve, nearly pushing him off the log they were sitting on.

"Oh my God, Steve, what was that? It didn't sound like the animal from before."

"She's right, Steve," Billy said. "That yell sounded higher, a wolf maybe?"

"I don't think they have wolves up here," Kelly said, looking around the campsite, her eyes trying to pierce the gloom.

Steve quieted them off with a wave of his hands.

"Will you pussies stop fussing over a few animals? Christ, if you're all so scared, then why the hell did you come out here at all?" Steve snapped.

The others were quiet for a moment, shamed by Steve. Then Billy spoke up.

"You know, it's probably mating season or something. That's why we're hearing so many animals. What do you say we have supper?"

The others brightened at that. Between all the hiking and the weird sounds, no one had realized how hungry they were.

In no time they had gathered their supplies and had made a simple supper of hot dogs and beans; using the flames of the fire to heat the food.

Once supper was finished and the forest had continued to remain silent, everyone sat back and enjoyed the night.

The sun had completely set, wreathing the entire glen in perpetual darkness, now only the fire left to stave off the night.

Everyone laid back and talked about the different things that seemed to matter in their life, whether it was that new flat screen television they bought or the speeding ticket they had received and were going to fight at traffic court.

The night continued on until it was nearly midnight. With no television or other outside influences to keep them awake, they all soon agreed to go to bed.

Billy added more branches to the fire, hoping it would burn into the night and keep away predators. Some of the embers floated on the heat waves and were caught by the wind to be blown skyward, the tiny fire-points looking like more of the stars in the night sky.

Then he and Kelly went off into their tent and Steve and Carla went to theirs.

It broke his heart to know what they would be doing in that tent this night, but he knew there was nothing he could do about it.

With Kelly pulling him into the tent, he knew at least he'd be able to take his mind off of what was happening with a little meaningless sex of his own. Kelly was a nice girl, but he knew their relationship was doomed to failure, but at least it would be a nice ride until it ended.

The campers all crawled into their tents and with a wave to each other, zipped them up for a night of peace and quiet, secure in each others arms.

*   *   *

The half moon was high overhead in the night sky, the stars twinkling like a thousand diamonds.

Kelly unzipped the tent and crawled outside. She had to go to the bathroom. She'd been holding it for what seemed like hours, but had finally decided it was no use and had to go. Once she was standing up, she shrugged into her jacket to fight off the chill and walked to the perimeter of the campsite.

Her eyes darted around her nervously, every shadow perceived as a threat. Snoring floated on the air coming from Steve's tent. She assumed it was Steve, but knew it could also have been Carla. Kelly had known a few girls in her life that snored like a middle-aged trucker.

Finding a patch of leaves, she decided it was as good a place as any to do her business and squatted down to pee. While her bladder drained away the beer from the evening before, she stared out into the darkness, trying to pierce it with her will alone.

Then she heard a twig snap off to her right. She froze in mid-pee, too scared to move, while whatever was out there moved closer. If it was an animal, it was stealthy, with only the barest sound drifting to her ears while it made its way across the leaf-strewn ground.

For a second she wondered if she should stand up and run the six-feet back to the clearing, but remembered something about not running from an animal. She didn't know if it was correct, but it seemed like sound advice now.

Besides, she was so scared she didn't even know if her legs would move on command.

The animal moved closer and she was able to discern a large black shape, but no more. Then two yellow eyes pierced the darkness. The eyes were no more than a foot away from her and she couldn't imagine how the animal could have gotten so close without her seeing it better.

She felt its breath on her face. She tried to scream for help, but nothing came out of her mouth but a tiny squeak, barely discernable from the other sounds of the night.

The bear raised itself up on its hind legs, its once midnight-black fur now coated with a darker black, viscous substance. Kelly had the briefest sensation of seeing the paw come at her head, but terror and the darkness made it impossible to be sure.

Either way, one second she was staring up at this eight-foot hulking beast and the next second, she was knocked unconscious as the weight of the paw knocked her to the ground, her head striking a skull-sized rock imbedded in the earth.

The bear used its jaws to pull the unconscious woman across the loom, only the barest of blood dripping from her arm. The bear had other plans for Kelly than to rip her apart and feed on her. The essence inside the bear told it what it needed to do.

Bring her back to the pool so she, too, could become one with it.

As the crickets chirped and the night creatures scurried from their warrens, the bear dragged Kelly across the landscape; to a fate worse than death.

Twenty minutes later, Billy stirred in his sleeping bag. He leaned over, feeling for Kelly and was surprised to find her side of the tent was empty. He sat up, wiping sleep from his eyes and listened to the night.

Shrugging into his jacket, he climbed out of the tent. The fire had gone out, casting the entire clearing in gloom, only the half-moon giving any illumination at all.

Walking around the clearing, he called out to her.

"Kelly, are you there? What's the matter, you sick...Kelly?"

Nothing, no answer. He started to worry and so walked over to Steve's tent. Giving it a good shake, he waited for the angry voices within.

"It's me, Billy. Get up, will ya? Kelly's gone and I don't know where she is."

Steve's voice, groggy from sleep, came to him through the tent. "Shit, Billy, she's your girlfriend. What the hell do you want me to do about it?" He growled angrily.

"Well, for starters, help me look for her. If it was Carla missing, I'd help you," Billy pleaded.

A heavy sigh was heard in the tent followed by a rustling of clothes. A moment later the tent unzipped and Steve climbed out.

"Shit, it's cold out here," he said, pulling his coat on. His pants were already on and while Billy waited, Steve put on his boots.

"What's wrong, Steve, where're you going? It's night still," Carla's voice floated from the tent.

Billy was able to see past Steve into the tent. Carla was laying down, a sliver of moonlight bathing her upper body in its light. She was only wearing her bra and panties, and as Billy watched her, he felt a fluttering in his stomach, seeing the woman he loved half-naked.

Then Steve blocked his view and the moment was over.

Steve leaned back inside, "Kelly's missing and Billy wants my help to look for her, you can stay here if you want."

"No, wait for me, I want to help," Carla said, and then there was more motion in the tent while she struggled to get dressed in the small confines of the tent.

Three minutes later, she was standing in front of her tent waiting for the men to decide what to do.

Steve looked at Billy, his face barely discernable in the dark. "So what now, oh great white hunter? It's pitch black, I can't see shit."

"Come over to the fire pit, I'll get it started and we can use torches, plus, I have a small pocket flashlight for emergencies," Billy said, moving across the clearing to the campfire.

The others followed and ten minutes later the fire was burning bright, casting shadows across the clearing.

Steve looked around and yelled at the top of his lungs. "Kelly! Where are you! Come back to the campsite!"

"I already tried that, but she didn't answer." Billy said, worried about Kelly. She may not have been the love of his life, but she was a good person and he would never want anything bad to happen to her.

Carla stood closer to the campfire, her eyes reflecting the flame like she was a demon of the night.

"Look, no matter how bad we want to find her, there's no way we can do it in the dark, we have no choice but to wait until the sun's up. We can search for her then," Carla said rationally.

"She's got a point, Billy. It's pretty fuckin' dark out here, even if she's out there, how the hell could we find her?" Steve asked.

Billy wanted to argue, but knew they were right. To start running around the pitch black woods with not even a real weapon to defend themselves with was foolhardy.

Walking over to the log by the fire, he sighed.

"Shit, I know you're right, but I can't just stand here and do nothing. What if she's hurt?" Before Steve or Carla could answer, Billy continued. "Damn, this sucks, where the hell could she be?" Then he sat down, accepting his fate.

"Fine, we wait for sun-up, but the second there's light we go look for her, deal?" Billy asked.

Steve nodded yes along with Carla.

"Of course, little brother, the second it's light, we go."

Billy slumped on his seat, impatiently counting the minutes until they could start the search. As he looked up at the moon, slowly moving across the sky, he knew it wouldn't come soon enough to suit him.

Kelly came awake groggily, her body feeling every bump and rock as it was dragged across the forest floor.

It was still pitch dark and it seemed to her that she was being pulled by nothing more than shadows. Then the eyes looked at her and she knew she was in trouble. She screamed for help, but there was no answer. She had no idea how long she'd been out or how far away from the campsite she was.

She tried to pull her arm from the bear's mouth, but when it began to growl and squeeze her arm tighter in its jaws, she decided to stop, not wanting to make things worse.

Another hour went by and her back felt raw from being dragged across the rough landscape. Just as the sun was starting to rise, the large black bear stopped at a small, dark pool of water.

Lying on the ground, she had no idea as to the depth of the body of water. The bear dropped her arm and walked over to the edge and sat down.

She was about to try to get to her feet and run away when she was stopped in her tracks by a large deer. It, too, was covered from head to hoof in a black tar-like substance.

The deer's eyes flashed at her and from its mouth came a soft growl. The deer took a step toward her and she backed away, not realizing it, but moving closer to the depthless pool.

She thought about trying to run to the side of the pool, maybe she could run around the edge until she'd made it to the other side. Maybe then she could make a run for it or even just climb a tree.

The deer and the bear pushed her closer to the edge while in a nearby tree a large bird, covered in the same black ooze, squawked at her.

She took another step back; her foot only inches from the edge, when a black tentacle shot out and wrapped itself around her leg, knocking her shoe off.

She screamed in fright and tried to pull away, but the tentacle pulled harder, its elastic-like form starting to cut into her skin.

With blood running into her sock, her hands reached out for anything to stop her backwards progress, but there was nothing but loose leaves and gravel for her fingers to grasp.

Her lower body became immersed in the pool and she was surprised when it felt warm to the touch.

With arms flailing, she screamed for help, pleading that someone would come to her aid, but with the exception of the possessed animals, she was alone.

By now, only her head was above the surface, the black sludge surrounding her. She prayed to God that it would be painless and her head slipped under the black surface. Her eyes were open, though they saw nothing. She was holding her breath, knowing she only had a few minutes before her lungs would force her to exhale.

The liquid was warm and it reminded her of what it must have been like when she was still in the womb of her mother. Her eyes leaked tears that were lost in the blackness and she felt her lungs screaming for oxygen.

Despite knowing to breathe was to die, she had no choice and opened her mouth and sucked the dark fluid into her lungs.

At first she felt herself choking as the liquid filled her lungs instead of life giving oxygen, but then she felt a warmth suffuse her and she could have sworn she could hear someone talking to her.

The soft voice told her to relax, that she wouldn't be dying today, just simply transformed into something newer, better than she was. While she floated below the surface, she could now see through the eyes of the other animals. At first she was a deer, then a bear, and then she was soaring through the sky as an eagle.

Her inhibitions gone, she opened herself to the essence of the pool and let it fill her.

Soon she felt whole, like she had never felt before, when she was alive.

Slowly, the tendrils brought her back to the surface. Once there, she stood on her own legs again and walked out of the dark liquid.

She had a new purpose now; to find others like herself and bring them to the pool, so that they, too, could experience the joys of the darkness.

And if they resisted, she would kill them.

The sun was finally starting to rise, the night being banished from whence it came. Billy was on his feet, ready to go find his girlfriend.

Steve and Carla had actually managed to get more sleep despite the missing girl and to say Billy was upset about that was an understatement.

Walking to the edge of the clearing, he turned to the other two.

"All right, it's daylight, let's go. We've wasted enough time as it is," he said. "You two start over there and I'll go over here," he pointed across the clearing. "Walk back and forth and try to see any signs of a scuffle or blood or something like that."

Steve held his hand up in a salute. "Sure thing, Matlock."

Billy turned and walked back to Steve with fire in his eyes.

"You better cut that shit out right now, Steve, because so help me, I'll knock you on your ass. My girlfriend is out there somewhere and I have no idea if she's hurt or worse, so shape up and start helping or shut the fuck up."

Steve backed down, not used to seeing his mild brother so riled up.

"Whoa, little brother, I'm sorry. I didn't mean anything by it. Don't worry, man, we'll find her."

Carla stepped in and placed her hand on his arm. Despite everything he was feeling about Kelly, he still couldn't help but relish her touch.

"Don't worry, Billy, I'm sure she's okay, she probably just wandered off and got lost. That's all."

His anger exhausted, he calmed down a little, not the least because of Carla.

"Okay, I'm sorry, It's just....where the hell did she go last night?"

"Well, let's go find out," Steve said, moving off in the direction Billy had just directed him to go."

Billy looked askance at Carla and she smiled. "Don't worry, you'll see, everything's gonna be fine." Then she went off to catch up with Steve.

Billy watched her walk away, admiring her figure as it swayed under her jeans. Then he came to his senses and focused on the problem at hand, namely Kelly.

He started off to the perimeter of the clearing to try to find any signs of where she could have disappeared to.

Fifteen minutes later, Steve yelled to the others that he'd found something. Seconds later the others were all gathered around the site where Kelly had been knocked out by the bear.

"What could have done this, a wild animal?" Carla asked, looking at the disturbed leaves and the bloody rock, where Kelly had banged her head.

"Don't know, but it looks like she was dragged that way," Billy said, pointing deeper into the woods.

"The trail's easy enough to follow, so come on, let's go," he said, starting off.

Wait a sec, Billy. Let's pack our stuff up and follow the trail, that way we won't have to worry about coming back this way if we don't want to."

Billy mulled it over for a moment and then nodded. "All right, let's pack it up so we can go, we've wasted enough time as it is." Then he rushed back to the campsite to start gathering their things, with the others following.

Twenty minutes later, they were all packed and ready to go with Billy in the lead.

The trail was easy to follow; the leaves and branches pushed to the side like a giant had swept a two-foot path clear with a broom. Every now and then Billy would spot a maroon drop or two of blood on the leaves or in the path. His heart started to quicken at the thought that she was bleeding.

Steve came up behind him and rested a hand on his shoulder. "Don't worry buddy, we'll find her," he said.

Billy looked at him, the worry clearly evident in his eyes.

"Oh, I know we'll find her," he said. "The question is: what condition will she be in when we do?" He picked up his pace, leaving further discussion of the topic moot.

They walked in silence for a while, Billy feeling tired due to the fact he was carrying both his backpack and Kelly's and his lack of sleep.

Time went by and the sun rose higher into the sky, shining down on them with a cool light. The temperature continued to hover in the low fifties and the hikers were at least comfortable in their climate, although the sweat of exertion still made them warm. Billy could feel the sweat trickling down the small of his back, feeling like an insect under his shirt. It reminded him of a time when he was younger and a beetle had gotten under his clothes when he'd been playing in the grass. Brushing the distasteful memory aside, he picked up his pace a little more.

"Hey, Billy, how 'bout slowin' down some, my feet are killing me." Steve said through gasps.

"Come on, ya big baby, Kelly needs us," Carla said, passing Steve on the trail.

With Billy and Carla continuing up the trail left by Kelly, Steve sighed. Then he sucked it up and picked up his pace to catch up to the two of them.

An hour later, Billy slowed, his eyes scanning the forest floor nervously for signs of Kelly; the trail seeming to disappear. Moving closer on the trail, he saw a copse of trees surrounded by scattered boulders. Inside the depression in the land was a black pool of what must be water.

He stood watching it as his brother and Carla caught up to him.

They both saw him staring and their hopes went up.

"What do you see; is it Kelly?" Steve asked, but his expression changed when he saw the pool. "What the fuck is that, oil?" He said, moving closer to the pool.

"Don't know what it is," Billy said simply, his attention focused on looking for Kelly.

Carla followed Steve to the pool, making sure not to step in any of the black ooze on the ground near the edge. Then she saw Kelly's shoe and ran to the edge.

"Look what I found. It's Kelly's, isn't it?"

No sooner had Carla finished her question then a black tendril shot out of the lake and wrapped itself around her leg. She screamed when it starting pulling her into the water, her shoes losing purchase as she fell to the wet earth.

"Carla, oh my God, hold on!" Steve screamed and ran to her side. The second he was near the edge another tendril shot out and wrapped itself around his thigh, the pool pulling him toward its black depths.

Carla was forgotten now, Steve worrying about himself while he was pulled deeper into the dark water.

Billy was still at the edge of the boulders, never getting a chance to help Carla, Steve had moved so fast, but once he'd seen the second tendril wrap around his brother, he knew if he got too close then, he too, would be captured.

Spying a large tree branch that had fallen from a storm, he dragged it as close as he dared.

"Steve, grab this and I'll pull you free!" Billy yelled.

Steve reached for the branch, his hands wrapping around the bark and Billy started to pull. Carla gave one more scream and then her head disappeared under the surface.

"Carla no!" Billy screamed, watching her go under the obsidian surface. Then he had to focus on his brother. Heaving with all his might, he managed to pull Steve out of the black pool. Slowly, inch by inch, his brother was able to crawl free until he was totally out of the black fluid. With one final heave, Billy pulled him away from the edge and hopefully, safety.

Steve crawled on his hands and knees away from the pool, his breathing coming hard from exertion and fear. Another tendril shot out, searching for him, but missed him by inches as he continued to move farther away from the edge of the pool.

Then, from the other side of the pool, Billy saw Kelly. She appeared from behind a tree and started to walk towards Steve. Steve was too busy catching his breath to notice her yet, though, and she was able to come up behind him unannounced.

"Kelly, oh my God, I was so worried, are you okay?" Billy asked her when she was close enough. But she ignored him. She, too, was covered in black slime and she reached down and picked Steve up, holding him like he weighed next to nothing.

Steve let out one scream of shock, and then found himself flying through the air to land in the middle of the pool. He didn't actually sink, but seemed to be absorbed into the black water.

Billy screamed, watching the tableaux before him, helpless, but it all happened so fast there was nothing he could do. Then Kelly started towards him. He started to back away from her, wary of his feet tripping over a stray branch or rock.

"Shit, I don't believe this," he muttered to himself. "Kelly, you stay the fuck back, or else," he warned. "I don't know what's going on, but I know you just killed my brother!"

She ignored him and kept coming, an evil grin on her face. As she moved closer, Billy could see her once blue eyes had turned yellow. Why this had happened, he had no idea, but it still added to the weirdness of the situation.

Billy reached down and pulled his survival knife. The six-inch blade wasn't much, but it was all he had.

Behind Kelly he heard a growl, it sounded like a bear or a large cat. Something he definitely didn't want to mess with. And then the bear showed itself from the copse of bushes surrounding the pool. Even if he got away from Kelly, the bear could easily track him down and do God knows what to his body.

"I'm warning you. If you don't stay away, you'll be sorry!" He yelled at her.

She was only a few feet away and still advancing. Billy was debating if he should turn and make a run for it when his foot caught on an exposed root and he went tumbling backward. With a startled cry, he fell to the soft earth with Kelly jumping for him at the same time.

The woman expected a standing opponent and was thrown off-guard when he fell backward. She fell on top of him and Billy let out another scream.

Four heart pounding seconds went by and Kelly didn't move.

Finally, Billy pushed her off and discovered when she'd fallen on top of him she had impaled herself on his hunting knife.

Pushing her away, Billy noticed the one inch gash in her chest. Instead of blood pouring from the wound, a black slippery substance shot forth into the air with the beating of her heart. As more of the liquid left her body, the lesser the deluge, until only a trickle was left.

Kelly looked at him with her yellow eyes and tried to speak, but it was too late. Her head dropped down into the leaves and moss and she remained still.

Billy lay there next to her, not believing what had just happened, when the bear roared again.

That broke him from his stupor and he climbed to his feet and ran. The bear chased him, its large legs eating up the distance between them and Billy knew any second he would feel the weight of the bear on his back when it pulled him to the ground.

Up ahead was open sky and Billy realized he was running towards a cliff.

With a quick look over his shoulder, he saw the bear closing the distance between them and he ran a little faster, his heart pounding in his chest like a jackhammer. The only reason he was still moving so fast, and at speed, was because of all the adrenaline pouring through his system, but he knew that wouldn't last forever. He needed a way to lose the bear and with the cliff fast approaching, an idea struck him.

Seeing the edge of the cliff come into view, he only hoped his idea would be enough.

Running as fast as he could until he neared the edge, he slammed on the brakes, his boots sliding in the turf until he was almost directly at the edge of the cliff. Looking below, he saw only jagged rocks and broken trees that had fallen when the soil had eroded at the edge.

The bear was still coming, the black slime covering it seeming to absorb the sunlight like a sponge. He watched the bear's fur ripple as the powerful muscles propelled the animal forward at top speed.

Just when the bear would have clawed him or tried to bite him, he stepped backward and fell straight down. As soon as his head passed the edge of the cliff, he reached out with his hands to grab something, anything, which would prevent him from plummeting to the rocks below.

The bear flew into the air; unaware until it was too late that it had run out of earth. It soared out over the cliff and then curved downward to land on the rocks below.

Billy had managed to grip some tree roots and he looked down to see the bear plummeting downward. The bear exploded on impact, the weight of it, plus the height, more than enough to break open the bear's rough hide.

Black fluid shot into the air, the bear's organs covering the surrounding rocks, the animal dead on impact.

With his breath rasping in his throat, he hung there and watched, barely believing his trick had worked. Then with arms that felt like lead pipes, he started the arduous task of climbing back up the cliff to the edge above.

He still needed to check on his brother and Carla, maybe they had made it out of the pool and were okay.

With the sun shining high in the sky, he continued to make progress up the cliff face, confident in himself that he had the determination to make it.

*　　*　　*

A few minutes later, a dirty hand shot over the edge of the cliff, followed by another hand. Then a head popped up and with a grunt of pain, Billy pulled himself over the lip and back onto solid ground. He lay there panting, relieved to be safe again. Still not believing what had transpired in the last hour, even though he had experienced it first hand.

He lay there for the next five minutes, until he felt confident that he had his breath again.

Standing on wobbly legs, he started back to the pool. On the return trip, he came across Kelly, the blade still in the dirt where he'd dropped it. He reached down with his free hand and closed her staring eyes, thinking it was the least he could do.

Standing back up, he wondered what the hell he was going to tell the police when he returned to civilization. Personally, he didn't want to spend the rest of his life in jail for murder nor did he want to try to explain how a pool of water sucked his brother and girlfriend down under its surface.

He decided to compromise. Picking Kelly's body up, he carried her back to the pool. Though it broke his heart, he got as close as he thought he could and tossed her body at the dark surface, his toss coming up short.

No sooner had her body landed in the mud then a tendril shot out and wrapped itself around her neck. Then with pulling motions, the tendril pulled Kelly back into the pool until nothing remained but a small ripple on the surface.

Billy sat on a boulder and sobbed now that he finally had a chance. He didn't know what he was weeping about exactly, he had so much to choose from, but he knew he needed to let it out before he went mad.

The tears rolled down his cheeks and he thought about his brother and the woman he loved, and even Kelly. She didn't deserve to die.

From across the pool, a deer showed up and an eagle settled on a neighboring tree branch.

Billy took one look at them and knew they were one of the others, like the bear...and Kelly. He stood up and waved the knife at them.

"Fuck off, ya hear me! If you screw with me I'll do to you what I did to them!" He screamed, pointing to the pool.

The deer held its ground, for whatever reason, Billy had no idea.

He sat on the boulder, watching them as they watched him. Then the surface of the pool rippled and small bubbles formed on its surface. As Billy watched, two heads broke the surface and started to move towards him. The faces were covered in black slime, but it was still easy for Billy to tell who those faces belonged to.

It was his brother and Carla.

Slowly, their shoulders broke the surface, the two bodies walking out of the pool in torpid movements.

Billy watched in horror, knowing that it was impossible. They had been under water for almost an hour.

He hated to admit it, but they were dead.

The couple stepped fully out of the water, their shoes standing in the mud at the edge of the rippling fluid. Slime dripped from their bodies to collect around them, and then the slime would flow back into the pool where it had originated.

Both faces turned to look at Billy and their eyes flashed yellow in the sun.

Billy slid off the boulder and backed away. The two slime covered corpses followed. He was preparing to run when the deer blocked his path, its antlers more than enough to slow him down, if not seriously hurt him.

Other animals appeared from the woods around him.

A raccoon with a black slime covered coat and a group of squirrels, their dark black fur glistening in the sunlight. Even a small field mouse sat on a nearby rock; its nose twitching in his direction. It moved across the rock, leaving a black slime trail in its wake, small yellow eyes watching him.

He was surrounded and though he might have escaped the bear. He knew he'd never escape the combined gathering of dozens of the forest creatures, plus the bodies of his brother and Carla.

But run he did. There was a small hole in the line of animals to his right and he ran for it. The deer was closest and it lowered its head to maul him. At the last moment, he twisted his body like an acrobat and avoided the point of the deer's antlers.

Then he was free with nothing but woods in front of him.

With the adrenaline pumping again, his aches and pains forgotten, he ran as fast as he could, hearing the animals behind him.

He ran for as long as he could, sometimes losing them and sometimes not. It seemed unlikely that he could outrun a deer in its own habitat, but it seemed he was.

He idly wondered if they were playing with him.

He slowed down for a moment and listened to the forest. There was nothing behind him. He didn't know how he'd lost them, but he was just glad he had, still too tired to really think it through.

He continued walking deeper into the forest, further away from any signs of man.

Hours later, the sun was starting to set and he decided he needed to find shelter for the night.

Looking while he walked, he soon found a small cave hidden from view amid a copse of bushes. Checking to make sure he wasn't followed, he climbed inside and wrapped his arms around his knees for warmth. The sky darkened and night fell. He awoke to realize he'd fallen asleep, the day's events catching up to him. Feeling safe in his warren, he figured he'd just stay put for as long as he could. If they didn't find him, in another day he could leave and sneak back to his car and civilization.

He sat in the cave, listening to the crickets surrounding the outside of the cave opening. His heart slowed down and he let himself relax, finally feeling he was truly safe, that the terrible ordeal was over.

He thought about his brother and Carla. Kelly floated into his thoughts and he realized she really had been a wonderful woman and maybe he could find happiness with someone other than Carla. He'd have to now, as the woman he'd loved so deeply was some kind of demon.

Sitting there in the dark, he realized how short life was and that you had to live every day as if it was your last. He felt himself drifting off to sleep again and he let it take him.

The darkness covered the land, the forest growing still for the night, the birds and animals bedding down for the night.

While Billy lay sleeping, the crickets grew quiet, a preternatural silence descending on the forest.

Outside the cave, shadows began to form around the opening and the sounds of snapping twigs cracked through the silent forest.

Inside the cave, Billy remained asleep, oblivious, dreaming about future possibilities.

Three Days To Die

James Masterson woke up screaming.

Looking around the room, he realized he was in a hospital room, complete with a heart machine and pumps. A tube went into his mouth and down his throat and an IV unit dripped into his right arm. A thin plastic oxygen tube sat under his nose. Most of the wires trailed off the machines and then ran along the floor until they plugged into his body. There were more holes in him than he'd care to count. His right leg and left arm were in casts and if he was correct, then the bandages wrapped tight around his middle meant that he had at least one broken rib, although he was pretty sure it was more than one.

One of the monitors had a picture of his lungs on it. Every time he breathed in or exhaled, the lungs would show a blue or red color, depending upon intake or exhales.

The funny thing was he didn't feel any of the pain you'd usually associate with being in a hospital bed with the amount of damage he seemed to have suffered.

He tried to sit up in bed, but his body didn't respond. That was strange.

"Oh my God, I'm paralyzed," he gasped. But if he was paralyzed, then why could he talk even with a tube in his mouth?

He tried again. "One, two, three, four, the mouse went out the door," he said. He'd spoken the first thing that had popped into his head. It was part of a nursery rhyme his mother used to sing to him before bed. He could hear himself clearly. He looked in the reflection of one of the machines, the polished metal acting like a mirror.

There he was, lying in bed. His eyes were open, seeing nothing, his chest rising and falling in a steady rhythm.

Or at least that's what the doctor's must have thought. Although it seemed hard to believe, he seemed to be in some form of astral projection. He was still connected to his body, though. He was still stuck in this hospital room, but he could see and hear everything that was going on around him.

Then a nurse walked into the room.

Seeing her, James went back into his body and tried to sit up again. "Oh, thank God, there's something seriously wrong with me. Can you help me please?"

The nurse ignored him. She was checking his readouts on one of the machines and acted like he wasn't even talking to her.

"Hello? What the hell is going on around here? Why won't anyone answer me?"

It was at that moment that his wife walked into the room, followed by a doctor.

"Oh, God, honey, I'm so glad to see you, these quacks won't talk to me?"

That was when he noticed she was crying.

"Honey, what's wrong? Why are you crying? Look, I'm fine," he said, trying to wave his arms in the air. But no matter how hard he tried, they just wouldn't move.

The doctor was talking to his wife. Amy looked horrible, the bags under her eyes making her look like she hadn't slept in days. He stopped trying to move and talk and just listened to what the doctor was telling her.

"I'm so sorry, Mrs. Masterson, but I'm afraid your husband has suffered a terrible head trauma. His brain function has almost completely ceased. The swelling in his brain has gone down leaving irreparable brain damage. Though not *actually* brain dead, for all intents and purposes he's as close as someone can be without actually being brain dead. The odds of him waking up are too high to even calculate. Do I make myself clear? I know it's a little difficult to swallow." The doctor placed his hand on her shoulder, consoling her.

"What! Brain dead, but that's impossible!" James screamed, but no one could hear him but himself.

Amy nodded, understanding. "So there's no chance of him waking up?"

"No, I'm afraid not. He'd have a better chance of hitting the million dollar lottery." He gestured to all the machines connected to James. "See all these machines? They're the only thing keeping your husband alive." He looked down at the floor, seeming to inspect his shoes. "Look, Mrs. Masterson, I don't want to sound callous, but have you decided what you want to do about keeping him on life support? As you know, your insurance is picking up the tab, for now, but they usually fight cases where the patient has no hope of recovery"

Amy nodded, wiping her nose with a tissue. "Yes, Doctor. James always told me if he was ever in a state like the one he's in now, with no possible hope of recovery, that he wanted me to pull the plug."

"*I did what*!" James ranted. "I never said that, hell, I said that *no matter what, don't pull the plug*. If there was ever a chance I could come back, I wanted it," he ranted to no one but himself.

"All right, Mrs. Masterson, but there's still a three day waiting period before we can cease all life functions by shutting down the machines. Until then, I'm afraid you'll just have to wait. Also, you'll need to contact your attorney. You need to find out if James had a living will, items such as that."

"But he would have wanted me to pull the plug as soon as possible, Doctor, isn't there any way around it?"

The doctor shook his head no. "I'm sorry, Mrs. Masterson, but its hospital policy.

"It's only three days. I'm sure your husband would understand."

Wiping tears from her eyes, she smiled wanly. "I guess so. Rules are rules, I suppose. I'm sure they're in place for a good reason."

"Exactly, if your husband was to miraculously regain consciousness, it usually happens in the first seventy-two hours." Checking his watch, the doctor moved to the doorway. "Well, I'm needed elsewhere. If you have any questions, please don't hesitate to call me. Unless I'm in surgery, I'll be more than happy to talk to you. Once again, I'm so sorry for your loss."

Then the doctor walked out of the room, leaving James alone with his wife.

The second the doctor was gone, Amy's tears dried up like a puddle in the desert.

With her face set in stone, she looked down at James. With a voice filled with venom, she whispered into his ear. "Three days my love, and then it's the great beyond for you. Until then, enjoy your stay. After all, it's your insurance that's paying for it." Then she turned around, her hair swinging over her shoulder and walked out of the room, her sadness gone like a birthday cake at a fat kid's birthday party.

He watched her go with eyes that shouldn't be seeing. That was when reality flooded back to him and he realized that he was in a hospital.

How the hell did that happen? He tried to remember the last thing he'd done before waking up in the hospital bed, but it was all a blank.

Did Amy have something to do with it? Was that why she was so eager to pull the plug?

Why was she acting so cruel? She was like a badly written character in a murder mystery. Until waking up in bed, here, today, he had thought he had the perfect marriage; but he was wrong.

Dead wrong, to coin a pun.

Trying to remember what had happened, he still was drawing a blank. Must have something to do with his head trauma, he guessed.

He'd just have to go back to the last thing he remembered doing, and then hopefully, he could move forward with the timeline until he came to the part where he had some kind of catastrophic accident and wound up brain dead in the hospital.

Trying to think back to his most recent memory, he failed miserably. He decided he better work harder at it.

He was on a deadline. He had seventy-two hours to piece together what had happened to him, before they put him to sleep forever like a sick pet. He had to concentrate.

He had only three days to solve his own murder before he died. If that wasn't a motivator, then he didn't know what was.

DAY ONE

The day was already more than half over. James had racked his brain for hours, but nothing would come back to him.

He remembered the morning of two days ago, though. He had risen at 7:30 in the morning, had gone for a quick two mile run and had then returned home. He had showered, shaved and had then gone to work, stopping at Dunkins to get a coffee and a bagel.

He was an office manager for a finance company in the city and had spent his traditional hour in traffic until arriving at work at 8:55 AM. Then he'd spent the day working. Nothing unusual there, though.

He did remember it was odd, how when he'd arrived home his wife had left him a note on the fridge, saying she was out with the girls.

But later, after he'd taken a shower, the phone had rung. It had been one of his wife's girlfriends. She was looking for Amy. He'd told her that she was out with the girls and that shouldn't she have been with them?

She said that she had no idea what he was talking about and to have Amy call her when she got in.

Around 11:00 PM, Amy had strolled in. James had questioned her, but she had brushed it off as a misunderstanding and had gone to bed.

He still hadn't given it much thought, although now that he thought back, he had tried to fool around with her later in the night when he had gone to bed and she had said she wasn't in the mood.

That was strange. They hadn't been intimate in more than a week. She should have been as horny as he was, but instead, she had gone to sleep, a pleasant smile on her face.

He was brought out of his reverie when a man in a suit walked in, followed by Amy. The man was talking to her.

"Let me say again how sorry I am about your husband, Mrs. Masterson," the suited man said.

Amy nodded politely. "Thank you, Lieutenant, and please, call me Amy."

"All right…Amy. There are still a few things I'd like to go over with you about your husband's accident. When would be a good time?"

Amy feigned sadness and started what James knew to be crocodile tears.

"Oh, Lieutenant, could I come down to the station tomorrow? Right now I'd just like to spend some of the last minutes I'll ever get with my James. Alone, if you don't mind."

The Lieutenant's eyes looked down as if he was studying his shoes.

"Of course, Amy, there are just a few follow up questions, that's all. A formality really. We've already ruled your husband's car crash as accidental, due to drinking while intoxicated."

"*A car crash while drunk*! But I have no recollections of a car crash and I've never touched a drop in my life. Well, except the occasional one at New Years or Christmas. But I absolutely never drink if I'm driving, not even one. The drunk driving laws are too damn tough in this state."

Now he knew something was off, even if Amy hadn't whispered deadly sweet nothings into his ear. But he had to figure out what had happened. If he was going to die, then at least God could give him that much.

Once the Lieutenant had left, Amy stuck around for another fifteen minutes. Then she leaned over and pretended she was going to kiss him, but instead, she whispered in his ear.

"I know you can't hear me, being brain dead and all, but it just gives me a tingle to think there's some part of you that might hear me. Two and a half days to go, dear. Now if you'll excuse me, I have a date." Then she stood up, fixed her dress in the mirror, checked her makeup and left.

Inside, James was fuming. "That bitch, I'm not even dead yet at her own hands and she's already running around on me," he hissed out of a mouth that wouldn't move.

He decided he needed to concentrate more, he had to; the clock was ticking on his death warrant.

The rest of the day and night were unexceptional. The nurse would come in and check his vitals and once another nurse came in and gave him a quick sponge bath. But it wasn't anything great, not like you hear about in stories about nurse's sponge baths. Frankly, he thought the nurse was just going through the motions, due to the fact that he was getting his ticket punched in less than three days.

Sometime in the night, they changed his pee bag and then it was lights out. He sat there in the dark, still racking his brain. He wasn't tired. In fact, he didn't even feel he needed to sleep at all.

That was odd. Here he was brain dead and he didn't even sleep.

He lay there in the dark, listening to the machines keeping him alive.

At least for two more days.

DAY TWO

The next morning was uneventful, at least until Amy showed up with his best friend and next door neighbor, Frank. Frank was wearing sunglasses with dark lenses.

Frank's face looked like he had just did five rounds with Rocky, the black eye the most prominent feature on his face; even the sunglasses not large enough to hide the shiner.

As they walked into the room, James saw that Frank looked solemn. He walked to the bed and leaned over and looked at James in the face. Snapping his fingers in front of James' face, he soon stopped and looked at Amy.

"He's really gone, huh? His brain is fried?"

Amy nodded. "That's what the doctors say. He's technically brain dead. The chance he'll ever come out of it is one in a million, or something like that. Let's just say the odds are ridiculous. He'd have a better chance of hitting the lottery."

"That's great, I like those odds. Once he's dead, we'll take the life insurance money and Aruba here we come." Frank reached out to grab Amy, but she slapped his hand away.

"No! Not here. Here I'm a grieving widow. When we get home, I'll be your sex slave," she said, with a wiggle to her nose.

If James was able, he would have dropped his jaw onto the floor. His wife and his best friend? It was like one of those really bad soap operas on television in the daytime. And to top it all off, they killed off the troublesome husband for the insurance money. You couldn't get any more cliché than that.

But the worst thing of all was they were going to get away with it. But how?

How he had wound up in his present predicament was still the mystery question.

After only ten minutes, they began getting ready to leave.

"Come on, babe, I've got to go down to the police station and talk to that cop again," Amy said, putting her jacket on.

"Oh, shit, there's not a problem, is there?" Frank asked, looking nervous.

She shook her head no. "No, babe, everything's fine. They said I have to answer some follow up questions, its all routine for this kind of thing."

Frank looked relieved. "Oh, okay, you had me worried there for a minute."

Amy walked close to Frank and leaned so close she could feel his breath on her face, then, glancing over her shoulder in the hall to check if the coast was clear, she gave him a sensual, but quick kiss on his mouth.

"Don't worry, baby, everything's moving along as planned. Just stay calm and let Mommy handle it."

Then she disengaged herself and walked out of the hospital room, with Frank following like a love sick puppy dog.

When James was alone again, he was fuming.

But no matter how much he ranted, he was still helpless.

Time went by and he calmed down a little. What choice did he have? Besides, he needed to stay focused if he wanted to remember what had happened to him.

He concentrated, trying to remember the events of the day before his accident and slowly, they came into focus.

The morning had been the same routine as always and his day at work was nothing unusual. Except for when he had called home to talk to his wife. He had gotten an idea that he could pick up some take-out and they could have a romantic dinner together, but when he had called, no one answered. He'd tried back two more times in the next ten minutes and finally, on the last ring, on the third try, she had answered the phone.

"Hello?" She'd said, breathing heavily.

"Honey? Hi, it's James. What's wrong? You sound out of breath?"

"Umm, hi, James. I, uh, was just out jogging."

"Jogging, since when?"

"Since this morning, I thought I'd do it, too, and then we could jog together."

"Wow, that's great. Listen, I thought I'd bring home some take-out and then maybe we could..." He stopped talking when he thought he heard a man's voice.

"Honey," he asked. "Is someone there with you?"

There was a flutter of activity on the phone, but it was all muffled due to the phone being jammed into Amy's chest. Within seconds, she was back on the line, acting as if nothing had happened.

"No, honey, no one's here, it was just the television. When the commercial came on, it was louder than the show. I turned it off, that's all," she answered.

James was about to ask her something else when one of his assistants had walked into his office and distracted him.

"Oh, damn, honey, something just came up here at work, I gotta go. I'll see you tonight, love ya," James said, hanging up the phone.

"Okay, James, bye."

When she'd hung up, he hadn't given it much thought, but she hadn't said I love you back. While that shouldn't have seemed odd at the time, it now sent a red flag in front of his eyes.

Coming back to the present, he started to put the puzzle pieces together. So there was someone in the house with her and that was why she was out of breath. They had just had sex in his bed. It must have been Frank with her, unless she was even more of a slut than he thought.

Now the rest of the day came back to him.

The rest of the work day had gone smoothly and he had returned home a little earlier than usual.

Two hours earlier to be exact.

He had picked up some Chinese take-out on his way home and had thought to surprise her. Instead he had walked into an empty house...or so he thought.

He started to hear a faint banging sound coming from upstairs and he placed the food down on an end table and slowly walked up the stairs.

The noise grew louder the closer he came to his bedroom. The door was open a few inches and he walked up to it and looked inside.

When he did, it felt as if his heart had been pulled out of his chest by an icy hand.

There was his wife, on her back and his best friend was on top of her going to town.

She was yelling in pleasure and for just a moment, James realized that she had never been that animated when they had made love together.

He pushed the door open a little more and as it swung inward; his body cast a shadow onto the two grinding bodies on the bed.

Amy's head moved to the side and that was when she saw him.

"Oh, shit, James. What the hell are you doing here? It's only three?"

James was in his own world, too shocked to think clearly.

"Thought I'd come home a little early, surprise you. Guess I'm the one who got the surprise, huh?" He said quietly.

Frank had jumped off the bed and was hastily getting dressed. Then the man walked over to James and smiled.

"Hey, buddy, I'm really sorry about this. This stuff just happens sometimes, you know?"

James turned to walk out of the room. Despite feeling betrayed, he still had a level head and his analytical mind took over.

"Fine, if you two want to be together, then it's fine with me. I just wish you had had the morals to tell me what you felt about each other instead of sneaking around behind my back. Unless that's what made it fun, knowing you were lying to me."

He walked out of the room and started down the stairs.

"I'll start the divorce papers tomorrow, but be assured by cheating on me; you'll get nothing; especially not alimony."

Amy threw on a nightgown and followed him downstairs.

"James, wait. Be reasonable," she pleaded.

He stopped at the bottom of the stairs and looked up at her. "Reasonable? How the hell can you say that after I just caught you screwing in our bed?"

Frank slipped by Amy and walked down the stairs until he was face to face with James.

"Now, hold on. I said I was sorry, there's no reason to treat her like that," Frank said.

"What! Are you really serious? You don't even care that I caught you, do you? Don't you even feel guilty?"

James turned away and started for the door with Amy running after him.

"James wait, I'm sorry," she said, grabbing his arm before he could open the front door.

"Get away from me!" James yelled.

Disgusted, he pushed her away. A little harder than he would have preferred, but he was angry. She fell away from him and hit the hardwood floor with a smack, her nose bouncing off the polished hardwood floor.

The impact was just enough to give her a nose bleed. She sat up with blood running down her face, where it dripped from her chin to pool on the shiny wood surface of their custom-installed floor.

James saw the blood and was about to apologize when he saw stars and his head was rocked back against the front door. His head bounced off the door and he leaned against it, dazed and confused.

Frank had seen the woman he loved on the floor, bleeding and the man had jumped into action. He had sent an uppercut into James face that had stopped him cold.

James swayed like a drunk at last call until his faculties came back to him.

Thoughts of reason were gone and he saw red. He charged at Frank, his head down like a bull. The two men fell to the floor with a crash of furniture, their arms and legs flailing around them. The take-out was knocked to the floor from its perch on an end table, the boxes becoming crushed and broken. The smell of fried rice and chicken fingers filled the room.

James was able to get the upper hand and managed to straddle the dazed Frank. James sent punch after punch at the man's face.

Suddenly, James felt something strike the back of his head and he went down like a felled ox.

He lay on the floor, barely conscious, watching his wife and Frank.

Frank raised himself from the floor and when he looked up, he freaked.

Amy was standing over James, holding a hammer she'd found across the room.

James had left it there after deciding he'd hang the new picture he'd bought the other day. Now as he lay on the floor with a concussion, he wondered if he'd ever get that chance.

"What the hell did you do?" Frank yelled, taking the hammer from Amy and moving away. There was some blood on the tip and as Frank pulled it away, some of the drops fell to the floor. He looked at the weapon in his hand and then went over to the couch and shoved it under one of the cushions.

He'd deal with the tool later. One thing at a time.

Frank knelt down on one knee and checked James, sighing with relief. His pulse was weak, but stable.

"We've got to call an ambulance. He's hurt. Why'd you do that?" Frank asked of Amy.

With tears in her eyes, she just shrugged. "I don't know, I saw him on top of you, beating you, and then I saw the hammer. I didn't think; I just didn't want him to keep punching you." She started to cry harder and Frank pulled her close, hugging her.

Meanwhile James was floating in and out of consciousness on the floor.

Frank moved away from her and reached for the phone. He started dialing. He'd pressed 9-1, but was stopped before he could press the last number when Amy pressed the button on the phone, canceling the call.

"Wait," she said. Her tears seemed to be stopping and she was starting to get control of herself. "If we call the cops, you or me or both are gonna end up in jail for assault, or worse. Do you want that?"

Frank shook his head. "Hell, no, besides, you know I got in that bar fight a few years ago. They'll use that against me."

She smiled. "Exactly. We have the perfect opportunity here to fix a problem." She thought for a moment, her finger tapping her chin; then she smiled.

"I got it, I know what to do. We can make his injuries look like an accident."

"What, are you serious? You mean kill him?"

She moved closer to him and being careful not to touch any of his bruises, she caressed his face while her other hand moved under his pants.

"You want to be with me, don't you?" She purred, while giving him little kisses.

"You know I do," he said simply.

"Then help me do this, and we'll be together forever. And best of all, we'll get the life insurance money when he's dead."

Franks one good eye lifted in interest, the other swelling up, thanks to James. "Oh, yeah, how much?"

"One million dollars," she said, emphasizing each word with a kiss to Frank's neck.

"We took out the policy a few years ago, so it won't look fishy when I collect it."

James groaned on the floor and Frank looked down at him.

Amy was rubbing him hard and he couldn't believe despite what had happened in the past hour that he was now erect. But it was when she lowered herself to her knees and started to really give it to him, that his hesitation vanished.

As he exploded into her mouth, he gasped. "All right, I'm in. Oh, God that was great."

She stood up and wiped her mouth. "There's plenty more where that came from, baby. I promise. Now here's what we'll do."

James lay on the floor, falling in and out of consciousness, but he had managed to hear almost the entire twisted plan to kill him.

Now, lying in his hospital bed, the night before came into focus, as if a trap door had finally been opened and the memories were flooding through.

He remembered the night his wife and best friend put into motion the events that would eventually kill him. He lay in his bed, staring up at the ceiling, knowing that they were going to get away with it, too.

The nurses had changed shifts and darkness had fallen outside his one window.

Tomorrow they would disconnect the machines keeping him alive and he would die. Despite saying God this and oh my God that, he wasn't really a religious man, although now, as he waited to die, he sure as hell hoped there was something to go to after his body ceased to function.

He wondered how many other atheists changed their tune when it was their time to go. As he lay in his bed and the nurses out in the hallway went about their business, one small tear rolled down his cheek.

No one saw it and even if they had, it would have been dismissed as non-relevant, but James knew what it was.

It was him crying. His soul was crying, even though his body wouldn't let him.

DAY THREE

The morning of his last day on earth was unexceptional. The nurses went to and from the nurse's station, delivering medicine and changing bedpans.

James passed the morning remembering what had happened the night his wife and friend had plotted to kill him.

After Amy had explained what she wanted to do, Frank, like the good little lackey, had nodded his head and picked James off the floor, a small amount of his blood spreading on the floor.

James groaned some more, trying to tell them to stop what they were doing, but all that came out of his mouth were moans and wheezing.

Carrying his body to the garage, Frank placed him in the passenger seat, and then he returned to check on Amy.

He had no idea how long he'd sat there waiting for them to return, but finally, Amy had shown up again. She was carrying a brown shopping bag and when she set it on the floor next to his feet; he heard the distinctive sound of rattling glass bottles.

Opening the garage, she pulled out onto the street. It was late fall and the sun had set hours ago. Starting down the street, she paused in the road and waited while Frank pulled out of his own driveway and then followed her. What James didn't realize was that it was well past midnight, the roads quiet in their little piece of suburbia

They drove for about a half hour, until Amy pulled over to the side of the road and turned off the engine.

The stretch of highway she'd picked was empty, the road leading up to an abandoned electrical transformer. In the distance, the twinkling lights of the city could be seen, looking like stars that had fallen to earth and had decided to hover above the ground.

Frank pulled up behind her and jumped out of the car with the slamming of the vehicle's door. Amy opened the bag she'd brought with her.

Inside were empty beer bottles, which she tossed around the car, then she pulled out a bottle of Rum. She made him drink more than half of it. He was too dazed to stop her and just swallowed out of reflex. When she was satisfied, she poured a little on his shirt and then dropped the bottle on the floor where it promptly rolled under the front seat.

A car's headlights came around the bend in the road and Amy pulled Frank to her and started to kiss him passionately. The car slowed a little as it passed them, but once the driver saw the two of them making out, the old woman in the car stepped on the gas and sped away down the road, a disgusted look carved on her face.

Amy pushed Frank away and then went to James.

"Help me put him in the driver's seat," she called to Frank.

Frank went to the passenger side and in a matter of minutes; James was behind the steering wheel.

He moaned again, louder this time, and Frank got nervous.

"Oh, shit, I think he's comin' around."

"Doesn't matter," Amy said. "In a few minutes he's gonna be toast. Just make sure the coast is clear. I didn't do all this to get caught now," she snapped.

Then she started the car again and put the vehicle in drive. She ran with the car for a few seconds, making sure the vehicle was lined up with the yellow line in the middle of the road, then she let go and watched. Her chest heaved with the exertion of her present activities.

James was starting to come around, although the half bottle of Rum wasn't helping. He opened his eyes just as the car reached the end of the road, where it curved sharply to the left. The car, without anyone to steer it, continued going straight, until it went over the side.

James felt his body being thrown around like a rag doll, the car turning over and over; descending the two stories down the embankment. The grade of the hill was enough to keep the car connected to the earth, but not enough to keep it from rolling like a child's matchbox car.

With the sound of crunching metal and shattered glass, the car came to rest at the bottom of the ravine. James was unconscious again and this time he wouldn't be waking up. His head had taken a beating. His brain had been slammed against the front and back of his cranium like a bad case of shaken baby syndrome.

He lay there with half his body hanging out of the shattered driver's window, his breath coming in shallow gulps. A bird flew by, ignoring the mangled car beneath it, the starlight reflecting off the spinning hubcap still attached to the rear wheel of the car.

Frank pulled up with his car and Amy hopped in. While Frank drove off, away from the accident, she smiled.

"Now to go home and play the worried wife. I don't want to see you for a while, at least not until they find him."

"You mean if they find him. That ravine's pretty steep. No one will see him unless they know to look down there."

"Not to worry," she grinned mischievously. "I left his cell phone on in his jacket pocket. The cops should be able to find him by that. Once I get home, I'll start making calls to him. You know; the worried wife and all that."

Frank looked at her. For just a moment he saw who she really was.

"Jesus, Amy, you're evil, you know that?"

She smiled at him, her eyes reflecting the headlights as another car passed them on the other side of the road.

"Not evil, smart, and don't you forget it. Listen to me and we'll be fine. Now, let's go home. I want to be there so I can call his cell."

Frank nodded and stepped on the gas just a little more. His hands gripped the steering wheel so hard his knuckles started to turn white. Amy didn't seem to notice, since she concentrated on looking out her window at the world flashing by.

While driving, frank wondered if he had just made a deal with the devil that he would eventually regret.

DAY THREE—THE END

That afternoon Amy arrived with her lawyer. A few minutes later two doctors and a nurse arrived as well. The Lieutenant was there also and Amy started to talk to him.

"Thank you for coming, Lieutenant, you didn't have to."

The man smiled. "It's okay Mrs. Masterson, I wanted to be here, besides, we had a mugging this morning and my victim is upstairs in emergency. I need to get a statement from her."

"Oh, I see. Well, thank you anyway." Amy looked out into the hallway and saw another uniformed policeman. For just a moment her heart skipped a beat.

The Lieutenant saw her looking at the uniformed officer and smiled at her.

"He's with me; for the mugging victim."

Amy nodded and breathed a sigh of relief inside.

She looked at the doctors. "Well, can we get this show on the road?"

The doctor nearest her was taken aback by her callousness, but he had seen different people deal with loss in different ways. The hospital staff prepared to turn off the machines.

James was screaming inside. *"They can't kill me!"* He screamed. *"I'm not ready to die yet! Wait, I'm still in here!"*

He was thrashing inside, his mind fighting with everything he had. He fought with all of his being to somehow wake up.

Fingers were reaching for buttons, the doctors preparing to kill him.

James let loose a scream that would have shaken the hospital to its core if he could have vocalized it with his corporeal mouth. Then he lay back exhausted. Waiting to die.

Suddenly the machine that read his brainwaves started to beep. Hands were removed from switches and the doctors gathered around the machine.

The men stood there conferring with each other, while Amy looked on nervously.

"What, what's going on, what's happening. Is he dead?" She asked.

"On the contrary," one of the doctors said with a wide smile. "It's a miracle, he has brain function. His brain is coming back online, so to speak. Nurse, turn off those machines, we need to let his brain take over. The conflict could be catastrophic."

"Yes, doctor," the nurse said and proceeded to start disconnecting tubes.

Amy looked around the room. "What? No, this can't be happening, not now."

The Lieutenant looked puzzled. "Why, what's wrong, aren't you happy? Your husband is going to live."

She looked up at him. "What? Of course I'm happy, just shocked, that's all."

Then one of the doctors spoke up. "He's coming awake. Hello, James, do you know where you are?"

Everyone in the room stood around him, amazed that he was awake. Then he saw Amy over the shoulder of one of the doctor's and next to her was the police detective he'd seen earlier.

He raised his hand, shakily and called the man over to him. At first the doctors thought he was gesturing for his wife, but as Amy moved closer, her face a mask of nervousness, James waved her away and pointed to the detective.

Confused, the man moved closer, until he was standing over James. The man smelled like cigarettes and fast food and it smelled wonderful to James.

The Lieutenant leaned over until he was only inches from James mouth.

"Not drinking...wife...best friend...neighbor...tried to... kill me...weapon under couch...hammer...my house...blood on it." Then James passed out, the effort too much for him.

The doctor leaned in and checked his vitals.

"He should be fine, just the exertion of coming to. He must have really needed to say something."

The Lieutenant frowned. "If it's true, oh, yeah, I'd say so."

The Lieutenant called the policeman in the hall into the room. "Officer, arrest her on possible attempted murder charges."

The policeman went to Amy and gently handcuffed her.

"What, what's happening, what did my husband say to you?"

"You'll find out soon enough, if it's true. I want to search your house. Do you consent or will I need a warrant," the Lieutenant asked.

"A warrant, why? Go ahead; I've got nothing to hide."

"Fair enough."

Turning to the uniformed officer, the Lieutenant started to leave the room. "Take her to the station. Once I get back-up, I'm going to her house. Oh, and call headquarters and find out who her neighbors are. If one of them is a man, then I suspect we'll need to talk to him, too."

The officer nodded, and with Amy struggling, dragged her from the hospital room.

The doctors fussed over James for a few more minutes after all the commotion was over. Once assured he was doing well, the room was emptied, until only James remained.

Lying in his bed, James smiled from ear to ear.

This time his real true face smiled...and it was wonderful.

101 Ways To Get To Heaven

PART1: Just Another Morning

The morning alarm screeched its wakeup buzzer, sending Jerry deeper into the folds of his bed.

His hand reached out to hit the snooze button for the third time, but he missed, knocking the alarm to the floor.

"Damn it," he mumbled into his pillow.

At least now the small speaker was buried in the carpet and if he really tried, he might be able to squeeze a few more minutes of sleep from the morning sun.

With a deep sigh, he decided he might as well get up and join the world.

Besides, he had to be at work in less than an hour and if he was late again he would probably get written up.

Throwing the blankets off himself, he sat up in bed and scratched his head. His mouth tasted like he had chewed shoe leather all night and he decided the first thing on the morning agenda would be to brush his teeth.

His foot came down onto the carpet, but instead of feeling the soft plushness of carpeting, his foot sank an inch deep into a hairball.

But not a regular hairball, oh, no. This one had about half a bowl of cat food in it, and then just a tuft of wet hair. It seems when his cat Fluffy needed to *worf* it up, whatever else was in his stomach would come up first.

And it never failed; he would always eat a heaping bowl of food before leaving him a present. His foot now fully entrenched in the cold spit-up; he sighed and looked for the cat.

Just to throw a few imprecations at its face, not that the big fur ball would care.

What a life, to lie around all day and eat and sleep and... well you get the rest, right?

Slipping his foot out of the gooey mess, he reached for a tissue and wiped off the slime. Then making sure the rest of his path was clear, he stood up and started over.

The routine in the bathroom went smooth and soon he had made it to the kitchen. He was relishing eating the last donut from the day before. The sweet confection was sitting on his kitchen counter, patiently waiting for him to devour it.

Or so he thought.

Instead of what he wanted, what he got was a half-eaten circle now lying on the floor. Little teeth marks covered the baked good and it glistened in the morning's rays from too much cat spittle.

"Fluffy, if I get my hands on you!" He screamed to the house. The damn cat was probably sleeping under the couch or sunning himself in the living room, now content and full on his donut, he thought.

Deciding it wasn't worth finding the cat, he just called into the living room, hoping the animal was in there.

"Hope you enjoyed my donut, ya jerk. I hope it gives you worms."

Then realizing the futility of fighting with a dumb animal, he slipped on his coat and left for work. There was a coffee shop on the way to work; he'd grab a muffin or something there.

On his way out of the kitchen, he saw the note he had left on his refrigerator. **CALL BROTHER** was written in bold letters so he would remember. Both he and his brother were orphans. Despite all the odds, they had managed to stay together through all the foster care and orphanages. When he had reached eighteen, he had left and never looked back, his brother right behind him.

Still, Jerry always wondered what it would have been like to grow up in a real family, with real parents.

While he walked down the street to the bus stop, thoughts of a blueberry muffin floated into his mind. Without realizing it, he started to smack his lips.

Checking his watch, he realized it was well past eight. He needed to be at work by nine, so he should be fine.

He had ten more minutes before his bus came, so he entered the coffee shop on the corner, looking forward to that blueberry muffin.

"Hi, Jerry, what's up?" Inquired Susan, the perky young woman who worked the counter this morning.

"Morning, Susan, how's Rick?" He asked, regretting it the moment he said it. He had accidentally opened Pandora's Box. From past conversations with her, he knew she was having some romantic problems with him.

"'Bout the same, he just won't commit. Every time I try to get close, he just pulls away. I try to…"

That's all Jerry heard, after that, he would quickly tune out for the next two minutes. She was sweet, but she was like a broken record. He wanted to tell her to just dump the guy, but knew that like a lot of other women, she craved the drama, even if it drove her crazy.

He kept nodding and uh-huhing until the appropriate time and then he would cut her off.

"Look, that's great, Susan, but I'm running late for work so could you just help me, please?"

"What? Oh of course, I'm sorry. What would you like?"

"A blueberry muffin would be great," he said.

Her face went into a pout and she turned to look at the back wall where all the pastry was supposed to be.

"Oh, I'm so sorry; we're all out of pastry. We got wiped out today."

"Well, what do you have left?" He inquired.

She turned around and bent down to the bottom rack on the wall. With a piece of wax paper, she picked up a day old cruller and held it under his nose.

"We've got these. They're left over from yesterday; otherwise they'd be gone, too." She frowned just a little. "They're kind of stale, though."

Jerry was about to give her an answer when he heard the rumbling of an engine, a bus engine, coming from the street outside. He turned around quickly and his heart sank as he watched the number 10 bus driving off. He checked his watch and saw the bus was four minutes early. He knew the bus company had a five minute window and he had just blown it.

"Ah, forget it, Susan, I gotta go, that's my bus," he said running out of the coffee shop like a marathon sprinter.

Susan waved and then went back to cleaning the counter, Jerry already forgotten.

Jerry hit the doors and pushed through them, jarring his arm as he went. The bus had just pulled away and he ran after it, his briefcase flying next to him like he was trying to make it hover on its own accord.

He made sure to get behind the bus, so that the driver could see him, waving frantically and calling for it to stop.

For just one brief moment the bus driver's eyes and Jerry's met in his side-view mirror. Jerry saw recognition in the man's face. The bus driver now knew he had a passenger running behind the bus.

But instead of stopping, the driver stepped on the gas pedal and the bus surged forward with a burst of oily smoke and a revving of the engine. As Jerry watched the bus pull away, he distinctly caught the driver's face in the mirror for the second time.

His mouth fell open when he saw the man was smiling. One of those mischievous grins that are best seen on ten year olds.

Jerry stopped running and stood in the street, watching his ride to work moving farther away.

With his head down, he started back to the bus stop. He hadn't realized how far he'd run. He had a good seven or eight minutes left of walking until he returned to the closest bus stop. The next bus should be by to the pick up spot within the next ten minutes before it would head into the city, but that few extra minutes would make him late for work.

He started back, walking slowly. Now he would be late for work and get written up. While he walked in the gutter, he paused.

His shoe felt funny.

He looked down and bent the sole of the shoe up so he could see it better, leaning against a fire hydrant, his body still standing in the gutter of the street. As he examined the shoe's bottom, he realized that the stitching had come undone and the entire shoe was threatening to fall apart.

"I don't believe this, I just bought these shoes," he mumbled to himself, wondering if his morning could get any worse.

Looking up into the clear blue sky, he sighed.

"What else are you going to do to me today, God? My pants are still intact, how about splitting them up my butt? Or I got it, how about making it start raining. That would be fun if I showed up at work with one shoe and soaking wet."

He looked back down at his shoe again, standing in the street with one leg in the air. Struggling to see if there was any hope for the fractured footwear at all.

Two-hundred feet away a sweet old woman was driving her car. She was at least eighty and frankly should have stopped driving when Clinton was in office. But she loved her independence and so continued driving long after her expiration date.

Like a lot of older women who were trying to keep up with the times, she had a cell phone. Her daughter had given it to her on Christmas, that way she would always be able to call for help if there was a problem or she was feeling sick.

So this little old lady with the coke bottle eyeglasses, with her head barely peeking over the steering wheel and her left blinker still on from the turn she'd made about two miles ago, drove down the road.

Her cell phone began to ring.

It was her daughter, checking to see if she was coming to the house for lunch today.

The sweet old lady, who could barely see, turned her head to pick up the cell phone. As the little thing rang, she tried to remember how to answer it, forgetting in her age that all she had to do was open it.

Her attention was fully focused on this one small task and she didn't realize the nose of the car was drifting into the gutter of the street.

With one hand on the cell phone and one on the steering wheel, her driving chores were all but forgotten as she tried to discern this new marvel of technology, the cell phone.

Jerry gave up trying to fix his shoe, it was hopeless. And the best thing of all was that they were brand new and he had thrown out the receipt. Normally, if that happened, you just go out in the trash and get your hands dirty, right? Well not this time, good old Jerry's luck was holding this morning and he realized it had been trash day this morning, as well, the barrels having gone out the night before. By the time he returned home this evening, the barrels would be empty, and probably rolling around half-way down the street for good measure.

With a big sigh, he turned around to head back to the bus stop, wondering what else could possibly happen to him today.

As soon as he turned around he saw a big car coming straight for him. In that split second before impact, time seemed to slow and he noticed the small tuft of gray hair behind the steering wheel. If there was a head belonging to that hair, he couldn't see it. A bird flew by, overhead, seeming to pause in mid-flight as he studied its wings. An ant was sitting on the curb below him, deciding if it should chance the long drop to the street and try for the piece of donut someone had dropped out of their car window in passing a few hours ago.

All this was taken in, in the blink of an eye. His mind saw what was about to happen and he couldn't help but chuckle in his mind. His eyes turned upward and he looked into the sky once again.

"Good one," he said under his breath and then he was flying over the hood of the car, his legs bending one way, his torso the other. The world went topsy- turvy for the briefest of moments and then nothing but darkness.

The old lady became startled by the noise of Jerry's bouncing body and hit the brakes, her car swerving more and striking the fire hydrant, sending a surge of water into the air. In a second the street was a river, Jerry's shattered body becoming soaked as the small amount of blood was washed away by the flowing water.

Susan and a few others ran out of the coffee shop to see what had happened and a man in an overcoat ran over to Jerry's prone, supine form.

"Out of the way, I'm a doctor," the man screamed, pushing through the street gawker to reach Jerry's side. The man touched two fingers to Jerry's neck, but after seeing the position of the neck and body, he already knew what the result would be.

Standing up, he looked at a few of the faces surrounding him and shook his head.

Susan brought her hands to her mouth and let out a shout of surprise.

"Oh my God, I was just talking to him," she said as one of the other regular patrons took her by the shoulder and helped her back into the coffee shop.

The sweet little old lady climbed out of the car, the water soaking her to the bone.

She stood there, scratching her wet hair, wondering what had happened and what all the commotion was about.

As for Jerry, he lay in the street, dead. His briefcase floated away down the street on the current of water, his left hand seeming to float next to his body in the pool of water, as if he was trying to hail a cab, still worried about being late for work.

PART 2: So This Is Heaven?

Jerry opened his eyes.

Disoriented and feeling a little woozy, he was surprised to see he was in a waiting room. Old magazines littered the small coffee table in front of him and a water dispenser sat quietly in the corner, being ignored.

The strange part was the other people that shared the room with him.

In the rows of chairs lining the wall across from him sat four people, all in a state of undress and dishevelment.

The first was a woman in her middle forties or early fifties. She was wearing nothing but a towel and her hair continued to drip water onto her seat. The second individual was a man, late forties if Jerry was correct. He looked like a construction worker with the brown jacket and jeans and the heavy work boots that had metal sewn into the tips.

What was shocking was the man had what looked like half a brick lodged into the top of his head. What was even stranger was the man barely seemed to notice; he just sat there quietly reading a People magazine and sipping from a small cup of water.

The third individual was a young man in his early twenties. He had the look of a metal head or some kind of punk rocker. He sat quietly with his legs crossed. In the skin of his left arm a needle dangled, complete with the rubber hose tied off at the top. The rest of the arm looked like a bird with sharp claws had run up and down his arm leaving tracks.

The fourth and last person was a man about Jerry's age, he seemed normal enough with the exception he was in his pajamas.

Jerry was feeling nervous and so wanted to talk a little, still not understanding where he was.

"Hi there, I'm Jerry, I was wondering if you had any idea what's going on here?"

The man in the bathrobe turned to look at him, a look of almost boredom on his face.

"Hey there, Jerry, name's Clyde, I'm in computer software. And what do you mean by *going on*?"

Jerry leaned a little closer to Clyde and lowered his voice more. "I mean, I have no idea what the hell's going on here. That guy has a brick in his head."

Clyde casually turned to look at Brick Head. "Yeah, so what else is he supposed to have in his head if not a brick?" Clyde inquired with a smile.

Jerry shook his head back and forth. "No, you don't understand, he has a brick in his head. Shouldn't he be dead, or barring that, in a hospital?"

Clyde really looked at Jerry as if seeing him for the first time.

"Jerry, old pal. What's the last thing you remember before you came to be here with me in this room?"

Jerry had to think about that one for a moment. He had gotten up for work and had walked to the bus stop where he wanted a muffin, but they were out. The bus had left him and then he had...

It hit him in a rush, the memory flooding back. "Oh my God, I was hit by a car."

Clyde nodded. "There you go, that's right. I have to take your word for it, but it sounds right enough." Clyde pointed to the other people in the waiting room with Jerry and himself.

"You see that woman there? She slipped in the bathtub and cracked her head; skull fracture. That guy with the brick? Took his hardhat off on the job and walked under one of his buddies a few stories up. Brick came loose and the rest is obvious. That kid there? Overdose, if it isn't blatantly obvious. And I had the misfortune of having a heart attack. Happened in my sleep, never woke up after I went to bed the night before." He tapped his chest over his heart. "Too many fast food burgers I guess."

"And I was in a car accident?" Jerry asked, still quite shocked.

Clyde nodded. "You bet, welcome to the waiting room of the afterlife."

Jerry's mouth fell open and his mind raced. How could this be? He couldn't be dead, it wasn't fair.

He sat in that chair for hours, then days, and then weeks, the others with him. Then one by one they were called through the door at the end of the room. The door would open and a bright light would shine through. Each person would wave goodbye and then walk into the light, the door closing after they were gone.

Finally Jerry was alone in the room. He sat there for how long, he had no idea and slowly he began to accept what had happened to him.

On that day, on that moment, the door opened and Jerry heard his name.

"Jerry McDonald, step into the light," a disembodied voice told him.

On shaking legs, he stood up and moved towards the door. With his pulse pounding in his head, he stepped into the portal and the door closed behind him. So this was Heaven, he thought, at least he'd made it.

PART 3: Take Your Pick

Jerry couldn't see anything, his eyes blinded by the bright white light in his eyes. From somewhere in front of him a voice called to him.

"That's right, Jerry, keep walking forward, you're almost there...and...stop."

Jerry did as he was told. Waiting, nervous and worried.

The light flashed off, leaving his eyes with little pinpoints of light swirling around his vision. Slowly they faded and he found he was looking at a man in a three piece suit, sitting behind a glass desk. On the desk was a spotlight, now off and turned away from Jerry's face.

The man noticed Jerry's look of surprise and he chuckled.

"Sorry about the light in the face, Mr. McDonald. It's just my little joke. You know, step into the light, and all that," he chuckled softly.

Jerry just stared at the man.

The man had a folder in front of him and he browsed through it, nodding his head every so often.

"So," he said. "Car accident, huh? Tough break."

Jerry had finally found his voice. "Who are you and what am I doing here?" He asked quietly.

The man stood up and walked around his desk, sitting on the corner. He looked at Jerry.

"You're in luck, Jerry, you might be dead, but if you want, you can get another chance to play the game."

Jerry blinked a few times, trying to let it all sink in. "Excuse me? The game?"

The man blinked. "Sure, the game of life. Didn't you ever play the board game? Listen, Jerry, most of the junk you hear about religion is crap. People say and believe what ever suits their own purposes and agendas. Now according to your file, you're nothing, no actual faith in anything."

Jerry stood a little straighter. "Now hold on, I have faith. I have faith in myself and my fellow man, as corny as that sounds. I believe we make our own destiny, not have to wait for some divine being to dole out what's good and bad once we're dead."

The little man nodded briskly. "Exactly, that's what I meant. You're an independent. We like that around here, Jerry. You're just what we're looking for?"

Jerry's eyes creased. "And just where exactly is here, anyway?"

The man waved the question away. "Irrelevant, Jerry, totally irrelevant. You can call this Heaven, or limbo or whatever you feel comfortable with. To tell you the truth, I'm not really here either. I'm more of an ephemeral being. I've just taken this form so you can understand things better."

Jerry nodded slowly. Then his eyes started searching the room and the corners of the walls as if he was searching for something.

"May I ask what you're doing?" The man asked.

"I'm looking for the cameras. This is a practical joke right? I'm on one of those television shows where you fool the guy and then everyone jumps out and laughs and the guys humiliated."

The man shook his head slowly. "I'm sorry, Mr. McDonald, but this is as real as it gets. Look, I've got a thousand more appointments today, literally, so let's move this along. We're sending you back. You can be any animal you'd like, with in reason, of course. Just don't ask to be Paris Hilton's dog or Britney Spears' cat. It can't be done. It just doesn't work that way."

"Right," Jerry said, stretching the word out. "Anything I want? Any animal on the planet."

"Within reason, Mr. McDonald. It has to be one of the higher forms of life, such as a horse or dog. Oh, and birds are fine, too. Cats are fine, also. In fact, that's our most popular choice."

Jerry thought back to his last morning on earth and his ruminations on being a feline; and grinned ear to ear.

"All right then, I'll take a cat."

The man nodded. "You're sure now. Once we're done here, that's it. No back takes. This contract is solid. Set in stone. Solid as a rock. Ironclad..."

"All right, I get it, Jesus," Jerry said.

The man waved his finger in front of Jerry's face.

"Please don't use that name here, we're equal opportunity in this office."

"Fine, whatever. So when does this happen? How long does it take?" Jerry asked, curious.

The man smiled at that. A smile a child gives when he's taken the last cookie from the jar, but looks you in the face and denies it innocently.

"That's the easy part, Mr. McDonald."

The man snapped his fingers and a trapdoor opened below Jerry's feet. Before he could even scream, he was falling through the hole.

Below him was blackness. He craned his head upward to see the small square of light quickly receding as he plummeted downward.

With the sound of a maelstrom in his ears from the passing air and his clothes flapping around him like he'd just jumped out of an airplane, he managed to take in enough air to let out one piercing scream.

He continued falling, to be enveloped in the blackness, until he was gone.

PART 4: Welcome Back!

Jerry's eyes opened just a fraction. All he could see was black. Something warm and soft was next to him as well as other shapes similar to his own. The smell of mother's milk tempted him and he used his new olfactory senses to seek the warm fluid out.

He began sucking from one of the many nipples his mother had bared for him and his siblings. Contentment suffused him as he filled his small stomach.

Time went by and soon the dark of his vision became small blurs and as more time passed, he began to see.

His soul was now inside a cat.

He looked down at his gray and white paws and turned to see his fluffy tale. He had an amazing sense of balance now, as if he could walk a tightrope blindfolded.

He had brothers and sisters to play with and a mother who loved him. Things were pretty good, he had to admit. He was just thinking he could get used to this until the third month had rolled around.

Suddenly his brothers and sisters were being taken away to never return. The part of his mind that was still Jerry realized him and his siblings were being given away to good homes.

When it was his time, he found himself being held up in the air by a pretty woman in her early thirties who looked back at him and made cooing noises and baby talk.

Before he knew it, he was in a cardboard box and being taken to his new home.

Once he had arrived, he immediately explored the new house. It was neat and clean and had many windows for him to lie in and soak up the sun.

Life was good. He thought back to when he had owned his own cat and was pleased to see he was right.

Being a cat is pretty sweet. He still got to watch television, his new owner always leaving it on when she was around.

Her name was Brenda Stevenson and she had been married for a little over five years. Her husband, Bill Stevenson, was a heavy set man who loved his wife dearly. Every morning, Bill would get up and leave for work at around six. He wouldn't return home until around eight that evening.

You see, Bill was a workaholic and while he was able to buy Brenda whatever she wanted, he was never around to give her the attention she so sorely craved.

About six months after Jerry had arrived in the Stevenson home, things began to get interesting.

It was around ten in the morning when Jerry heard Brenda talking to someone at the front door. He had jumped down off the couch where he had been lounging and he moved to the hall to hear better.

"So yeah, I lost my job the other day. They said they were downsizing. Stuff like that happens to people everyday," A man's voice said.

"Oh, Kevin, I'm so sorry. That's too bad," Brenda said.

"Thanks, Brenda, that's nice of you, but it's not so bad. I get to collect unemployment insurance for a while. So until then, I guess I can just relax and take a little vacation here at home."

Jerry saw Brenda's eyebrows go up just a little at that last remark.

"Oh, really, you're going to be home a lot now, during the day?"

"Yup, you bet, maybe I'll write that novel I always said I'd write but never had the time. I've got plenty now."

"If you have some free time, do you think you might come over one day and help me fix a few things around the house? Bill works all the time and told me I should just get a handyman, but I just don't like the idea of strangers in my house, seeing all my possessions and such."

Kevin gave it some thought, his lip moving a little as he reasoned out the question.

"Sure, why not. Just tell me when you want me and I'll come over. You've got my number, right?"

Brenda nodded energetically. "Sure I do, it's probably in my phonebook."

"Okay then, I'll talk to you soon," Kevin said and left the door.

"Bye," Brenda said and closed the door. She saw Jerry sitting on the floor and looked down at him.

"What are you looking at?" She asked him. Jerry just stood up and walked away. The couch was calling him back.

One week later, Kevin was at the front door. Brenda had called him and he had quickly accepted. Brenda had him working all over the house. He fixed everything from peeling paint to burnt out light bulbs. He nailed down the old wooden stairs on the back porch and then fixed the floor molding in the living room.

By the time he was done, he was hungry and tired. The clock read a little past twelve in the afternoon and Kevin was shocked to see he had been working for four hours straight.

He sat down at the kitchen table and Brenda handed him a glass of lemonade.

She was wearing a tight button down shirt with just one too many buttons undone. The pair of white shorts she wore led nothing to the imagination.

And as Kevin's eyes took her in, he was glad of that.

She was beautiful.

She sat down next to him and they talked for a while. Jerry lay on the kitchen floor watching and enjoying the show. As they talked, Brenda inched closer, her cleavage easy for Kevin to see.

He swallowed hard and then drank half his glass of lemonade in one gulp.

"How is it?" She purred.

"It's fine, thank you," he stammered. While he was no way afraid of a woman's advances, he knew she was married and therefore, off limits. And on top of that, Bill had been his friend for years and he would never try anything with his wife.

Brenda leaned a little closer and Kevin could smell her perfume.

"You know, my husband works all the time. He never pays any attention to me," she said.

"Oh, really, well I find that hard to believe, Brenda. If I had a beautiful wife like you, I'd give her all the attention she wanted."

She blinked at him, more of a batting of the eyes. "You think I'm beautiful?"

He nodded. "Sure, you're one of the best looking women on the street."

She sat there quietly, biting her lip in thought. Then she stood up and with a gesture pointed to the stairs that led to the bedrooms on the second floor.

"Kevin, I have one more thing that needs a good fixing. It's upstairs. Just give me a minute and then come up, will you?"

Then she glided to the stairs and was up them in a flash.

Kevin sat there, tapping his hand on the table. Could she be talking about what he thought she was talking about?

He shook his head. No, that would be ridiculous. This wasn't some trashy romance novel where the lonely housewife needs some attention from the handsome handyman.

It was impossible and frankly, he wouldn't be that lucky.

It was always the other guy who got the hot housewife.

He realized a few minutes had passed and so he stood up, finished off the rest of his lemonade and went upstairs.

"I'm in here," Brenda's voice said, coming from the room at the end of the small hallway.

With his heart in his throat, he walked to the door and opened it. Brenda was laying on the bed in nothing but a white, see-thru lingerie. Her head was propped up on the pillow and her feet were curled up under her body.

She looked beautiful and sexy.

"Come here, handsome, and take care of what really needs to be fixed," she purred softly.

Kevin ran his hand over his chin, rubbing the small stubble there. He was undecided. On the one hand there was a really hot housewife lying partially nude in front of him just waiting for him to ravish her. On the other hand Bill had been his best friend for years.

Brenda rolled onto her back, her perfect breasts calling him.

"Oh, the hell with it," he said, "I can always get more friends."

Then he jumped into bed with her and started their first bout of lovemaking.

Jerry sat in the doorway getting an eyeful. This was one of the times he regretted not being human, because Brenda was wild. She did things to Kevin that day that the poor man had only read about in magazines.

Finally it was four o' clock and Kevin got dressed and ready to leave. Brenda sat up in bed and kissed him gently.

"Same time tomorrow?" She asked sweetly.

Kevin's eyes lit up. This wasn't a one time thing!

"Sure, you bet," he said while getting dressed.

He left then, running down the stairs and then out the door.

Eight o' clock rolled around and Bill walked in the door, tired and grumpy. Brenda didn't mind. She fed him his dinner and then he went up to bed, while she stayed in the living room watching television. Jerry sat on her lap and kept her company. Only he knew the truth of what was happening and he couldn't say a word to Bill, even if he wanted to.

The next morning, Bill left for work and just as soon as his car had disappeared at the end of the street, Kevin was already on the move. He slipped in the back door and before Bill's side of the bed was cold, he was having sex with the man's wife.

Off and on all day they had sex and just hung around the house.

This went on for days and then weeks, until finally they had become so complacent, they barely thought about Bill anymore.

They were in love and the fact that she was betraying her husband and he was betraying his best friend meant nothing to them.

Everything was wonderful, Jerry had something to keep him occupied, and the show was always great. Sometimes he would hop up to the foot of the bed and get front row and center.

He knew one thing, Kevin had stamina.

Two months and five days into the affair, the two of them were going at it in the bedroom. They were making so much noise neither of them heard the front door open.

Downstairs, Bill had come home from work early. He had thought he would take off for a half a day and surprise his wife, maybe take her out for dinner. Despite the fact that he worked constantly, it wasn't because he enjoyed it. In fact, he hated it, but he loved his wife passionately and wanted to give her all the things she deserved.

He tossed his keys onto the table and stopped when he heard a soft thumping sound coming from upstairs. Not knowing what it could be, he moved to the stairs.

"Honey? Is that you? I'm home early, surprise," Bill called up the stairs.

No one answered.

He started to climb the stairs and then he heard it again. A thumping sound and then what sounded like his wife screaming.

"Oh my God, there's someone in the house. A burglar?" He mumbled to himself.

As fast as he could, he ran to the den closet and retrieved a small black box about as big as a shoe box. The box had a push button combination on its side and Bill quickly punched in the numbers. It was easy to remember, it was Brenda's birthday.

Opening the box, he pulled his .38 Smith and Wesson revolver from the black mold that perfectly conformed to the weapon. Snapping open the cylinder, he double checked it was loaded and then closed it and hurried back to the stairs.

If his wife was in trouble, then he had to save her.

Taking the steps two at a time, he stopped at the top. The bedroom door was closed and he moved slowly across the hallway, the gun in his hand leading the way.

The sounds of moaning and banging grew more intense and with a deep breath to prepare himself for the worst, he turned the doorknob on the bedroom door and kicked the door in.

His wife sat up in bed, Kevin having to roll off Brenda in the process. Bill just stood there, transfixed. He couldn't believe what he was seeing.

"Now, honey, its not what it looks like," Brenda pleaded from the bed. Her bare breasts shone with sweat, her hair in total disarray.

Kevin covered himself with a sheet, his eyes going wide when he saw the gun in Bill's hand.

"Now, buddy, don't do anything hasty," Kevin said, his hands raised in front of him as if he could ward off a bullet with the palms of his hands.

Bill only saw red.

"Shut up! Both of you, just shut up!"

They did as they were told, too scared to move.

Bill was slowly falling into a rage that he couldn't control. After everything he'd done for her. This is how she repays him? And with his best friend, no less.

Bill snapped, the rage overwhelming him and his sanity falling away.

"Fine, you two want to be together? Then you can be together forever!"

Before either of them could do anything but hold up their hands and turn away, Bill shot them both in the chest. The bullets tore apart their hearts and struck main arteries, the two adulterers dying within seconds of each other.

Kevin fell onto Brenda and lay still.

Bill stood there not understanding what he had just done in his anger. Then as time went by and the sun's shadows crossed the window, he slowly came out of his stupor and saw what his own hands had wrought.

He sat on the bed, looking at his dead wife and grief overwhelmed him. He had killed two people in cold blood. One of them being the love of his life.

He looked down at the gun in his hand and without giving it more thought, let his grief take him.

He placed the gun in his mouth and pulled the trigger, his body falling over to lie at his wife's feet.

Jerry sat in the hallway looking at the carnage.

Great, he thought. Now who's going to feed me?

Four days later, Brenda's sister called the police when her sister wouldn't answer the phone and Bill's work didn't understand why he hadn't come in. The police arrived shortly and found the grisly scene.

The house became awash with detectives and crime scene techs and soon it was decided that it was a murder suicide.

As for Jerry, well he wound up at the pound. He was a full grown cat now and no one wanted him. All everyone ever wanted was kittens.

Time passed and poor Jerry reached his time limit at the pound. They had no room for unadoptable animals.

Jerry was taken from his cage and brought to the back room. He tried to fight, but they tied his paws.

"Sorry, buddy, but I guess no one wants you," a voice said from above him, the plastic gloved hand coming closer with a needle.

He felt a slight pinch under his fur and then he felt sleepy. His eyes closed and he cursed his luck. To be reincarnated only to be killed a year later.

This really sucks, he thought, drifting back into the void of death. His heart stopped beating and his muscles relaxed.

Then blackness

PART 5: Let's Try That Again

Jerry opened his eyes to find himself in the eternal waiting room again. This time he was alone, the other seats vacant. He had no idea how long he waited, time being irrelevant, but he looked up when the door across the room opened and a bright white light appeared.

"Step into the light, my son," a disembodied voice said in a haunting voice.

Jerry wasn't amused. He stood up and strode straight into the doorway. A moment later he was standing in the office of the man with the three piece suit.

When he saw Jerry, his eyes lit up and he shut the spotlight off.

"Oh, Mr. McDonald, I didn't expect you back so soon," he said while pushing the spotlight over to the end of the desk.

"Sorry about the light, just having a little fun. I wouldn't have bothered if I knew it was you, though."

Jerry sat down without being asked. He crossed his arms on his chest and frowned at the man.

Three Piece Suit came around his desk and sat on the corner.

"What's the matter, Jerry, feeling down?"

"Well, yeah, a little. I get a chance at a new life and I die in less than a year. They put me to sleep for God's sake! Do you know how humiliating that was, not to mention painful? Doesn't feel a thing, my foot. That crap they pumped into me hurt like hell!"

Three Piece Suit man nodded, agreeing with everything Jerry said. "Yes, Jerry, I know all about it. We do get satellite up here, although sometimes there's some interference. We even get the Spice channel, but don't tell anybody I told you." He winked casually with his right eye.

Jerry looked at the man like he was insane.

"What are you talking about? I don't care." Jerry sat there for a few more minutes and calmed down. Now that he had gotten it all out, he was starting to feel a little better.

"Sorry about that, it's just dying really pisses me off. So what happens now?"

Three Piece Suit walked back to his chair and sat down. He opened a folder and started flipping through the pages.

"Well, it seems from what I have here that we have an opening for a dog or a bird, a parakeet to be exact."

"A parakeet?" Jerry said. "No thank you. I'll take the dog and it better not be one of those ankle biters, God I hate those things," he finished, making a face of distaste.

"I assure you it's not one of those, Mr. McDonald. It's a German shepherd I believe," Three Piece Suit said with a smile.

Jerry's eyes lit up. "Okay, that sounds great, thanks."

Three Piece Suit put up his hands in a 'stop' gesture. "Please, Mr. McDonald. I'm just doing my job."

He reached out with his right hand and flicked a switch on his desk.

"Well, good luck and I hope it works out better for you this time," he said.

Jerry was about to answer when the trapdoor opened and his chair tipped forward. He slid out and into the black abyss.

This time he was a little calmer, knowing what to expect. He closed his eyes and enjoyed the ride.

He felt himself losing consciousness and he rolled with it. His mind drifting away until he knew no more.

PART 6: It's A Brand New Day

Jerry opened his eyes to find he was a puppy. He was cute and fluffy and everyone who met him said how adorable he was.

He didn't mind. The part of him that was still Jerry liked the compliments. When he was old enough, he was adopted by a skinny black man named Lamar Johnson.

Lamar needed a watch dog to keep an eye on his various business ventures. You see, Lamar was an opportunist.

At the moment Lamar had ventured into the profitable world of bootlegging movies. His cousin Jerome would sneak into the movie theatre with his small digital camcorder and tape whatever movie was playing. Then he would bring the copy back to Lamar who would burn it to a DVD disc and then start burning them on his computer.

At the moment, Lamar was small-time, only having one computer and one burner. It would take him all day and all night, having to get up off the couch where he'd fallen asleep and change the burnt disc for a blank one.

It was hard work, probably harder than most people thought. He had to burn the discs and write the name of the movie on every one of the covers, (the long names being the worst), then he had to make a copy of some picture he found from a magazine so his customers would know what movie was what.

Then every disc had to be put into a white sleeve to protect it.

But he wasn't done yet. He still had to inventory everything he had so he would make sure he had enough of whatever was popular for the week.

While he did all this, Jerry would sit on the rug near him and watch him work till the wee hours of the morning.

Lamar was usually exhausted when he was finished. For the thousandth time Lamar wondered why he just didn't sell drugs like the rest of his friends. They made more money and got to sleep at night.

Lamar figured he may have been breaking some copyright laws, but he felt he worked damn hard for his money. And who the hell was he really hurting anyway?

What, some Hollywood star might make a little less on a movie and could only afford to buy one Hummer and one Porsche instead of two.

Boo-hoo. Lamar could barely make enough to pay the rent for his tiny one bedroom apartment and hopefully have enough left over for his car insurance.

Lamar packed up all the movies in two small boxes and put all his ruminations behind him.

It was morning and it was time to get to work.

He left his apartment, taking Jerry with him and packed all his movies into his beat up Dodge Caravan. The van had ripped window tint on all the windows and more dents than should be allowed on one vehicle at a time. The driver's door had to be pushed in at the hinges before he could open it at all. And one of the back windows was gone, replaced by some cardboard and duct tape.

Yes, sir, he was livin' the dream, he was.

Starting the van, it wined in protest for a second and then gave in and started.

He pulled out of his parking spot and headed to his first destination. He did most of his business with body shops and a few car dealerships on the auto mile.

Most of the people he dealt with were just blue collar guys, mechanics mostly.

They were in the same boat he was, except they had a real job where his was a little more improvised.

Jerry sat in the front seat with Lamar, enjoying the wind in his face.

Lamar left the van and visited with each customer. Some bought a few and some bought nothing. No matter what you sell, you're still subject to the customers whims. It was still supply and demand.

Lamar came home that night with a few bucks in his hand, still feeling good about his day. He put the money he made into buying another computer, this way he cut his work time in half. He made some more money and he bought a machine that would let him copy eight discs at once.

Now he was able to make all he needed in a few hours, and that gave him more time to see more people and hopefully, sell more movies.

Lamar was doing great. His cousin was getting him all the new movies and he had to admit they looked pretty good.

He continued to get bigger and bigger and Jerry watched it all from right in the center.

There was only one problem that Lamar had forgotten. According to the law, he was breaking the rules.

Despite how hard he was working and how well he was doing, he forgot one very important thing.

Jealousy.

His cousin Jerome saw how much Lamar was making everyday and he decided he wanted it all for himself. Jerome picked up the phone one day and made a quick call to the MPAA. The Motion Picture Association of America.

The next day Lamar had some visitors. They barged into his apartment and seized all his computers and equipment. They took him away, as well, and he had to spend the night in jail.

The next day he posted bail and he returned home to find his apartment stripped of everything he had worked so hard to build.

After that Lamar had no choice but to go into the drug business. He had to eat and he had to live. But he had no other marketable skills.

He actually made more money in the drug game than he ever had making movies, and it was easier.

But Lamar wasn't happy and it was just a matter of time before he started to sample his own supply to try and take some of his own pain and sadness away.

He had found out that Jerome had started up his own little bootleg business and was now seeing all of Lamar's old customers.

Lamar was betrayed by his own family, even if he was just his cousin.

After that Lamar was shooting up everyday until the end result finally happened.

He had received a bad supply and had ended up overdosing.

Jerry sat on the floor and watched him in his death throes. There was nothing he could do. He tried licking his face and pulling on his shirt to wake him up, but it was too late.

Lamar had died, overdosed on his own supply.

Jerry had been his dog for almost two years, the time passing in the blink of an eye. Now Jerry found himself in the apartment of a dead man. The other apartments around Lamar's were empty, only the very poor mixed in with some illegal immigrants living there. The immigrants could hear a bomb go off in the apartment next door and they would keep quiet; not wanting to call attention to themselves and wind up being discovered by INS.

Jerry had no food and soon had drunk all the water from the toilet.

Days went by and Jerry started to feel tired as starvation set in. There was no food in the house and he wouldn't eat his master. By the time he might have changed his mind, poor Lamar was nothing but rotten meat, his corpse bloated from internal gas.

Jerry howled day and night, but there was no one to hear or the other drug addicts in the building didn't care, they themselves in their own world of misery.

Outside the apartment's windows, people walked by on the sidewalk, unaware of what was happening only a few yards away.

Jerry laid his head down on the floor and whimpered. He had not had food or water for almost a weak and his bones shown through his now dull fur coat.

He couldn't believe this was happening again. He was going to die, and this time it was a hell of a lot more painful than just being put to sleep with a shot.

With one more gasp of breath, he slid into death, joining his master at last.

More than a week would pass before someone would complain about the smell and kick in the door to find two desiccated corpses, one human, the other a dog.

The story of Lamar Johnson was over before it had truly started.

PART 7: Welcome Back, Again

Jerry opened his eyes to find himself in the waiting room again. This time he wasn't alone. There were two other people occupying the room with him. One was a middle-aged woman with a bottle of sleeping pills in her hand. Her other hand still held the suicide note she had written before killing herself.

The other was a young man; a teenager really. He had half his skull bashed in. He sat quietly with a skateboard on his lap.

Jerry watched the kid for a few minutes and then couldn't help but comment.

"Hey, kid," he said to the teenager. "Bet you wished you had worn a helmet now, huh?"

The teenager merely made a rude face and then turned the other way.

Jerry grinned at that. The stupidity of being young. It was a damn shame this one kid would never grow up to realize the folly of his youth.

The door opened on the other side of the room and the white light shone into the waiting room. Jerry didn't even hesitate for a moment.

As soon as the door opened he stood up and then walked into the office like he owned the place.

Three Piece Suit's eyes lit up when he saw who had walked into his office, the man standing up to greet Jerry.

"Ah, Mr. McDonald, it's so nice to see you a..."

Jerry put up his hands for the man to stop talking and Jerry bullied forward with his tirade.

"Save it, pal; I'm not interested in you're niceties. I'd just like to know what exactly I did to deserve this kind of punishment. I mean, I never killed ants with a magnifying glass when I was in elementary school and I never went around kicking dogs when I was in high school. I'd just like to know why exactly you're making me suffer like this."

Three Piece Suit seemed to stutter for just a moment as he tried to get an answer together. To stall further, he sat down behind his desk and started rummaging through some folders.

Jerry stood in front of the man's desk. Arms folded with a stare that could cut stone.

Finally Three Piece Suit closed the folder he'd been perusing and then cleared his throat.

"I don't really know what to tell you, Mr. McDonald. Usually we have a one hundred percent soul placement. The fact that you are standing in front of me simply defies the odds."

Jerry's frown actually went into an even deeper frown. "Then send me to Vegas, because right now I'd like to see if I can get away with kicking your butt."

Three Piece Suit held up his hands. "Now, now, Mr. McDonald, there's no reason for violence. I have an immediate opening for you. Do you accept?"

Jerry's face changed from a frown to a grimace. "That depends, where's my soul going exactly?"

"That's a surprise, bye now," Three Piece Suit said and then pressed the button for the trapdoor.

The floor dropped away and Jerry felt himself falling. He barely noticed this time. He just closed his eyes and waited for the ride to end.

Part 8: You're So Tweet

Jerry opened his eyes to find his soul was now in a parakeet. After the first round of humiliation, he had gradually learned to accept his new place in life. A little old lady named Millie had bought him from the pet store.

She had brought him home and had placed him in a tiny cage situated in the living room.

For the first few months things had gone pretty well. His cage gave him a good view of the television and he would watch Millie's soap operas everyday.

In fact, he couldn't wait until next week when Susan's twin sister Sally was supposed to return from the hospital where she had been in a coma for three months and still had amnesia, but now didn't realize that Susan had stolen her husband while she had been asleep.

He still couldn't believe how fast he had become hooked on those day time soaps.

The next month had gone well, until old Millie started to get the onset of Alzheimer's. While it was tough for her, it was even tougher on poor Jerry.

You see, the poor woman kept forgetting about him, literally, and Jerry was slowly starving to death.

He hadn't had a fill-up on his water bottle for more than a week and he was circling down the drain fast. He managed to hold out for yet one more day, but finally succumbed to dehydration and lack of food.

Jerry finally fell off his perch and with his small legs sticking up in the air, became still.

He would have liked to think Millie would miss him, but the truth was, the old bat didn't even remember him anymore.

His small eyes closed for the last time and he was off to the eternal waiting room once again.

PART 9: Let's Make A Deal

Jerry opened his eyes and guess where he was? In fact, he had made this round trip so fast that Skateboard Kid and Suicide Woman were both still in their chairs, not having been called yet.

Jerry was fuming. He planned to march into Three Piece Suit's office and kick his butt all over the place.

After an undefined amount of time had passed, the door across the waiting room opened. The same white light poured out and Suicide Woman stood up, preparing to go in.

Jerry beat her to it.

"Sorry, hon', but I get next. Me and him have some unfinished business to attend to." Then Jerry charged into the room.

Three Piece Suit stood up and backed away from his desk.

"Now, wait a second, Mr. McDonald, I can explain, just let me send you back one more time. I promise you, you'll be pleased."

Jerry shook his head back and forth vehemently and started to chase Three Piece suit around his office.

"No way, that's it for me. Just send me to Hell or limbo or wherever souls go, because I'm tired of playing your sick game. What kind of entity are you to keep sending me back, only to have me die in a year or so? And guess what?   I remember every second of every death. Give me one good reason why I don't mop the floor with you and kick your butt to boot?"

"Well, for one thing, I don't really have a butt. Remember, this form is just for your benefit," Three Piece Suit said.

That statement made Jerry hesitate for a moment. He had forgotten that despite present appearances, the man in front of him wasn't really a man. He was some kind of angel or something like that.

That made him calm down just a little and he stopped chasing the man around the room.

"Oh, yeah, guess I kind of forgot about that. But that still doesn't change what you're doing to me has to be stopped. I want out," Jerry said and crossed his arms to make his point.

Three Piece Suit moved back to his desk and sat down.

"Look, just do one more and I promise you'll be satisfied."

Jerry's left eyebrow went up just a hair, showing his curiosity.

"Really? You promise. No more screw ups."

Three Piece Suit nodded quickly, reminding Jerry of one of those toys some people put in the back windshields of their cars. The ones with the bobble heads.

"Yes, Jerry, I promise." Then he quickly pressed the trap door button. But this time Jerry was ready and he jumped into the air, his feet landing on both sides of the opening.

"Not this time buddy." Jerry said, giving him a look as hard as stone.

"I'll go, but I'm warning you. If it doesn't work out, you better send me somewhere else, because this is it for me. Got it?"

Three Piece Suit leaned back in his chair and smiled. "Relax Mr. McDonald. I'm a professional. This time will be for keeps."

Placated for now, Jerry nodded. "All right then. Wish me luck, will ya. Because the way things are going, I'm gonna need it." Then he stepped out over empty air and let himself drop into the trapdoor.

Jerry fell, disappearing from view and the trapdoor snapped shut with a soft hiss.

Three Piece Suit grinned at his empty office.

"Don't you worry, Mr. McDonald, this time will be the right one."

PART 10: Welcome Home

Jerry opened his eyes, but instead of seeing light, it was still dark. He started to panic, but realized it would get him nowhere, so he calmed down a little. Wherever he had arrived it was dark and cramped.

There was almost no sound, but sometimes he thought he could hear someone saying something to him.

He had started to wonder if maybe Three Piece Suit had screwed him and sent him to limbo after all. Where he was now had almost no sensation and he was all alone. He couldn't imagine a worse place to spend forever.

He made due trying to keep himself occupied, thinking of things from his past and what his future might hold.

That usually didn't take too long, because at the moment, things were moving pretty slow. At least he never felt hungry or cold; he had to be thankful for that, anyway.

Time went by slowly and his limbo became even more cramped until he felt he would end up being crushed by the walls of his prison.

When he thought it would become so unbearable he couldn't take it anymore, he found his world collapsing in on itself.

Like an earthquake, his prison heaved and threw him about. He felt himself moving and he went with it, not strong enough to fight.

Suddenly a bright light hit him in his eyes and he wondered if he was back in the eternal waiting room again. Then he felt a pain in his backside and he let out a scream, his new lungs working for the first time.

He blinked up at a man in a white mask and was passed from hand to hand until he was finally cleaned and wrapped into a blanket.

He was handed over to a woman lying prone in a bed. She looked down at him and smiled.

Her smile was captivating and Jerry had already decided she was the most beautiful woman in the world.

Then he felt another consciousness with his and for some reason he knew it was okay to take a back seat and let this other consciousness take the steering wheel.

He knew he would always be in the backseat, making sure the consciousness was steering them in the right direction.

For the first time in as long as he could remember Jerry was at peace.

He looked up at the woman's face and just before he let go for good, to be absorbed into this other consciousness, he heard the woman say something to him.

"Hello there," she whispered. "I'm your mommy and I love you so much. I want you to know right now that I will love you and protect you with every fiber of my being. No one will ever hurt you."

Jerry heard it all and somewhere deep inside what was left of his soul, he knew it was the truth. He knew he was finally safe and would be happy, for as many years as God or whoever would give this new found life.

A man walked over to the woman and looked down at him.

"So what are we going to name him?" The man asked.

The woman's smile grew wider as she stared down at him.

"Let's name him after your brother, in his honor. That way we'll always remember him," she said.

"Okay honey, that would be great," he said.

His new mother moved him to her face and kissed him gently on the forehead.

"Welcome to the family, Jerry, we're so glad you finally arrived," she said.

Inside Jerry smiled back at her, agreeing with her sentiments.

He was finally home and the feeling was indescribable. He closed his soul's eyes deep inside the new baby and let himself float into the other consciousness. He knew he wasn't going away, only joining with the other half to make a whole.

And that was fine with him.

He had finally found his Heaven

Dead Endings: A Zombie Short Story

William looked out the front window of his small, one family house. They were still out there...the walking dead people.

They just stumbled around, not really doing anything; that is until they got a live human being in their sights. Then they would charge the person, surrounding him, using their greater numbers to corner the poor human. By that time it was usually too late to run. That was when mouths full of swollen tongues and blackened nails would attack the soft, pink flesh, rending it from the bones and devouring it whole.

The screams would usually continue for a few harrowing moments until the person would mercifully die.

But in time, the ravaged body would rise and join the others on the street, one more soldier joining the undead army from Hell.

William would usually turn away from the window once that happened. He had been hiding in his house for quite a while now, hoping and praying he wouldn't be discovered. So far his food was holding out, but he knew in time it would run out.

He tried not to think about what he would do after that.

Better to stay focused on the present and let the future work itself out.

Not that there appeared to be much of a future for him or anyone else on the planet. He walked back to the light-brown sofa that sat against the living room wall and fell onto it with a muffled cry. His voice was dampened by the pillow now pushing against his mouth and he screamed into it, letting out the fear and despair he felt.

When he felt he was a little better, he sat up, his back falling against the rear cushions. He wondered how it had all fallen apart and how he had arrived in this pit of despair.

That was when his mind would bring him back to the beginning, back to when it had all started.

Two months ago he had been a cashier at a local video store. The money wasn't great, but he was able to rent all the movies he could watch for free. His favorite had been horror movies, especially the end of the world stuff. Zombie movies were at the forefront of his choices. In almost every zombie movie he would watch, the world would end as the undead overran the living. Usually the hero would survive, but in some of the more depressing ones, the hero bit the dust on the last frame. He didn't much care for those. Even if the world was coming to an end in those old movies, he liked to have at least a little hope that mankind or the hero would survive.

When everyone died, it was just too depressing.

Like now.

Now, as he wiped a tear from his cheek, he thought back to all those movies, still not believing he was now living in one of them. Maybe the writers to all those apocalyptic movies had been more than just simple writers, but prophets. Modern day Nostredamas'

Two months ago to the day, the world had ended. Not with a bang, but with a moan from undead lips.

Two states over, an eighteen wheeler had overturned and had spilled its contents across the highway and had infected a nearby cemetery. The haz-mat cleanup crew arrived and with their white body suits and breathing apparatus, had quickly cleaned up the mess.

There were a few stories on the news about what the chemicals might do to the ground water supply or to the local plant and animal life, but after a day or so there had been a celebrity murder in Hollywood and the news had gone crazy trying to cover the new, more popular story.

After that, the chemical spill story was forgotten, one more trivial footnote in the cable news game. He always thought it was amusing how fickle the news stations were.

Thinking back to it all now, though, maybe if they had covered the story a little longer something could have been done to stop the outbreak; or at least people might have been more prepared when it happened.

About forty-eight hours after the chemicals had leached into the earth of the graveyard; the first newly revived corpse had thrust desiccated hands through the topsoil and climbed out into the light. Something in the toxins had revitalized dead organs and had breathed a form of un-life into the rotting cadavers of the graveyard.

After that, the disease had spread like wildfire. Once bit by one of the infected, victims would turn into the undead themselves in a matter of hours.

Husband would attack wife, wife would attack husband. Parents devoured children as they cowered in the corner of their bedrooms, pleading for their parents to stop scaring them.

A trucker had been infected and not realizing it, had continued across the United States, thinking he had nothing more than a bad case of the flu. When he had finally succumbed to the disease, he had managed to infect more people than could be counted.

Those people in turn infected others and like the worst case of the domino effect, more than half the United States was infected in days. That was when the government realized the infection couldn't be controlled and martial law had gone into affect.

The only good news in such a horrific situation was that the disease only seemed to affect humans. The animals seemed to be immune to reanimation, although not immune to being torn apart for their meat and blood by the undead hordes.

Almost all the dogs and cats were extinct in the United States now, all of them ripped apart and devoured for their flesh. Some tried to run, being quicker than the walking corpses, but they couldn't outrun the simple overwhelming amount of undead and were always cornered and then taken down. Those dogs and cats that tried to hide were only found as well, the zombies able to almost sense the life force of the living.

Before the outbreak had become out of control, his mother had been attacked when she had gone to the grocery store to stock up on canned goods and bottled water. The news was still trying to get a handle on what was happening and his mother had decided stocking up on supplies would be a good idea. She had been bitten on her arm as she exited the store. She escaped, but the damage was done; she was infected.

William still remembered the screams from his mother while she thrashed in her bed, the infection slowly taking over her body. His father had sat with her for as long as possible, until he was absolutely sure there was no hope. Then with sadness in his eyes, he had walked William to the kitchen and asked him to wait there.

His dad had patted him on the shoulder briefly, and with a sadness in is eyes William couldn't understand at the time, his father turned and walked back upstairs, a few of the steps near the bottom creaking under his weight as he slowly plodded up each one. When he reached the top landing, he seemed to pause, hesitating about moving further, but after a second or two his father had moved on to the end of the hallway.

William could hear him rummaging in the hall closet and he felt a sinking feeling in his stomach. His dad was retrieving his revolver. That was the only time he ever went into the hall closet, there was nothing else there he would have needed.

Above William on the second floor, he could hear the creaking floorboards as his father moved across the hall floor. He heard the bedroom door open and his mother's wails of pain drifted down the stairs until the door was closed once more.

Another anguished hour ticked by agonizingly slow, his mother's sounds of pain filling the house, far too loud for the bedroom door to muffle. Then her screams stopped and she succumbed to unconsciousness.

Hours went by, his father standing a silent vigil over her bedside.

William remained at the bottom of the stairs, waiting for what would come next.

Then she died.

Only to return minutes later.

The house was silent, only the sirens from outside drifting into the house to break the quiet. Most of the shrieks of panic and terror had fallen away from the street outside, most of the people either moving on or just retreating to their homes. William stood at the bottom of the stairs for what seemed like days, but was in fact only hours. His legs ached from standing too long and he decided he should just sit down and give his muscles a break.

Then he jumped when the sound of a single gunshot drifted down the stairs. The shot seemed to echo forever while William contemplated what that shot meant.

He was about to head upstairs when another echo of a gunshot bounced off the walls of the house.

With eyes wide in panic, he ran up the stairs, taking them two at a time. Pushing through the bedroom door, he stopped in horror at the visceral scene in front of him. His breath lodged in his throat and he started to shake his head in denial. What was in front of him couldn't be real; it must be some kind of nightmare. He must have sat down on the couch and fallen asleep and was even now dreaming.

But something deep inside himself told him that he wasn't dreaming; that what was in front of him was the end of a large part of his world. One of the reasons he enjoyed living so much was now gone, shattered to never return.

His mother's brains covered the back wall behind the bed, the blood and gray matter already starting to slip down the painted wall to disappear behind the headboard.

On the carpeted floor next to her was his father. At first glance, William knew he was dead, as well. The smell of gunpowder and copper filled the room and he slowly moved closer to what were once his parents. His legs felt weak and for a moment he wondered if he was going to faint, but after taking a few deep breaths, he began feeling better.

He looked down to see something next to his father's left hand. It was a small piece of notebook paper. Small red dots covered the white page and William leaned down to pick it up.

The words I'm sorry, were written hastily in his father's handwriting. William let the paper fall from his hand. It drifted down to land in the spreading puddle of his father's blood, the thin carpet not absorbent enough to hold the viscous fluid.

He stood there quietly, listening to the sirens wail outside the window. The sound of crunching metal and shattered glass floated into the room from an accident on the street in front of his house.

After a moment a muffled explosion filled the night, only to fall away a few seconds later.

He barely noticed, caught up in his own internal grief for his family. He was angry at his father for what he'd just done. The selfish bastard had taken the easy way out. What the hell had he been thinking?

When he put a round through his head, William's father had also resigned to abandon his son.

Now he was alone in a dying world.

Time went by slowly. William didn't notice. He stood in his parent's bedroom for another hour before coming out of his stupor. He realized he couldn't just leave his parents to rot where they lay, so he started the arduous task of burying them. One after the other, he wrapped each one in a blanket and dragged them down the stairs. With muscles screaming from the weight of the dead bodies, he pulled and pushed his parents to the backyard. His father's head wound was so bloody the blood leaked through the sheet William had wrapped him in, and as he dragged the corpse through the house, a red trail appeared behind him.

He sighed at that. With the world going to hell he now had to scrub his kitchen floor.

He dragged his father outside and laid him down next to the sheet covered corpse of his mother. He felt like he should be crying, but for whatever reasons the tears wouldn't come. He idly wondered if he was in shock and later, after they were buried, it would all hit him even harder than when he had first walked into the bedroom and found his parents dead.

After retrieving a shovel from the shed in the corner of the yard, he started digging. The whole time he was outside, the sounds of the city falling apart could be heard. Sirens wailed, gunshots sounded and smoke from numerous fires floated on the horizon.

Once two shallow graves were dug, he gently rolled his parent's into the holes, and quickly covered them up.

When he was finished, he wiped the sweat from his brow and made the sign of the cross. While he wasn't overly religious, it felt like the right thing to do.

He said a few prayers and then tried to cry a little.

He managed to squeeze out only a few tears, but soon gave up. He wiped his eyes and then walked back into the house.

With a heavy sigh, he opened the back door and stepped into the dim interior of his now empty home, making sure to secure the door with the deadbolt.

The house was deathly silent with the absence of his parents. Not knowing what to do, he sat down on the living room couch and zoned out. He was in shock. His father had just killed his mother and had then taken his own life. Not the kind of thing one thinks will happen when they get up in the morning.

That was where he had stayed while the world outside his windows had continued to deteriorate. He was alone now. He had no brothers or sisters and most of his extended family was out of state.

He sat there on the couch for hours, until his growling stomach would not be denied. Despite the fact he was starving, he still didn't want to actually eat, so he made a quick cold cut sandwich and washed it down with some tap water.

Absently, he turned the television on. The anchorman for CNN was droning on about the epidemic and how FEMA was being called in to help. Rescue stations scrolled across the bottom of the screen as well as all the school and business closings. He watched it all in a daze, still finding it hard to believe. No matter how bad it was becoming, the government still wanted people to act as if everything was fine, that this was an isolated thing.

So far no one had used the word *zombies*. The news had only referred to them as the *infected*. But William knew better, all the signs were there, if only they would accept it.

But he knew they wouldn't.

Just like every other emergency, such as with Louisiana and Hurricane Katrina, the government was always slow to react. And this time would be no different.

By the time the politicians stopped arguing and deciding on a course of action, the world would probably be overrun.

He turned the television off, deciding he'd heard enough for the moment. So far the power was still on and he could only pray it would stay that way. He picked up the phone on the kitchen wall, pleased to hear a dial tone. If only he had someone to call.

William had always been somewhat of a loner. His movies and books enough to keep him company. Still, it would have been nice to have at least one person to call or to have someone call him, checking up on his welfare.

He turned to the stairs that led to the second floor, still expecting his parents to come down from their room and yell at him for having the television on too loud or some such thing.

He let out a long sigh, the sadness welling up inside him again. He felt tears and decided he needed to occupy himself before he started crying. He wasn't quite ready to go down that road at the moment.

A scream floated into the room, coming from the front of the house in the direction of the street and William ran to the window to see what was happening out there now.

A woman and a man were running down the middle of the street, their car left where it had struck a telephone pole. The pole lay on its side, half of the top lying on the front lawn of a nearby home. The other accident he had heard earlier remained where the vehicles had collided, immobile. Steam drifted from under the hood of one of them, a Honda he thought, not that it mattered.

The man and woman darted by the front of his house and continued running, darting and weaving between the few undead bodies that tried to grab them as they passed to close to reaching arms. The two easily avoided the zombies, much too quick for them and soon disappeared at the end of the street and out of William's line of sight. William craned his head against the window to see what they were running from and let out a gasp.

Five new zombies shambled down the street, each in a state of disrepair. The first one in line looked to be a middle-aged man. His stomach was torn open and his intestines dragged along behind him like a child's jump rope. His head had a deep gash in it and William could have sworn he could see some white of bone peeking through his matted hair.

The zombie behind the middle-aged man kept stepping on the ends of the guy's intestines, causing the man to jerk as he was stopped for a moment, then he would continue on when the pressure was released. The second zombie in line, the one that kept stepping on intestines, was a woman, or used to be a woman.

136

Now she was nothing more than a mess of ripped flesh and exposed tendons and muscles. While she walked, her muscles and exposed, moist organs glistened in the sun. Every now and then a piece would fall out of her and land in the street with a meaty *thwap*. Despite this, William was able to tell that the clothes she wore had once been reasonably expensive.

The zombies behind the woman didn't mind her pieces falling away to hit the sidewalk, though, because every time a piece fell, one of the others would bend over and pick it up and start to chew merrily.

The other three zombies in line were in a similar state. Except their torsos seemed to be intact.

The last one in line looked to be a teenage boy, seventeen years old or so and was probably only a few years younger than William. The boy was wearing one bloody, high top sneaker on his right foot, the other missing. He walked at a slant due to the height of the one piece of footwear. He bobbed up and down as the higher foot would move him forward and then he'd drop down when his barefoot struck the pavement.

The boy stopped when he was directly in front of William's house. He seemed to sniff the air while he looked around the street. Then the head turned to look at William. William jumped back, hoping he hadn't been seen. After waiting only a few seconds, he peeked out the side of the curtain and let out a sigh of relief when he saw the boy was gone. His heartbeat started to slow down and he was about to continue on with his day when the front window shattered, sending splinters of razor-sharp glass into the room.

William jumped to the side, acting on instinct. The sun's rays shone into the room as he rolled around on the carpet, his arm over his eyes. When he pulled his face clear, he was looking out the window at the zombie boy; the boy's blackened teeth grinning malevolently.

Evidently he had seen William and had scurried up the front lawn to get at him. The zombie was trying to climb through the window, its clothes catching on the exposed shards of glass in the window frame. William rolled to his feet and looked over the zombie's shoulder to see the other four walking cadavers now walking on his front lawn toward his house, and behind them, others started towards the house, as well, attracted to all the commotion.

In less than a minute a crowd of the undead was heading straight to William's house looking for a free meal.

He was in real trouble.

The boy zombie had managed to climb into the room, leaving large chunks of flesh behind it on the window sill. The blood covered shards reflected the light and covered the side wall with a dull red-glow from its reflection.

Climbing into the room, now minus more skin, the boy moved closer to William. It didn't seem to mind the extra wounds on its body.

William backed up against the far wall of the room, shock and panic freezing him to the spot. His heart felt like it was on the verge of exploding, while slowly the zombie moved closer to him, with the others not far behind.

He looked for a weapon, but there was nothing close to his hands. A lamp was at his feet and he picked it up and threw it at the first zombie. The weighted base of the lamp struck it in the temple, leaving a pinkish, red dent in its forehead, but still it came at him. Near his feet was a heavy bookend, one of his father's favorites. William picked it up and after hefting the heavy object, tossed it at the zombie boy. His aim was off and he managed to strike another zombie a grazing blow across the shoulder. The book end fell to the floor with a loud thump and was forgotten.

He tried to run, but they surrounded him, hands pulling him every which way, while the sheer weight of their bodies forced him to the floor. He cried out, screaming for help, but there was no one to hear his plaintive cries. Though he knew what was coming next, his mind refused to believe it.

Surely someone would come and rescue the hero of this story; the story that was his life and he the main character.

He felt the first teeth sinking into his right arm and he let out a shriek that hurt his own ears. Blinding white light flooded his vision and another set of rotted teeth sank into the meaty part of his thigh. He tried to kick the face away, but only ended up opening another piece of his leg to more teeth.

Then a face was leaning over his and he stared up into the eyes of death. White mucous covered the eyes and even in his pain he wondered how the infected could see anything. Then he was screaming again as that face dove onto his, blackened teeth clamping down on his nose and ripping it off. He tried to yell again, but blood from his shredded nose poured into his nasal cavity, causing him to choke. He was totally covered in bodies, each one vying for a piece of his tender flesh. He tried to turn his head to the left or right, attempting to spit the blood out of his throat onto the carpet, but legs and arms prevented it.

He realized he was drowning in his own blood and with each spasm the pain from the feeding zombies grew less, as if it was happening from far away.

His vision faded to black and he twitched one last time under the mass of bodies. Then he remained still, despite the feeding frenzy still being perpetrated on his person.

An unknown time passed and his eyes opened once more. The second his eyelids fluttered open, the undead backed off. His life-force was gone and he had become unappetizing to them. Now he was one of them.

One at a time they shambled away from him, some climbing back through the shattered front window, others moving deeper into the house; not knowing where they were going, but feeling the need to move in any direction.

William sat up; his head swiveling around like an owl in a tree.

He climbed to his feet, unsteady. Large amounts of his flesh, muscles, and tendons were missing, but he was still able to move slowly. One of his Achilles tendons had been severed by a pair of teeth and his right leg dragged behind him.

He barely noticed.

He shambled towards the window with treacle-like movements, his limbs barely functioning. Something from his past life was telling him he had spent time there recently, gazing out the window. Once he had made it to the frame, he accidentally leaned out, his body tumbling forward to fall onto the grass that covered the front of the house.

His missing nose allowed dirt to become lodged in his sinus cavity, the moist smell filling his head. He blew most of the soil out, the brown mucus dripping down his mouth and over his chin.

His arm became broken from the fall, but he barely felt it. The sharp sliver of fractured bone that now pierced his arm near his elbow was irrelevant.

Rolling to his feet, he shuffled out into the street to join his brethren.

He was hungry and he knew what would satisfy him. He joined his fellow undead in the road as they started up the street, searching for prey.

Sometimes they would find some foolish person who had ventured out into the streets, ignoring the warnings on the television. When that would happen, he and his fellow undead would feed and then add another soldier to their increasingly growing army.

In his addled brain he felt serenity. He was a part of something now. He had friends now. Though they didn't speak, he still felt their presence.

He may have been dead, but he was at least happy now. The group continued to grow, feeding as they moved through the city. Hundreds of humans were slaughtered and quickly added to the undead ranks.

Nothing could stop them, they were unbeatable. They would cover the earth and devour everything, until the earth was nothing but an empty candy dish with a few crumpled wrappers in the bottom of the bowl.

Then he heard a noise, like a rumbling. All heads turned toward the sound, eager to see if it was more prey.

From around the street corner a Humvee and an army issued tank rolled onto the street. Sitting on the back of the Humvee was an M-60 machine gun, the gunner already preparing the weapon for fire into the crowd of walking corpses.

William saw all this and a faint grin creased his face. They would overwhelm these vehicles and then consume the humans inside. Then, they too, would join the undead. That is, unless there was nothing left to come back.

As one entity the rotting crowd of human flesh turned and moved toward the Humvee, no fear or terror lived in their dead hearts or showed on their slack-jawed faces.

When the first walking corpse was no more than eight feet away from the vehicle, the gunner opened up with the M-60. White hot tracers floated over the heads of the undead for a moment and then the gunner got his height and range.

One after another heads began to explode as the high caliber rounds shattered skulls like soft melons. Skull fragments peppered the street like shrapnel, multiple shrapnel impacts striking William in the face and arms. He shrugged them off and continued over his fallen comrades. He knew they would be victorious. None had stopped them before, and why would now be any different?

One after another, the animated cadavers were mowed down, like wheat stalks in a high wind. Less than two minutes had passed since the first shot was fired and William realized he was one of the only few left standing. Something inside him, something that remained of his old self, screamed for his body to turn and run, that there was no hope of victory; but the part of him that was now fully in charge ignored him.

The hunger drove him forward and it would not be denied.

William and the last of his brethren charged forward, climbing over their dead comrades like they were attacking the beach at Normandy. One after the other they were continually mowed down. William looked to his left and his right and realized he was the last one standing. The machine gunner had stopped firing, the gun pointed at the sky, the heat of the muzzle clearly visible in the light of the day.

William grinned. He was immortal, undefeatable. He was the last one standing because he was the best, which was why the gunner had stopped shooting. He had cringed when he had seen William's face.

From around the back of the Humvee a man in a green uniform moved to the front of the vehicle. He had an army issued helmet on and the three stars glued to the front of the helmet glinted in the sun.

The man walked until he was only a foot from the first prone, dead body on the road. William watched for only a moment, then dove forward, crawling over the others to get at this man who would defy him.

The soldier reached down to his holster and unfastened the strap keeping his sidearm secured. William didn't notice; he just wanted to taste the man's blood when it flowed into his mouth from a torn out jugular.

William was only a few feet away and he knew in another heartbeat of his non- functioning heart he would be in reach of this foolish man.

Like lightning, the soldier whipped out his 9mm pistol and aimed it at William's head. William saw the weapon buck in the man's hand and a wisp of smoke floated from the barrel. Then he felt some kind of impact on his forehead. His head jerked back and he tumbled head over heels to land on the road amidst the arms and legs of his brethren. His vision blurred and then went out, like a light switch turning off, casting a room into darkness.

The soldier turned to his men and waved them onward, climbing back aboard the Humvee when it drove by him. The soldier had a slight grin on his face. They were slowly making progress and if things stayed the way they were, then this city would be cleared of infected people by dawn.

The tank rolled over the prone bodies, churning the corpses to a red mush. William's body was one of these and despite what was happening to his corpse, William would have been happy.

As his body blended with dozens of others, he could have taken solace in knowing that he would never be alone again, his body mingling with others for all of eternity.

Death On A Mountain

Karen ran through the darkening woods, her breath coming in ragged gasps.

She had no way of knowing how many miles she covered since she awoke in the middle of the forest; all alone in the mountains. Night was falling fast and as the light diminished, she realized she would be helpless once the last rays of the slowly fading sun finally disappeared.

Something whizzed by her ear, and she swerved to her right, away from the projectile.

An arrow had narrowly missed her head, and it was either blind luck or that her captor was playing with her, that she was still breathing.

She saw a path through the trees after swerving from the arrow's path and she took off in that direction. For all she knew she was only moving deeper and deeper into the Colorado mountains, but at the moment that didn't matter.

The only thing that mattered was escape.

She heard laughter coming from behind her, but she didn't look. If she did, she knew the chances of her tripping on a fallen tree or spraining her ankle in a gopher hole would only intensify. Even now, with the light almost gone, she knew the odds of her falling over some unseen object and cracking her skull open was growing every second.

While she ran, gruesome images of her falling into a crevice or just plain running over the edge of an unseen cliff flooded her mind. She imagined her body plummeting over the edge, falling the hundreds of feet to the jagged rocks below, where her fragile human form would shatter into a hundred pieces of flesh and muscle and gore. Her blood would paint the rocks scarlet only to disappear as it was absorbed into the earth.

And no one would ever know what had happened to her.

That was one of the scariest things to think about. The fact that her mom, dad and her friends would never know what was happening to her right now, on this mountain.

If she died up here, no one would ever find her body.

She imagined a small newspaper article appearing in one of the local papers, somewhere near the back of the periodical. **LOCAL WOMAN MISSING, POLICE FEEL NO WRONG DOING. HUSBAND IN SHOCK.**

That made her almost laugh if she had wanted to expend the energy to do so, but instead, she continued running.

She could still barely accept the reality she was now thrown into. And who could blame her? Only two days before, she had been sitting in her home, watching television and enjoying a few days off from work; and now she was running for her life in the middle of nowhere.

Reaching a large tree with a massive trunk, she leaned against it and tried to slow her breathing. She had always been an excellent runner, running more than five miles a day and six on the weekends. In her reality, she should have left her hunter far behind by now.

Yet he was so close, and if she stopped and strained her hearing, she could hear his footfalls crackling on the forest floor. The only reason for this strange occurrence had to be that her pursuer knew these woods far better than she could ever know them and by that fact alone, he was able to keep up with her, knowing when to take a shortcut and using the paths of least resistance, while she had to barrel and force her way through the overgrown underbrush.

Realizing she had stopped for long enough, she took off at a steady jog. There was almost no light left, the darkness nearly complete. She knew she needed to find a place to hold up for the night. She needed to rest and plan.

Her arms stung from the dozen or so small scratches she had already picked up from the foliage and low hanging branches.

She was a smart woman and she knew if she was given a chance to work out what was happening she would be able to figure out a way to get out of her present predicament.

Running down a slope and almost falling forward, she managed to regain her balance. It was a good thing, too. If she had lost her footing and started to fall, she would have ended up falling head over heels and the chance of preventing herself from crashing into a tree or breaking her neck on a low branch would have been nearly non-existent.

Reaching the bottom, she ran on. She knew her hunter wouldn't shoot her now, though. He liked the sport, the challenge. Once darkness would fall he would keep an eye on her, but would not shoot her.

No, he wanted her to see it coming.

Karen slowed down now, walking more slowly while the darkness descended in force. She looked up at the cloudless sky to see a blanket of twinkling stars.

Despite this, the solid overhead roof of the forest kept all but an insignificant amount of light from filtering down to the leafy earth, the illumination not strong enough to penetrate its leafy tops.

Karen slowed as she came upon an open clearing. A few scattered boulders were in a rough semi-circle and a few pieces of debris were scattered around the area. From first glance it was obvious this was a sight frequented by campers and hikers. Unfortunately, tonight the area was devoid of all life, except for her, of course...and her hunter.

Dropping down onto the spongy sod, she curled up into a ball and cried. Whether the tears were for her or for Brian, she did not know. But she cried none the less.

Rolling onto her back, she gazed up at the night sky through the opening in the tree tops. Closing her eyes, she thought back to only one day ago and to how it had all started and what had brought her to be all alone in the mountains with a killer on her trail.

*   *   *

Karen moaned in pleasure for the hundredth time since her lover, Brian, had joined her in bed. Though she was a married woman, her husband had grown so distant and devoid of feelings for her that she had completely given up on him.

In fact, the man seemed to love hunting in the mountains more than making love to his wife.

Despite this, she was certainly not going to ask for a divorce. Her husband, Martin, was rich and she'd be damned if she was going to throw away almost five years of marriage now.

No, instead she would just have a little fun on the side and let the marriage continue. She had taken a few days off, deciding with spring now here that she should enjoy a little of life. Though she worked, it wasn't for the money, but for the fun of it. Her fellow workers despised her for it, but she ignored them. It wasn't her fault that she had married well.

She had met Brian on one of her many late lunches in the cafeteria. He was tall and handsome with a boyish face and a muscular body. His eyes were a deep blue that reminded her of an ocean in the midst of a storm and though when she had first met him she had only said a few idle words to pass the time, she had already decided to sleep with him.

After the first time she had met him, they continued running into each other, if not at the cafeteria, then at the coffee shop near their office building. In less than two weeks they had become good friends and though Brian didn't know it yet, they were about to become closer.

She had made her move on him one day after work. Both of them were leaving at the same time and she had hinted that she had no plans that night and would love to go out on the town. At first the man was oblivious, but soon he understood what she was implying.

He had asked her out and the two of them had enjoyed a marvelous time on the town. That night she had returned to his apartment and the two of them had made wild, passionate love; the kind of passion that was so far removed from her own marriage that it seemed like a dream. She hadn't realized how much she had missed being paid attention to, the way he would caress her skin and nuzzle his chin into her neck as they made love. It drove her mad with desire.

The affair had gone on for weeks, the two of them happy in each others arms. Her husband never noticed a thing. Too busy working and going off on his hunting trips. That was where he was now. It was Saturday and he had left early the following day. She wouldn't expect him back until late Sunday night, so she knew both she and Brian would be safe to spend some time in her own house for a change.

Though she didn't mind his apartment, the other tenants had grown accustom to seeing her, but the way they looked at her, as if they knew she was an adulterer, bothered her.

No, she preferred to be in her own house, situated on a private drive where no prying eyes could see her or her guests.

Brian did something special with his tongue that caused her to moan louder. He was a wonderful lover, kind and giving, not to mention he was hung like a porn star.

Writhing in the bed in ecstasy, she reached up and kissed him, her arms wrapping around his head. Lips met in a lustful embrace and she felt herself reaching an orgasm.

Her eyes fluttered and she felt a wave of serenity flow through her. Brian orgasmed with her and the two of them lay together on the wide, master bed, panting and gasping together. She had her eyes closed, enjoying the feeling of utter relaxation when the bedroom door was suddenly kicked in; the door swinging so hard the doorknob lodged in the wall behind it.

Brian rolled from the bed, not understanding what was happening when Martin stepped into the room and raised the butt of his shotgun.

Before Brian could so much as yell in surprise, the butt struck him in the forehead, the man dropping to the floor unconscious.

"Martin, what the hell are you doing here? You're supposed to be hunting until tomorrow?" She asked, her voice frantic.

Below her on the floor, Brian groaned, a bloody head wound making a mess of the carpeting.

"Oh, I'm sorry, do you want me to come back tomorrow so you and your man-whore can keep desecrating my bed? You bitch, I had my suspicions that you were cheating on me, but I didn't want to admit it. So when my hunting partner took sick, I decided to cut my trip short and surprise you." He waved his hands around the room, his gesture referring to the house and its possessions. "Haven't I given you everything you've ever wanted? Haven't I been faithful to you? In all the years we've been together I never once looked at another woman and this is how you repay me?"

Karen stood up from the bed, her nakedness irrelevant to her.

"Yes, that's true, you never looked at another woman, but you never looked at me either. Too damn busy going on your damn hunting trips to pay me the slightest bit of attention. I have needs, too, and not just sexual. I'm not your damn property, Martin, I'm your wife!" She screamed at him, her eyes flaring with anger.

Martin stepped closer, his jaw set tight. He stopped when he was no more than an arms length from her.

Karen didn't flinch, but held his gaze, refusing to give in, though deep down inside she had to admit she was frightened.

Martin smiled then, his teeth flashing in the light of the room. Karen had never seen him smile like that. Though his mouth may have been curved slightly up, his eyes showed no amusement.

"So, you're my wife, and not my property, is that it?" He asked. "Well, I'll tell you this, you're half-right." Then he slammed the butt of the shotgun across her temple, causing her to fall back to the bed in a heap of limbs.

She lay there, on the verge of consciousness and passing out. Everything was a blur and though she wanted to get up and run away, her body ignored her.

From a blurry haze, she saw Martin pick up Brian and carry him out the bedroom door. She could hear his footsteps fading away and before she realized any time had passed, he was back, now picking her up as well. He grabbed some of her clothes from the closet and tossed them on her body, then carried her down the stairs. That was when she finally passed out; her mind falling into a black void that she could only hope wouldn't be permanent.

*　*　*

She awoke to the setting sun, the crimsons and violets causing her to wince. She realized she was lying on the ground and when she sat up, she saw she was in the woods. The redolence of the forest assailed her nose, causing her to want to sneeze.

Damn allergies, she thought.

"Good, you're up; lover-boy's been awake for almost a half hour. Now we can have some fun," Martin said from her side.

Turning her head, she winced at the sudden pain. She must have pulled something when Martin had struck her. Trying to sit up, she gasped when she realized she was hog-tied. Her arms and legs secured like she was nothing but a piece of cattle ready for the slaughter.

"What the hell are you doing, Martin? Let me go right now!" She demanded, outraged.

"Oh, don't worry, honey, I'll let you go. But first there are a few rules you should know about."

"Rules, for what? So help me, if you don't let me go right now, I'll see your ass in jail."

He chuckled, his chest heaving with joviality. For some reason, that made her cringe inside.

"Listen up, Karen; because it's just possible you might make it out of here alive."

"I'm not listening to a goddamn thing you say until you untie me, you sick bastard," she spit.

Martin sighed, standing up to his full height of six-two. When she had first met him she had been attracted to his height. He was taller than most men and therefore other men had to look up to him, and therefore by association, her. Now, as he towered over her, she felt herself starting to shake inside.

She was just starting to comprehend that things were very wrong.

"All right, Karen, I was planning to do this another way, but I guess I'll just have to prove to you that this is not a game. Doesn't really matter in the end, though, it's just that I would have preferred to drag it out a little longer." He strode over the leafy landscape, covering the few feet in only a few long-legged strides and stopped at the supine body of Brian. Picking the man up, he dragged him over to her, then Martin pushed him to a sitting position.

Brian was now only a hands-breath away from her. If her hands weren't tied, she could have easily reached out and caressed his cheek. Looking into his eyes, she saw fear in his; a few tears rolling down his cheek, his mouth covered with tape so he couldn't talk back.

She couldn't blame him, though; she knew what her husband was capable of. Brian was still naked, his skin covered in dirt and small twigs that had become imbedded in his skin while he lay on the forest floor.

"I think you need to see me do this to see how serious I am, Karen," Martin said, pulling a nine-inch survival knife from its leather sheath on his hip.

"Do what? What the hell are you talking about? Untie me dammit!" She screamed, struggling with her bonds.

Martin reached out with his left hand and grabbed Brian's hair in a firm grip. Then in one smooth motion, like he was casually slaughtering a pig or deer for supper, he brought the blade to Brian's throat and sliced the flesh open.

The razor-honed blade sliced into the skin like a hot knife through butter. Brian's carotid artery was cleanly cut, his blood shooting from his throat to shower Karen's body in scarlet.

Her eyes stinging from the warm fluid, she screamed, causing her mouth to become full. Spitting out the viscous fluid, she turned her head away from the ghastly scene.

The entire time Brian choked and gagged, his mouth covered by duct tape, he never screamed. He couldn't with his mouth taped shut.

Karen turned back to her dying lover and friend and looked into his eyes. That was where he was screaming, his pupils wide with fright and pain. At first he struggled, trying to free himself of his bonds, but as his blood drained from his body with every beat of his betraying heart, his actions slowed.

Karen watched the light go out of his eyes and she felt tears of sadness and loss flow down her cheeks, washing a miniscule amount of her lover's blood from her face.

When Martin knew the man was dead, the gash in his throat only seeping a small amount of blood, he tossed the corpse to the wooded ground.

Ignoring the body, he knelt down in front of her and with his right thumb, brushed some of her hair from her face. The strands were sticky with blood and he pushed them to her forehead, then he grinned.

"Now do you see how serious I am?" He asked, quietly, as if he was asking her what's for dinner.

Trying to hold back the sobs, she nodded, too petrified to talk.

"Good, now here are the rules. I'm going to untie you and you're going to run away from me. I doubt you'll have a problem with that rule. Now, we are all alone up here in the mountains, so there's no one to help you. You say I like hunting and spend more time doing that than spending time with you? Well, okay then. You also say we don't do enough together, so I figure this will be the perfect activity for the both of us."

Regaining enough of her composure to believe she could talk without crying or screaming, she asked: "What are you going to do to me?"

"Ah, well that's where the joint activity comes in." He pointed to his bow and arrow, leaning against a log a few feet away from the two of them.

"You see my bow over there?"

She nodded.

"Good, well I'm going to cut you free and you're going to run away from here," he said, repeating himself.

"What then?" She asked quietly.

He leaned in close to her, so close she could smell his breath. "Why, I'm going to hunt you down like the traitorous bitch you are and put an arrow straight through your black heart."

Her breath lodged in her throat and she shook with terror. He couldn't be serious? He wanted to hunt her down like one of the hundreds of deer he came into these woods to track and kill every year?

She was so shocked and appalled, she didn't realize he was cutting her bonds until her hands were free, then he did the same with her legs.

Finishing, he stepped back from her and retrieved his bow.

"Okay, bitch, I'm feeling generous, especially after putting lover-boy there out of my misery, so I tell you what...I'll give you five minutes head start." His head tilted down and his eyes looked up at her, gleaming in the slowly setting sun. "Then I come for you."

She stood there, not quite believing what was happening to her, then Martin brought up the bow and knocked an arrow.

"If you don't want to run, I can just kill you here and be done with it," he stated blatantly.

Karen backed away from him, moving to the edge of the clearing.

"Tick tock, tick tock," Martin said, waggling his index finger in front of his chest.

With one last look at Brian's body, she backed out of the clearing and began to run. Branches struck her face and she tried to duck, but they seemed to be everywhere, reaching out to grasp her in their embrace.

Muffling her cries and trying to conserve her energy for running, she kept moving, hoping beyond all possible hope she could somehow lose her hunter and somehow make it out of the mountains alive.

*   *   *

Opening her eyes, she realized the sun was coming up. Sitting up, she brushed leaves and twigs that had become entangled in her hair from her restless night in the woods. For the hundredth time, she thanked God that Martin had chosen to dress her after he had brought her out here to the middle of nowhere. That made her think of Brian, lying naked somewhere behind her, his dead body spread out on the forest floor. She wondered if Martin would bury him or simply let the wild animals dispose of the body.

She pushed such macabre thoughts from her mind. There would be time to think of Brian later, if she somehow survived this ordeal.

Standing up, she suddenly realized she needed to pee. Deciding every bush was a toilet; she stumbled over to the nearest bush and squatted down, her pants on her ankles.

She was just about finished, when an arrow flew by her head, so close she might have been struck if she hadn't leaned back at the last moment.

Jumping to her feet, and pulling her pants up as she ran, she took off down a small deer path. While she ran, she could hear the sound of laughter coming from behind her.

Evidently with the sun in the sky, she was a target again.

She ran all morning, having no idea how many miles she'd covered.

Slowing as she approached a small stream, she fell to her hands and knees, drinking greedily from the cold, clear water. Her throat felt soothed and when she had drunk her fill, she splashed her face and dunked her hair in the stream, trying to wash the blood from her hair and face.

Most of the blood had already dried and flaked off, and in no time she was feeling better. A bird cried in the towering branches, causing her to jump up and survey her surroundings.

Nothing but trees and rocks in every direction.

She tried to quiet her breathing, hoping to catch the sound of her hunter as he traversed the wooded landscape, but nothing came to her.

She frowned. Martin was a skilled woodsman and she considered sitting out in her backyard on the grass roughing it. No, if he was out there, the odds of her hearing him would be infinitesimal.

Deciding she had rested for long enough, she began crossing the stream, careful not to lose her footing on the slippery, wet rocks. Upon reaching the other side, she breathed a sigh of relief. One small hurdle down, only a thousand more to go before she was safe again.

She looked in front of her, trying to decide the best path. To her right the land curved downward, into what, she had no idea. To her left the land stayed level, following the path of the stream, or she could go straight ahead, the land slowly sloping upward.

She had always been one to make a decision quickly, dealing with the consequences later if she had made the wrong choice. This served her well now, not having time to debate the best way to run.

She decided to move up the slope, hoping once she reached the top, perhaps she could see something that could help her. Maybe a ranger station or a road.

She headed up the hill, only looking over her shoulder a few times. With Martin following her with a bow and arrow, he didn't need to get close to her to kill her. She quickly realized she would not see her death coming, instead a slim arrow would find her before she knew it was there, so she focused her attention on what was in front of her, concentrating on not falling or having her foot land in a gopher burrow or some other small creatures home below the ground.

With her breath coming in gasps, she continued climbing, praying her salvation was at the top of the ridge.

With the last of her strength, she climbed the few more yards to the top of the ridge. Breathing heavily, covered in perspiration, she looked out on the roof of the forest below her. Nothing but mountains and trees for as far as the eye could see.

She slumped and fell onto the hard earth and sat there wanting to cry, but knowing it would be a waste of precious energy. Turning her head to her back-trail, nothing moved behind her. If Martin was close, she had no way of knowing where he was. She let her upper body fall to the earth, her chest heaving as she took in breath after breath. The sky overhead was a clear blue with only a smattering of white fluffy clouds to mar its brilliance.

Though she was never one for nature, she had to admit it was beautiful up here in the mountains. The smell of the trees and wet earth filled her nostrils and she relished it. Every second her heart beat was one more than Martin wanted her to have.

Rolling over to her side, she sat back up. She had to think of a way to outmaneuver him, but how? The man was a trained woodsman, while she had never stepped foot in a true forest her entire life.

While she sat there racking her brain, she watched a family of birds in one of the branches. She wasn't good with types of birds, but she guessed they might have been some kind of swallow or sparrow, something small with wings, she thought. A bird was a bird.

She watched the two adult birds as they flew back and forth from the tree, looking for food for their young. Though she couldn't see the younglings due to the height of the tree branch, she could hear them chirping, exclaiming to the world that they were here to stay and that they were hungry.

Across from her, only a few yards away, a rabbit scampered across the path she had just left. The rabbit watched her for only a moment, its nose twitching as it tried to deduce if she was hostile, then it decided she was no danger to it and was about to scamper back into the foliage when an arrow ripped the air and the rabbit became transfixed. The small animal was dead before the arrow had finished its passage through its body, the small heart punctured.

The rabbit fell to the earth and with the exception of a twitching leg, was still.

"You're next, bitch!" Martin yelled from across the wooded landscape.

She tried to see where he was, but his voice only bounced off the trees. Jumping to her feet the moment the rabbit had been shot, she started to run again, anticipating an arrow through her back at any moment. Her arms pumped in front of her and she darted between trees, trying to move as fast as she could without tripping on the rugged terrain.

She never stopped or slowed, but kept moving.

Not knowing where she was going, she felt like she had left the earth, only to have been dropped in a world with nothing but trees and rocks for company.

She had no conception of how long she ran, but when the sun had reached its zenith, she slowed to take a break. Behind her, all was quiet. If Martin had managed to keep up with her than he was a better athlete than her.

Once again she thanked God, she enjoyed running for exercise; never realizing it might have been the thing that might just save her life one day.

Run to live, live to run, the jogger's mantra had never meant as much as it did right now.

Leaning against a rock, she decided she was probably okay for at least a few minutes. She figured Martin was tracking her, able to see her trail even when she did her best to leave no mark of her passage.

When she felt she could move again, she set off at a walking pace. Though every fiber of her being wanted to just keep running, she knew that was impossible. She had to slow her pace or he would easily catch up to her when she finally collapsed from exhaustion.

There was another slope in front of her, this one steeper than the last one, and using the surrounding trees for leverage, she climbed upward.

Upon reaching the top, she once again looked across the open mountain range. The sun was high in the sky and would be starting its descent soon. She wasn't relishing that at all. She knew there were bears and mountain lions out here with her, maybe even some cougars. Wouldn't it be the ultimate irony to be running from her husband only to be mauled by a wild animal?

As she looked out over the tops of the trees, she found herself smiling. If she had to die, then what a perfect way to deny her husband the pleasure of killing her. To take that away from him would almost be as sweet as escaping his clutches.

She looked off to her right and gasped when she saw smoke, a thin line coming from between the treetops. Someone else was out here. Maybe they had a cell phone or a radio and could call for help?

With no other venture feasible, she started down the hill in the direction of the smoke. She had no way of even believing she would be able to keep a straight line and reach the campfire, but it was all she had.

Deciding it was time to start running again, she started a quick jog, her steady rhythm quickly eating up the miles under her feet. She didn't know what waited for her at the bottom of the smoke trail, but it had to be better than what was behind her.

*   *   *

While Karen continued running toward the smoke she had seen in the distance, the actual campfire was surrounded by four people, blissfully going about their business.

"Tina, did you pack my razors?" Brad asked, in a frustrated voice.

Tina stopped digging in her own backpack long enough to look up at her boyfriend. "Brad, I've told you before, I'm not your mother, and no, I didn't pack your razors." She stood up and walked over to him, her slender figure swaying suggestively. "Besides, I like it when you don't shave," she said, rubbing his cheek with her hand, "it makes you look sexy."

Brad answered her by grinning mischievously and wrapping his arms around her and kissing her.

It was at that precise moment that the foliage parted to the right of the kissing couple and another couple walked into the small clearing.

The man and woman were holding hands, the woman chewing on a piece of grass, the small stock swishing back and forth while she chewed. Both stopped when they saw Brad and Tina kissing.

"Jesus, guys, do you ever stop? You're like a couple of dogs in heat," Chris said, stopping by the fire and sitting down. The woman plopped down on his lap, wrapping her arms around her boyfriend's head. "Oh, leave them alone, Chris, I think it's sweet. I wish you were more like Brad."

Chris's eyebrows went up in surprise. "Oh, yeah, since when? Jesus, Wendy, I thought you liked me for me, now you're comparing me with dumb and stupid over there?"

Wendy leaned over, kissed him and lowered her voice so only Chris could hear. "Oh, stop, I just wish you wanted to screw more often, that's all. I'm young and in my prime, baby, I have needs," she purred.

Chris sighed, pushing her off his lap. "Christ, Wendy, we've been through this before, once football season is over we can rut all night, every night, if you want, but until then I need to save my energy for the game. Coach said I can go pro if I just stay focused."

Wendy laughed. "Oh, please, that asshole says that to every player on the team."

Brad looked up from kissing Tina to look at his two college friends. "Will you two stop arguing, please? You're ruining the moment."

Tina leaned in close and nuzzled his neck. "Not for me, you've got me so horny I could do you even if they started talking about foreign politics or what they found dead on the path out there in the woods.”

“Oh, really? Well, what do you say we go to our tent and continue this conversation in private?”

Tina giggled, turned, and ran for their tent, already starting to undress.

Once the two disappeared in the tent, Wendy turned to look at Chris, her arms folded in front of her, a pout on her lips.

“That should be us, Chris; it’s been too damn long,” Wendy said.

Chris gathered her up in his arms and looked her in the eyes. “Relax, baby, the season’s almost over and once it is, I’m gonna rock your world.”

Wendy’s countenance softened and she sighed, leaning into his arms. “Oh, Chris, I don’t know why I put up with you,” she said softly.

He chuckled. “That’s easy, babe, because I’m so damn good looking and hung down to here,” he said, patting the side of his thigh with his hand.

She slapped him playfully and scooted out of his grasp.

“Fine,” she said

“Come on; let’s get something ready to eat. Once those two are finished they’re always hungry,” Chris stated while moving to the packs of food.

Wendy frowned slightly. “Oh, really? I wouldn’t know.” Then she moved to join her boyfriend. Tina and Brad made moaning sounds that floated out of the tent and into the surrounding woods, while up in the sky the sun began its downward descent, the woods soon becoming wreathed in perpetual darkness.

*   *   *

A few hours later, the four friends sat around the campfire talking about life and the future. All four of them were twenty or younger, that golden time in a person’s life when the entire world was open to them.

Tina was curled up in Brad's arms, enjoying his warmth. With the sun now down, the temperature had dropped almost ten degrees, causing them all to don light coats.

Wendy and Chris were huddled together on the other side of the fire, each one holding a stick with a burnt marshmallow on its end.

Bringing the marshmallow close to her face, Wendy tried to blow out the small flame that had erupted on it, the sugary treat burning brightly.

"I like them burnt, but not charcoal," Chris joked.

Wendy nudged him with her elbow. "I don't see yours fairing any better," she quipped back.

Chris looked at his marshmallow and grunted, then tossed it into the shrubs at the edge of the clearing. "Shit, you're right, it's burnt up. God, they make it look so easy on TV," he said, rising to go grab another stick and another bag of marshmallows.

It was while he was up, walking to his backpack, that a woman stumbled into the clearing.

"Help me, please," she gasped, falling to the denuded ground.

"Holy shit! Hey, guys, come here, you won't believe it, but we have a visitor," Chris said, moving to the woman.

Wendy was up first and when she saw the prone figure of a woman on the ground, she quickly ran over to her, only pausing long enough to grab a canteen full of water. Kneeling down next to the woman, Wendy placed her left hand under the woman's head and raised it off the ground. Then with her right holding the canteen, she gently poured some water into the beleaguered woman's mouth.

The woman sputtered out the water at first, but soon she was holding the canteen and drinking deeply.

"There you go, easy does it. Don't drink so much, so fast, they say it'll make you sick," Wendy said, pulling the canteen away.

The woman breathed heavily and blinked up at the faces looking down at her. By now, both Brad and Tina were next to her, as well.

"Who the hell is she and what's she doing way out here without any gear?" Brad asked the others.

"Maybe she got separated from her party or something bad happened," Tina suggested. "Is that blood on her shirt?"

By now the woman was looking a little better and was trying to sit up. Chris helped her and soon the woman was in an upright position. She looked at the canteen, wanting more, and Wendy handed it back. This time the woman drank more slowly.

"What's your name? What are you doing way out here alone? Are you hurt?" Chris asked her.

She stopped drinking and wiped her mouth on her dirty shirt-sleeve.

"My name's Karen, Karen Masterson. I'm fine, but we all need to get out of here, now," she said, gasping each word. All four friends could see the woman looked exhausted.

Chris stood up and looked down at Karen. "What the hell are you talking about, lady? We're not going anywhere. Do you have any idea how long it took us to hike up here?"

Karen shook her head. "No, you don't understand, there's someone after me, he's trying to kill me." She stumbled to her feet, Tina reaching out for her, helping her to stay upright.

"We need to leave before he catches up to me. He'll kill you, too, if he finds you," she stammered.

Brad made a disgusted sound and waved his hand in a 'forget it' gesture. "Lady, you're crazy. What the hell have you been smokin'? You sound like a bad horror movie."

Tina leaned closer to Brad. "I don't know, Brad, look at her. Look at her clothes; I think that's blood on her shirt."

Karen pulled her shirt away from her chest, sticking it into the other's faces. "Yes, this is blood. It's my boyfriend's blood. It got all over me when my husband slashed his throat in front of me."

Wendy took a step back, clearly unsettled. "Jesus, guys, what if she's telling the truth? What if there really is someone after her?"

Brad stepped away from them and moved back to the campfire. His body was silhouetted against the fire as he held out his arms to his sides.

"Are you guys for real? Jesus, there's no way a homicidal killer is running around the mountains slaughtering people. Christ, that only happens in the movies, and bad movies at that," Brad stated snide-fully.

The others were all standing together, watching him near the campfire. Tina was about to voice her objection to his dismissal when a strange sound filled the air.

A loud thwack sound was heard and Brad immediately gasped. At first the others looked around, not knowing what they'd heard, but then Tina screamed and ran to Brad. That's when the others saw a five inch arrow point sticking out of the upper part of Brad's chest.

The arrow had pierced his heart, slicing through the lower ventricle. Though Brad was still standing, his body was already shutting down in death.

With Tina at his side, Brad fell to his knees, looking down at the arrow which a moment before hadn't been there; a thin rivulet of blood dripping out of his mouth. He turned to look at Tina and tried to ask her what was going on, but his voice wouldn't work.

He saw Tina's mouth moving, her face shocked, but he couldn't hear anything. Then his vision grew dark and he fell over onto his face, dead to the world, forever.

Tina screamed again, shaking Brad, trying to make him get up. It was all some kind of joke, that's what it was. He was always playing pranks on her and this was just a really bad one.

As she knelt over Brad, her body illuminated by the firelight, she heard that odd sound again and all of a sudden her neck hurt.

Reaching her hand to her throat, she felt something sticking out of it. Her jugular had been pierced and as she tried to scream, to say something, blood flowed through her fingers and soaked her shirt and jacket, staining it a dark vermilion.

With both hands on her throat, she felt herself growing tired. She tried to stand, to go over to her friends, who hadn't quite figured out what had happened yet, but her limbs refused to obey her.

Then she dropped to the ground, landing on top of Brad, two lovers forever together in death.

It was Chris who seemed to break free of the numbness that had suffused them.

"Holy shit, the lady's right. Someone just killed Brad and Tina!" Grabbing Wendy by the arm, he pulled her to the edge of the clearing. "Come on, we've got to get the hell out of here, now, and find help before that sick bastard get's us, too."

Though dazed, Wendy let herself be pulled along behind Chris. Karen ran with them, not knowing where else to go. The three of them ran into the darkness, leaving everything behind.

With night having fallen, the woods were shrouded in darkness. Each of them wanted to run full-out, but they had to hold back, doing nothing more than walking fast, their hands out in front of them to keep from walking into a tree or falling down a slope.

They walked for hours, always looking behind them, wondering if the arrow that would mark their death was only a heartbeat away.

With the sunrise less than two hours away, Chris called a halt near a large boulder.

Breathing heavily, he tried to see the two women next to him, but their faces were nothing but lighter shadows in the darkness.

"Jesus Christ, who the hell are we running from? Who killed Brad and Tina?" Chris asked Karen.

"It's my husband. He brought me out here after he found me in bed with another man. He's an excellent hunter and woodsman. He wants to kill me, but he wants me to suffer. I'm so sorry, your friends just got in his way."

Chris stepped closer to Karen. "Are you telling me that if you hadn't found us, he wouldn't have bothered us? Christ, lady, you killed my friends just as easily as if you'd done it yourself. Get the hell away from us, maybe if we're not with you he'll leave us alone!"

"But, Chris, she needs help, we can't just abandon her," Wendy said.

Chris slapped his head with his hands, thinking he was surrounded by lunatics. "Oh really, Wendy, and what am I going to fight back with? This knife?" He said, pulling a small four inch knife from his waistband. The blade reflected the moonlight, only a lighter shadow mixed with others. "This won't do shit. No, we need to ditch her now and make a run for the ranger station."

Karen's head lifted at that. "Ranger station? Where, how far is it?"

Wendy shrugged; the gesture unseen in the darkness. "Don't really know. A couple of miles at least. It's over the second mountain. There's a deer path that cuts all the way to the front door if you know where to find it."

"Forget it; we're out of here as soon as it's light." He pointed his small knife at Karen's face. "But when we go, you better go the other way or I'll kill you myself. Got it?" Chris asked, looking at Karen.

Though she couldn't see his face well, the tenor in his voice told her everything.

"Yeah, I got it. I'm so sorry about your friends. I didn't even know who you were. I saw the smoke from the fire and ran to you for help." Her voice lowered until it was almost silent. "I never would've come to you if I'd known what he was going to do."

Chris spit. "Maybe so, but that still doesn't bring my friends back from the dead, now does it."

He climbed onto the boulder and stretched out. His legs were killing him, despite the great shape he was in, and now that his body was cooling down, he was becoming cold. Rolling onto his side and curling into a fetal position to try to conserve his body heat, he tried to get some sleep before the sun came up.

"I suggest you try to get some rest while you can, 'cause when the sun rises, it's balls to the walls out of here." Then he rolled over and was silent.

Wendy patted Karen's shoulder and leaned close to her ear.

"I'm sorry that you're in this mess, but I have to agree with Chris. Once the sun comes up you need to go your own way." Then she climbed onto the boulder and curled up next to Chris.

Karen slumped to the ground, wrapping her arms around her knees. She had no jacket, her light shirt hardly enough to fend off the cold. Still, she tried to sleep.

At first her mind kept right on running and her head was filled with scenes of Brian and later the other two kids getting murdered. She tried to push the images from her mind, but they wouldn't leave. She figured with all this worry and anxiety, there would be no way she would ever fall asleep, but ten minutes later her head started to droop and her eyes grew heavy.

With her adrenaline finally subsiding, she felt overwhelmed with exhaustion and without realizing it, she succumbed to sleep.

A few hundred yards away, Martin knelt down and raised his night-vision goggles to his eyes. The goggles were able to use even the smallest amount of ambient light and make the night become day.

Well not day exactly, more of an incredibly overcast day where the clouds blocked the sun. Through the goggles, the world was nothing but gray and shades of gray.

It took him less than five minutes to find the three people. The two campers were on the large boulder and his bitch of a wife was curled up on the ground.

He grinned, lowering the goggles. It would be far too easy to kill them now.

No, he would wait for sunrise, when they would think they were safe; then he would give them a morning surprise they would never forget.

Hunkering down in-between the two tree trunks he had picked for cover, he tried to get more comfortable. Sunrise was a little more then an hour away and he wanted to be prepared.

*   *   *

Karen was startled from her restless slumber, shaken violently awake by Chris. The sun had just started rising on a new day, the dew from the night still covering the boulder and forest floor around her.

"Rise and shine, lady, it's time for you to get the hell out of here," Chris said, curtly.

She wiped the sleep from her eyes and the small amount of drool that had accumulated on the corner of her mouth. Blinking herself awake, she slowly stood up. Though she had slept for less than three hours, she still felt somewhat refreshed.

Chris had backed away from her, Wendy at his side. Though Chris' face was hard, Karen could see Wendy's countenance was much softer. After what the girl had told her the night before,

Karen had the feeling it was Chris pulling her reins, the girl deferring to her boyfriend.

Brushing a few twigs and loose dirt from her pants, Karen prepared to leave.

"I'm so sorry for all that's happened, I hope you know that. If I could do it all over again I…"

She was cut off by Chris' hand in her face.

"Save it for someone who gives a damn, lady, just go."

Karen turned to leave, not really knowing where to go, but wanting to respect the couple's wishes. She felt a pressure in her bladder and decided she'd pee when she was a little ways away from Chris and Wendy.

Just before she was enveloped in the brush, she stopped, wanting to ask either of them if they had any idea where she might go for help, but before she could so much as get the first word out, Chris had covered the few feet separating him from her and pushed her to the ground.

"What the fuck's wrong with you, lady, I said to get the hell out of here!" Chris screamed at her, his forehead bulging with veins of anger. His right fist was clenched and Karen seriously thought he was going to hit her. She was about to try and explain that all she wanted was some kind of directions when an arrow appeared in Chris' left eye.

The eye exploded outward, like a hammer had struck it while it was lying on a table, the clear fluid shooting out of the socket and falling onto Karen's shirt. She screamed in shock and her bladder let go, her pants becoming warm and wet. From where Wendy stood, the young girl had no idea what had just happened to her boyfriend and was about to go to them when an arrow missed her by less than an inch, the shaft sticking out of a nearby tree, the end vibrating from the impact.

"Oh my God, he's shooting at us again!" Wendy screamed, looking around her, not realizing she needed to drop to the ground to present less of a target for the hunter.

Karen had stopped screaming, the initial shock of seeing a man shot through the head past now. Chris was still standing up, his body not understanding the trauma that had happened to it.

His left hand reached up to try to touch the intrusion and his brow seemed to furrow in concentration, as if he was trying to reason why he had an arrow in his head.

His one good eye was moving back and forth frantically, still in shock, when another arrow pierced his remaining eye. Chris may have been lucky on the first arrow, the shaft not piercing his brain enough to kill him, but the second arrow hit its mark.

The shaft slid through his socket, blinding him, and the point sliced through blood vessels and grey matter. Chris was brain dead before he knew he was brain dead. The man swayed on his feet, like a tree ready to topple after being chopped with an axe, waiting for all but the last strike; more than enough to send the tree falling to the ground.

His fingers danced a jig of their own, seeming as if they were trying to break free of his hand and find a new home before their present one was extinguished. Then his legs gave out and he fell over, falling on top of Karen. She shrieked again, her lap covered in blood and gore from Chris' shattered eyes.

Wendy was screaming, her hands over her face, not believing what was happening.

She was running around in circles, clearly losing it. Karen pushed Chris' body away from her, the arrows scraping her thighs through her pants. Chris fell onto his side and then onto his back, the two shafts pointing at the sky like he was waiting to play a macabre game of horseshoes, his face being used as the posts.

Staying low, Karen crawled across the ground, reaching Wendy and pulling the girl to the dirt with her.

"Are you crazy? You need to stay low or you'll get shot," Karen hissed, keeping her voice more or less at a normal tone, though the undertone said she was ready to lose it at the drop of a hat.

Wendy was crying, the tears running down her face. "Oh my God. Chris, he's dead, isn't he?" She asked, though Karen figured she already knew the answer.

"I'm afraid so, and we'll be joining him if you don't get it together."

Wendy nodded and seemed to regain a small amount of her composure. When Karen was satisfied she was better, she nodded.

"Good, all right then, that's better. Now my husband won't get close to us, he wants to kill us from a distance, so stay low and head for those trees," she said, pointing to the shadow infested forest.

Wendy sniffed and with one final look at Chris, her face showing she wanted nothing more than to go to him, she started crawling to where Karen had pointed.

Karen started to follow her, but then she stopped for a moment and glanced at Chris' corpse. She took a chance and duck-walked to him and quickly retrieved the small knife he had on his belt.

She was rewarded by another arrow and laughter floated over the terrain from her side. It appeared almost magically in Chris' torso and she backpedaled and moved as fast as she could from the boulder, leaving Chris' cooling corpse to lie under the sun.

Her damn husband was just playing with her. He probably could have killed her at anytime, but he wanted her to suffer. Moving down the small deer path, Wendy a few yards in front of her, she made up her mind that one way or another, she would turn the tables on him and make him pay.

Martin stepped into the small opening in the forest where Chris' body lay unmoving. The ants and other insects had already begun the cycle of life, crawling into the man's mouth and other openings.

Martin retrieved his arrows, disappointed that the one that had missed Wendy, lodging in a tree, had a broken tip. He wouldn't be able to re-use that one.

That was okay, though, he had a full quiver and with the ones from Chris' body, he had more than enough to take out his bitch of a wife and her new friend.

Leaning against the boulder Chris had spent the night on; he pulled a water bottle from his pack and took a swig, thinking back to the two well placed shots in the kids head. If only he could share those shots with others, that would be a tale worthy of telling at the bar he hung out at after his trips, but that would obviously be out of the question, no, he would have to enjoy these kills solely for himself. He screwed the cap back on the water bottle and carefully placed it back in his pack. The water was more precious than gold right now. They were high in the mountains and there were no streams for miles. Karen was in for a surprise when she became thirsty.

He chuckled at that, hoping she suffered even more.

If he was right, then the two women were trying to make it to the ranger station. It was only a few miles away and it was actually possible they could make it there before they died of dehydration or an arrow to the heart.

Shrugging his backpack onto his shoulder, he picked up his bow and headed off on their trail. The broken branches and disturbed leaves were so obvious it was like they wanted him to find them.

His face creased in an evil grin. Well, if they wanted him to find them, he wouldn't disappoint them.

*   *   *

After two more miles had passed beneath their feet, Karen called a halt. Both women were sweating profusely. Karen was dying of thirst and one look at Wendy informed her that the young girl was in the same condition.

The only bit of hope they had was the deer path they had been on was holding true.

Hopefully, if they continued to follow its meandering course, they might come upon a stream or small lake. Or even better, the ranger station. Wendy was morose, thinking about Chris. Then she looked up at Karen, her eyes glinting in the sunlight.

"Just what the hell did you do exactly to have your husband bring you to the woods and try to kill you?"

Karen looked away from her, humiliated. "He caught me with another man and I guess it pushed him over the edge, that's all, I swear."

"Let me get this straight, my boyfriend's dead and my other friends, as well, because you couldn't keep your legs closed?" Wendy said, angrily.

While hurt by the question, Karen knew it came from shock and fear, so she didn't argue with her. Instead, she just nodded in agreement, trying to placate the young girl.

Wendy had to be nineteen or twenty, more than ten years younger then Karen. Karen remembered those years well. The world had been her oyster back then, and if someone had told her where she'd be ten years after her twentieth birthday, she would have laughed incredibly hard and then probably would have taken another shot of Jack Daniels. In college she had lived on the stuff, sometimes going days with nothing but a bottle of Jack and a bag of potato chips.

Then she was pulled from her trip down memory lane by Wendy's voice.

"Hello, can you here me in there?" She asked yet again.

"Huh, what? Oh, sorry. Guess I zoned out for a minute, what did you say?" Karen asked.

"I said, what the hell are we going to do now?"

Karen only gave it the briefest thought, already knowing their only option. "Simple, we keep moving and hopefully make it to the ranger station before he catches us. And on that note, let's get moving; we've wasted enough time."

Before Wendy started moving again she looked into Karen's eyes. "And what happens if he catches us before we make it to safety?"

Karen's face was grim as she pushed a branch away from her face and started walking. "That's easy, I'm afraid. He'll kill us."

*　*　*

The sun was high in the sky when they took their next break. Wendy had stumbled onto a berry bush and after seeing a deer nibbling on them contently; she ran over to them and started shoving fistfuls into her mouth. Karen followed her and soon both women were gorging themselves on berries.

"Oh my God, I've never tasted anything as good as this," Wendy said, eating another handful.

Karen started chuckling and Wendy looked at her with eyebrows raised, asking the unspoken question: *What's so funny?*

Karen finished chewing and swallowed her mouthful of berries and smiled at Wendy, her teeth stained red.

"I was just thinking what a great diet plan we're on. All the berries you can eat and a homicidal killer on our trail to make sure we keep running. If we tried to sell this program, we could make millions."

Wendy's jaw fell open as she looked at Karen, stunned.

Karen thought her face was hilarious and started to laugh again, berry juice slipping out of the side of her mouth and bits of berry flying out to land on her shirt.

Then Wendy caught the laughter and started to giggle. Slow at first, but then it became full blown laughter.

The two women continued laughing and shoving berries into their mouths, feeling good for the first time since they had met, while only a few hundred feet away, they were being watched.

Martin lowered the binoculars from his eyes and leaned back against the waist high rocks behind him, grinning malevolently. He had just caught up to the women, their path easy to follow.

Though Martin was tempted to take the shot, killing them and ending the chase here and now, he decided to wait awhile and savor the moment. He could take their lives at anytime when he so decided to and knowing that was almost as much fun as actually doing the deed itself.

After finishing the berries, the two women started moving again. The path was only slightly less distinguishable from the rest of the forest, but once you knew what to look for, it was easy to see.

The air was warm, the treetops keeping the worst of the sun's rays off their exposed heads. Still they were hot and thirsty.

Less than ten minutes after leaving the berry bush behind them, they became thirsty again.

Karen picked up a couple of small pebbles, giving one to Karen.

"Here, suck on this," she said. "I saw it in a movie once; it's supposed to keep you from getting too thirsty."

Wendy popped hers into her mouth, but after less than a minute; she was looking for another pebble.

"What's wrong? Didn't you like the one I gave you?" Karen asked as they trudged down the path.

Picking up a new pebble, Wendy carefully placed it in her mouth. "What? Oh yeah, yours was fine. So fine in fact that I accidentally swallowed it."

Karen chuckled. "Don't worry, whatever goes in, must come out," she joked.

"Yuck, don't remind me." The two women remained quiet for the next hour, the simple act of hiking through the warm woods enough to hold their attention.

Karen didn't know how many miles they had covered, but if she had to guess, she would have estimated at least three or four.

Wendy let out a small shriek and Karen prepared to drop to the earth, expecting an arrow to fly by overhead, but that wasn't what Wendy had shrieked for.

Karen looked up to see Wendy pointing to a radio tower, its uppermost peak sprouting above the treetops like some weird kind of mechanical tree.

Karen hadn't realized it, but they had been slowly moving up a subtle slope in the landscape and they were now near the top of one of the smaller mountains. Below them, where the radio tower peeked through the treetops, was the ranger station.

"Oh my God, we made it?" Karen asked, not believing her eyes.

Wendy jumped up and down, relieved to see safety in sight. "We made it, oh, thank God, we made it. Come on; let's get going before something else happens."

Karen nodded and the two women started down the other side of the mountain, the ranger station less than a mile away.

*   *   *

The hike was difficult, the deer path having ended some time ago. Now they had to pick and choose where to place their feet, sometimes slipping on the loose soil.

The closer they got to the ranger station, the more Karen felt cooler. It didn't take long for her to realize they were near water.

She could almost feel the mist on her face the closer they got to the station.

Finally reaching the bottom of the mountain, they hiked across the relatively level landscape. Her calves needed the break and she was thankful for the flat terrain.

Though both women wanted to do nothing more than run full tilt to the ranger station, they both held back. They had no way of knowing just what or who was in the station.

For all they new, Martin had somehow gotten in front of them and was even now waiting to put an arrow in each of their hearts. When they were no more than fifty feet away from the small building, Karen held up her hand to stop Wendy.

Karen's eyes roamed across the building, the door, the one window she could see and the wooden roof. The one-story, one room building was made out of logs and had some form of glue in-between the logs to keep the weather out. Behind the cabin was the tall radio tower they had spotted from a distance.

Now that they were closer, they could see a small amount of smoke coming from the one chimney, almost invisible once the wind blew it away.

Wendy gave Karen a look of: *What are we waiting for*? Then she began walking to the building.

"No wait, it could be a trap," Karen hissed, but it was too late, Wendy was almost at the door.

"Hello in there, is anybody home? We need some help!" Wendy called.

At first there was nothing but silence in return. Karen was angry at Wendy's alacrity to be shot and backed away from the cabin. If the girl wanted to get herself killed than that was her business.

While Karen surveyed her surroundings some more, she realized the back of the ranger station overlooked a large body of water. Moving closer to the edge, she skirted the back of the cabin and looked down at the water below.

Just after the drop straight down, the water turned into rapids, the swirling, white water striking the sharp rocks. It continued on for more than she could see and she backed away from the edge, not wanting to fall over into the rustling waters.

Though she was too high to jump, it wasn't so high that the possibility of surviving the fall wasn't possible, but she still didn't want to take the chance.

Just as she turned to head back to the front of the cabin, Wendy appeared. She was holding a bottle of water in her left hand, her right, carrying her own bottle, already almost empty.

Next to her was an older man in a park ranger uniform, right down to the wide brim cap. Karen couldn't help but think of Ranger Smith from the Yogi Bear cartoons she had watched when she was a kid. Deciding it must be safe, she lowered her guard.

Wendy walked over to her and handed her the bottled water. Karen took it and cracked the cap and then drank greedily.

"Man, that's good. Thanks, Wendy, and you, too, sir."

"Call me Ranger Johnson," the man said.

Karen chuckled. "That's almost as good as Ranger Smith," she said to herself.

"Excuse me, Miss, did you say something?"

Karen waved it away. "No, sorry, just talking to myself. Thank you, really. Look, we need to get out of here. Can you help us?"

Ranger Johnson frowned. "As I was telling the young lady here, I only have a two-way radio up here and the damn things on the fritz. The cell phone tower behind the cabin isn't operational yet. But my relief will be here tomorrow. You can stay here until he arrives, then I'll take you down the mountain with me".

Karen stepped closer. "No, you don't understand, we need to get the hell out of here, now. There's a killer following us and when he finds us, we're all dead."

Ranger Johnson chuckled. "Now, Miss, I don't deny you've been through a lot, but you're safe here. If your killer comes near here I'll introduce him to old Betsy here," he said, brushing back his jacket to show an old World War 2 army revolver. "I know what you're thinking, but it's in perfect working condition. My father gave it to me before he passed away."

"Yeah, that's great, but…" Karen tried to say, but Ranger Johnson wouldn't hear any more.

"Now that's enough talk for now, why don't you two ladies come inside and we'll get you fixed up and get some food into you. I don't have much in the way of delicacies but it'll fill your stomach." Then he headed back to the cabin, whistling an old Army fighting song to himself.

Wendy moved next to Karen and shook her head.

"I know what you're going to say and I agree. The man is friggin' crazy. I tried to tell him what had happened, but he just waved it away. Said people get lost up here all the time and see things. Hallucinate when they're so hungry and thirsty they can't take it anymore. That's what he thinks happened to us. Won't believe a word I told him."

"Shit, this can't be happening. We actually make it here and the only other person for a hundred miles is a nut."

"What do we do?" Wendy asked.

Karen shrugged. "What can we do? All we can do is hope we can hold out until his replacement arrives, maybe that guy will have some common sense."

Then the two women walked to the front door of the cabin and stepped inside to finally get some food and more water.

* * *

After a hearty meal of bread, canned beans and more bottles of water, the two women thought their stomachs would explode.

The sun was finally setting, its descent in the sky more than breathtaking. Dusk was quickly falling on the mountain. Ranger Johnson lit a fire to combat the quickly dropping temperature and then sat back and stretched.

"You ladies can take the bed in the corner, I'll take the chair here," he said, patting the arm of the rocking chair. "Besides, I don't sleep that much anyway. I usually go for walks near the cabin. I love nature, that's why I became a ranger."

Karen nodded, listening. She had tried twice more to convince the man they were in real danger, but he refused to listen, just waved her story away as fiction. Karen had to wonder if this was the reason why Ranger Johnson manned a station in the middle of nowhere. Maybe the man had snapped and park services had shipped him up here to keep him away from other people.

She felt her eyes drooping and realized with her stomach full and feeling moderately safe for the first time in days, she wanted nothing more than to go to sleep. So she stood up from the small table she was sitting at and touched Wendy on the shoulder.

"I can't take it any more; I've got to go to sleep."

"Amen to that, sister, I'll join you," Wendy said, rising and sliding across the small room to the bed in the corner.

Ranger Johnson nodded and stood up. "Good, that's real good. You ladies get some rest and before you know it, you'll be heading home." He walked to the front door and opened it, letting in the cool mountain air with a hint of the moisture from the rapids below. "I'm going for a walk, now don't worry, I'll always be in hearing distance of you. Goodnight." Then he slipped through the door before either Karen or Wendy could answer, locking the door behind him.

Karen stretched out on the small twin bed, too tired to care if there was a family of grizzly bears prepared to rip her apart and use her skin for a coat on the other side of the door. Wendy lay next to her, and Karen put her arm around the young woman. Despite everything happening to her, she was growing fond of the girl.

She had heard the best of friendships were forged out of hardships.

Wendy snuggled close and the two women closed their eyes and drifted off to sleep. Though Karen figured she would have terror dreams of running through the woods in fear, death chasing behind her, the truth was even her subconscious was just too tired to even try to rustle up even the smallest nightmare.

*　　*　　*

Ranger Johnson lit his pipe while he strolled away from the cabin. This was the best time of the day, right after the sun went down, when the animals prepared for the night and the nocturnal animals awoke to start a new day.

The breeze felt good on his face and he breathed in the fresh mountain air. This was what it meant to be alive, to stand out in God's own country; away from the hustle and bustle of man's world. Screw the cell phones and fifty story buildings. Screw the fancy sports cars and open-all-night fast food restaurants.

This is what it meant to be human, what it meant to be alive. Like it was thousands of years ago, before man had become too full of himself to realize what he was doing to the earth with the pollution and chemical waste and nuclear bombs.

Ranger Johnson let out a deep breath and breathed in the fresh smell of the forest.

Yes, sir, out here he was truly alive!

Then he felt something pierce his chest and he looked down to see something thin protruding just below his shoulder blade. It had happened so suddenly he had yet to feel any pain and he reached down to touch the protuberance.

That was when another arrow came out of the darkness and pinned his reaching hand to his chest, the arrow puncturing his heart at the same time.

Ranger Johnson's mouth opened and a small ribbon of blood ran out of the corner of his mouth, the red rivulets covering his immaculate uniform.

As his brain shutdown from lack of oxygen, his heart having pumped its last, he realized the women had been telling the truth and how the hell was he going to fix the holes the arrows had made in his uniform?

Then he fell over, dead. He twitched for another moment, a few synapses still firing until he became motionless, just another shadow in the growing darkness.

Martin stepped out of the shadows and lowered his night vision goggles from his face. That had been too easy. After hunting people for the first time in his life, he realized that hunting an animal like a deer or a bear was infinitely more challenging than hunting humans. Humans were fat and lazy and didn't have the survival instinct of a wild animal.

But still, this hunt was special.

He walked over to the prone form of the ranger and kicked the man to make sure he was dead. Rolling the man over, he was upset to see the man had broken both arrows when he'd fallen over. Still, Martin took the revolver, a small consolation for the loss of his arrows. Martin didn't hunt with guns, preferring the natural silence of the bow. Any idiot could shoot a firearm, but only a hunter of skill used a bow.

Sliding the weapon in the waistband of his pants, he admired his kill shot. Pinning the man's hand to his chest had been a work of art. Once again he wished he could share his craft with others, but that was out of the question. He didn't have any plans for going to the electric chair anytime soon. That's why he had brought his slut of a wife and her boyfriend all the way to the mountains.

Up here in the mountains amidst the statuesque trees, they were all alone. That was the way he liked it.

With a sigh, he dragged the corpse of the ranger into the woods. He didn't need to hide the body too well. By morning he would have finished his task here and would be on his way.

Minus one cheating wife, of course.

*   *   *

The sun streamed through the one window in the cabin and Karen opened her eyes. The small clock on the wall—battery powered—said it was almost seven. Sitting up and stretching, she realized she had slept for more than twelve hours straight.

Then she came to her senses and realized she was still alive. It had been a full twelve hours and Martin hadn't arrived. Maybe they had lost him somewhere in the forest, the man now fifty miles away from them.

She could only hope.

Standing up and stretching, she walked over to the small cabinet and grabbed another bottle of water, then she went to the small bathroom in the back of the cabin. The bathroom was nothing more than a fancy outhouse, but it served her purpose well. Drinking the water and peeing at the same time, she finished and walked back into the small room. Wendy was waiting for her to finish, dancing back and forth, she had to go so bad and quickly went in after her.

Once she, too, had accomplished morning's most important task, she sat down and munched on a leftover piece of bread, washing it down with another bottle of water.

"Where's Ranger Crazy?" She asked Karen, munching happily.

"That's a good question, let's finish eating and see if he's outside. He said his relief will be here in the afternoon, so we still have a few hours to kill."

"Yay, more fun with Ranger Nutjob," she joked.

Karen shot her a semi-dirty look. "Oh, be nice, he's not that bad. He's just eccentric."

If he's eccentric, then I'm Hollywood's next big thing, he's nuts." Then her face grew serious.

"Look, Karen, I'm sorry I said those things to you before Chris died. I didn't mean them, well, you know what I mean, not really," she said ruefully.

Karen smiled wanly. "It's okay, Wendy, I understand. Let's just concentrate on getting out of here alive, okay?"

"Okay," Wendy said and pushed her plate away from her and stood up. "So what do you say we go check on Ranger Wackjob?"

"I think that would be a great idea," Karen said, moving to the door and opening it, with Wendy right behind her.

Karen opened the door of the cabin, letting the sun shine inside, momentarily blinding her for a moment. Instead of stepping out into the morning light, she stepped a little to the side and raised her hand to her eyes, shielding them from the sun's brilliance. She felt, more than saw, the arrow buzz by the half-an-inch void where her head had been only a fraction of an instant ago.

The arrow intended for her passed by her head and instead lodged in Wendy's throat. Wendy gagged on the shaft and panicked, pushing Karen through the open door and outside.

Both women fell to the earth, Wendy still clawing at the arrow. Karen's eyes were wide in fear. She needed to do so many things at the same time. She needed to help her friend. She needed to find where Martin was shooting from so she didn't stumble into him, and she needed to get the hell out of here before she was next.

Wendy had managed to get onto all fours, though the arrow looked horrendous, it wasn't fatal. She would live if she left it alone and waited for a real medical professional to extract it. But that was easier to say than have it done.

Wendy came to her knees, still trying to figure out what to do, when another arrow sliced through the morning air and transfixed her in the mouth.

The arrow bounced off her front teeth, breaking three of them and was then deflected up into her skull, piercing her brain and killing her. She dropped to the ground like a puppet with its strings cut and didn't move again.

Karen saw Wendy's eyes were still open; seeming to look straight at her, accusingly and she turned away, unable to keep looking. That's when she decided to run.

She prepared to run to her right when an arrow appeared in the ground in front of her. Sliding in the dry earth, she turned around and started running the other way, only to be stopped by another arrow appearing in front of her feet.

It was painfully clear what Martin was doing. If she tried to run away, he would put an arrow into her.

Though she knew what waited for her if she didn't run, her will to survive stopped her from moving. Every second she breathed was a chance she might live to see the sun rise tomorrow.

She started shuffling away toward the edge of the cliff, expecting an arrow for her trouble. When none came, she continued to move backward.

When she was only a few feet from the edge of the drop-off, she heard Martin's voice from the side of her, near the cabin.

"That's far enough, baby doll. Wouldn't want you to slip and fall off the edge," he said, strolling toward her almost casually. When he was less than twenty feet away she was able to see the gun in his waistband, the suns rays reflecting off the revolver's black finish.

She knew what that meant.

"You bastard, he was a harmless old man, you didn't have to kill him," she spit.

Martin stopped when he was ten feet from her. "Didn't I? I couldn't exactly take you down with that old fart in the way. Besides, thanks to you I've been having fun out here. You've helped me kill a lot of people since you got out here."

"That's bullshit and you know it. Don't try to put your sick fantasies on me to try to ease your conscious. I may have cheated on you, but I sure as hell don't deserve this! Christ, Martin, you've become a serial killer. Didn't you ever hear of divorce?"

He laughed at that, his voice floating over the edge of the cliff to echo in the valley below.

"Divorce? Are you crazy? Even with you admitting you cheated on me the damn courts would still give you half, they're so screwed up. No, my dear, better that you and I come out for a hunting trip and you wander off never to return. A bit cliché, I'll grant you, but without a body, there's no one to contest it."

Karen took another step backward, her hand reaching into her back pocket for the knife she had taken from Chris. She continued talking, keeping Martin occupied while her hand fumbled with the knife, getting it open, but managing to give herself a few shallow cuts for her troubles.

"All right, you bitch, enough talk. I'll admit you gave me quite a chase, despite the fact I could have ended it anytime I wanted. You've got more spirit than I ever gave you credit for." He raised his bow, an arrow already notched, ready to be fired.

"I wanted to take you down at the door, the second you opened it, but you moved at the last moment. That's all right, though. This way I get to see your eyes up close when I shoot you dead."

Karen saw the gleam in his eyes, the way he squinted. She could see his arm tensing, preparing to release the arrow.

She knew it was now or never.

Bending her knees, she pulled the knife from behind her and threw it as hard as she could at Martin. She was in no way skilled with knives and could only pray the spinning knife would strike Martin with the blade first.

She was half-lucky.

The blade whirled in the air at the same moment Martin prepared to release the arrow. Though the blade in no way threatened Martin, the handle struck the bow, causing Martin to be off from his aim by the minutest bit.

The arrow flew from the bow, covering the ten feet in less time than a heart could beat. But instead of striking Karen's chest, directly in her heart, the arrow was off.

Still, the arrow sliced into her shoulder, the impact causing her to step backward from the force of the blow.

She fell over the side of the cliff, her last look at Martin defiant to the last. She didn't scream, not giving him the satisfaction. If she couldn't kill him, then this would be the next best thing.

She had kept her word to herself and as she fell to the water below, she smiled.

Martin ran to the edge, watching his wife fall to her death. He saw her smile before she was too far away to see any detail and he screamed in rage.

He had been so close, only to lose her now.

Her body was lost amongst the white water, the corpse probably torn and crushed amidst the rocks and churning water.

Backing away from the edge, he cursed. If only he hadn't been so damn conceited and had just shot the bitch.

Oh well, he thought, dead is dead, after all.

He decided his hunting trip was finished. Retrieving his arrow from the corpse of Wendy, he dragged her body into the woods and left. No one would ever know he had ever been on that mountain and when he returned home, he would report his wife missing, acting the distraught husband.

All in all everything had worked out for the best.

Whistling a tune he had caught on the radio when he had been first driving his wife to the mountains to slaughter her and her boyfriend, he left the ranger station behind him. He had a long walk to get back to his car and he wanted to be there before the sun set that night.

THREE MONTHS LATER

Martin stayed perfectly still, not wanting to spook the deer that was no more than fifty feet in front of him. He had been hiding in the shrubs all morning, not moving, barely breathing.

The deer was nibbling on some berries, similar to the ones his late-wife had ate only a few short months ago. Martin decided the time was right and raised his bow.

Letting out a deep breath, he let his arrow fly.

The shaft spun through the air, perfectly designed, the simplest, long distance killing tool he knew. His aim was true and his arrow took the deer down with one shot. Standing up and stretching cramped muscles, he prepared to go down and retrieve his arrow and skin the deer.

His mouth watered as he thought of the venison he'd be having that night, alone in his million dollar house.

With his wife dead, lost in the mountains, he had collected on her accidental-death insurance policy. So on top of getting rid of the traitorous bitch, he had collected a million dollars.

Not a bad way to handle your problems, if you asked him. Whistling a tune, he shifted the revolver to a more comfortable position on his thigh. He knew he was foolish to carry it, the gun being evidence that he had been at the scene of a murder sight, but he couldn't help himself. Every time he touched the weapon it made him think of that day on the cliff.

It always made him smile.

Upon reaching the deer, he knelt down and prepared to skin the animal, removing his arrow from the still carcass.

Suddenly, a flock of birds took flight, and the forest seemed to become preternaturally quiet.

Standing up, he placed his hand on the revolver for a different reason. The previous owner had lovingly taken care of it and Martin had continued the tradition. If there was someone out there that wanted to mess with him, they were in for a rude surprise.

He stood perfectly still, his ears listening for the slightest sound, his eyes scanning everywhere, using his peripheral vision for signs of movement.

Nothing.

Deciding it must have been his imagination, he started stripping his kill.

Less than an hour later, he was finished. After stripping the carcass clean, he'd tossed the entrails aside, leaving them for some lucky cougar or some other carnivorous animal.

Pulling some plastic wrap from his bag, he wrapped the meat tightly and stuffed it into his backpack. Then he stood up and prepared for the long walk back to where he had parked his new SUV, bought with the spoils of his wife's murder.

Walking back up the slight incline, he slowed as he came to a cluster of trees that had to be at least fifty years old each, the wide trunks huge.

Though it was a tight fit, it was the only feasible way to move up and down the slope.

With a tensing of leg muscles he started upward.

When he was passing the second tree, something long and slim flew through the air and sliced into his left shoulder blade. The timing had been perfect, the arrow easily sliding through flesh to pierce the tree behind him.

He let out a yowl of pain and dropped his backpack. For the moment he was stuck to the tree, the pain unbearable.

Sending curses to whoever was out there in the woods, he tried to control his breathing. Evidently some novice bowman had shot him by accident and would be along shortly to help him.

He would kick the guys ass after he was let free, he knew that. Maybe even sue the bastard.

Leaning against the tree, his back touching the rough bark, he was mortified when another arrow shot out of the leaf shrouded shadows and pierced his other shoulder to the same tree.

His yell of pain was excruciating, the arrow piercing muscles and tendons. Now every time he took a breath his new wound pulsed with pain, his body felt like it had lava flowing through his veins, the pain was so bad.

"Jesus Christ, you idiot, I'm not a goddamn deer! Stop shooting or so help me!"

His hands were hanging loosely by his sides, free for the moment, at least until another arrow screamed through the air and pinned his right hand to the tree. He screamed in pain, almost blacking out. Before the pain in his hand could even start throbbing another arrow pinned his left hand to the tree, as well.

Martin shrieked and passed out for a few moments, exactly how long he didn't know, but when he opened his eyes he saw who his attacker was.

"You! No fucking way, you're dead!" He exclaimed, believing he was seeing a ghost.

The hunter said nothing, but merely stared at him. Then the person leaned over and twisted the arrow in his right shoulder.

Martin screamed as nerve clusters sent the agony to his brain.

He started to black out again, but a slap in the face brought him back to reality.

"Oh, no, you're not getting off that easy," Karen said soothingly. "I want you to see everything. I want you to feel everything."

Breathing heavily from pain, sweat pouring off his face and into his eyes, Martin gasped.

"But how? I saw you fall over the cliff, you died; drowned and crushed on the rocks."

Karen chuckled. "Is that what you thought? Well, you were wrong. I was lucky and hit the water in a deep spot. True, I did hit a few rocks, but I was pushed to the shore a ways down where I lay there unconscious for half the day. Luckily, some white-water rafters saw me and rescued me. After that, I recuperated at a hospital. I have a few bank accounts you don't know about, dear, and I paid cash for my medical expenses. Let me tell you they should be the one's who're killed, the way they bled me dry. I emptied one bank account just to pay the hospital bills." She started walking around the tree, Martin trying to move his head to follow her. Karen talked in a soothing voice, like she was sitting in a bar, meeting a friend over drinks.

"When I was recuperated enough to leave the hospital; I did a few weeks of therapy. One of the therapists recommended I take up a sport to help me tone my muscles. So I decided on archery. I practiced everyday for hours, honing my skill, thinking of what would happen when I finally met you out here again."

She made a disgusted face, thinking of something distasteful. "I've been sitting up there on that hill all damn day, waiting for you to kill something and leave. I really don't know what you see in killing a defenseless animal for the hell of it. Christ, Martin, if you want meat so badly just go to the damn supermarket like the rest of us."

"What're you going to do to me?" Martin asked hesitantly.

Karen chuckled. "My dear husband, that should be obvious, even to a simpleminded fool like you."

"Oh my God, you're going to kill me, aren't you?" He asked, tears forming in his eyes.

"Oh, really, Martin, take it like a man. I promise you this, I myself will not kill you; does that make you feel better?"

Though he found it hard to believe her, he took her at her word. "If you're being truthful, then yes, it does. Look Karen, I'm so sorry about what happened. Maybe we could start over, you know, fresh?" He suggested.

"Oh, Martin, I think we're way beyond that, don't you? Ah, good, my friend is here," she said, looking behind Martin. Pinned to the tree, he couldn't see what she was looking at, not that he thought he would want to.

Karen turned away from him and started to rummage in his backpack, taking out the venison he had so carefully wrapped.

"Ah, this should do nicely," she said while unwrapping each piece. She took each bloody piece of meat and shoved them in his pant's pockets, inside his shirt and down his pants.

Martin struggled, the smell of the bloody meat turning his nose.

"What the hell are you doing, Karen? Let me down now, you said you wouldn't kill me!"

Karen wiped her hands on Martin's shirt and stepped back from him, picking up her bow and quiver as she moved further away.

"Ah, now you weren't listening, were you. I said that I wouldn't kill you, not that something else wouldn't." Then she turned and started walking back up the slope, easily moving between the trees.

Martin called after her, pleading to be let loose, but she ignored him. With her plan of revenge finished, she hiked away from the Martin, relishing the fact that he now had become the hunted.

She chuckled to herself while she strolled away, Martin's calls for help music to her ears. Despite what they say in movies about revenge not making her feel better was a load of bullshit. She had been dreaming about this day for three months and now that it was over, she felt wonderful, like a weight had been lifted off her shoulders.

Besides, revenge was nothing more than rough justice and anyone who said otherwise was full of shit.

Whistling a tune, she headed off back to her car. She would be returning to her million dollar home tonight after a long disappearance and once she was proved to be alive and well, despite what Martin had told the authorities, she had a trip of her own to make.

Martin, too, had a hefty accidental insurance policy on his head.

Martin called after her, begging for her to return, but she ignored him, and just kept walking. After only a few minutes he got some of his courage back and decided if he wanted his freedom, he would have to do it himself.

Did she really think these small arrows would hold him? They hadn't even struck any vital arteries or veins. He could easily escape and when he did, she would wish she had died on that cliff months ago.

He tried to pull his hand free and screamed in pain. Maybe it wouldn't be as easy as he thought, but he knew sooner or later he would summon enough courage to free his hands and when he did, it would be child's play to pull free the other arrows pinning his shoulders.

He was about to try again when a low growl caught his attention. He turned his head as far as he could and his eyes locked with those of a giant cougar

The animal's nose was twitching, smelling the venison covering Martin's body.

He let out a scream, his heart stopping in fear; the cougar snarled and raised its claws. The large cat was hungry and dinner was right in front of it, the fragrance of the venison driving it crazy with hunger. Pickings had been slim lately, all the hunters taking the meat it so surely needed to survive.

With one final snarl, the cat pounced on Martin, muffling the man's shrieks as it gouged his chest open.

Martin continued screaming much longer than he would have thought possible with his insides exposed to the elements and a giant, man-eating cat chewing on his organs.

The tranquil forest absorbed the screams of the dying man and soon all was silent once more, the trees waved in the wind, the majestic mountains standing the test of time.

The forest had existed long before man and would be there long after man was gone.

2044

The alarm clock shrilled its piercing siren, demanding he give it the attention it so sorely needed.

Reaching over his still sleeping wife, Thomas Jones slapped the off button to the small clock radio.

Rolling out of bed, he stood up, his back sore. Whether it was from sleeping wrong or something more serious, he had no idea.

Forty years ago he might have considered going to a doctor, perhaps receiving a physical, but now, that wasn't much of an option.

Healthcare was almost nonexistent in this day and age and he just thanked God that he was still relatively healthy.

Walking out of the bedroom, he stumbled into the small, dingy bathroom. The tiles were missing in far too many places to count and as he sat on the toilet, he noticed another small hole down by the floorboards.

Yet another uninvited guest had decided to make his home its own residence.

He didn't quite understand why the filthy rodents even hung around. As for food, he had almost none and the prospect of receiving more was highly unlikely.

He had received his rations for the week, for both he and his wife, so if he was unfortunate enough to run out, then it would be hard luck for him.

True, there was always the black market, but the prices were usually much too high and the risk far too great.

If one of the soldiers caught you, it was very possible you could be shot on sight, and labeled a terrorist.

He chuckled at that, while he used one of the few pieces of toilet paper left on the roll, the last roll for almost another week.

It had been almost forty years since the fabled day the World Trade Center towers fell. At the time, no one would have ever imagined that it would be the beginning of a new world order, where one's human rights meant nothing and freedom of speech meant even less.

Where the Patriot Act of 2001 would become the new constitution for the United States of America, where if the government so much as even thought you were a terrorist or a malcontent, you would find yourself thrown into a cell where it was very possible you could spend the rest of your natural life.

Standing in front of the bathroom mirror, Thomas Jones stared back at his gaunt face. His cheekbones stood out, making him look like a Halloween skeleton. His eyes were set deep into his head and dark bags hung below each socket.

His nose was slightly bent from an automobile accident a few years back. He had to set the break himself, not quite doing it properly. His wife teased him and told him it gave him character, but secretly he had just wished he could have gotten it fixed by a licensed medical doctor who knew what the hell they were doing.

Brushing his teeth with baking soda, he felt yet another sore tooth. Sighing, he tried to ignore it for now. When the time came and the pain became too great, he would retrieve the set of pliers from the kitchen drawer and pull it out; but only after drinking half a bottle of Gin.

He shaved quickly, not wanting to be late for work again and combed his thinning hair; still there, but disappearing day by day.

He was still one of the lucky ones and had a job to go to. In the last twenty years, unemployment had doubled, and then tripled, until there just weren't enough jobs for everyone. If Thomas had to say what the reason for it was, he would have had to say it was when America absorbed Mexico as one of its new states.

The talks with the border between Mexico and the United States had been settled once and for all almost twenty five years ago.

Now every Mexican citizen was a United States citizen with all the rights and privileges. Perhaps it might have looked good on paper, but in reality it had been a nightmare as thousands upon thousands of Mexican immigrants had flooded America, looking for more jobs and the ones that couldn't find one immediately went on welfare and state aid.

Walking through the small hall that separated the bedroom from the kitchen, he opened the beat-up, old refrigerator, looking for his lunch to take to work with him. The old machine whined and sputtered and Thomas knew one of these days it was going to finally give up the ghost once and for all. He didn't know what he would do when that actually happened, as neither he or his wife had enough money to purchase a used one, let alone a new one.

Just one more worry to add to the list, he thought.

Pushing the door closed, making sure the fraying gasket didn't sit the wrong way and let out the cold air, he grabbed his lunch and set it on the table.

A large rumbling could be heard coming from the street outside the window and he opened the shade enough to peek outside.

A Homeland Security Control Unit was driving by, its five antennas and radar dishes spinning in circles. The unit's job description was protecting the masses from infiltration from unsavory elements, but the truth was, they were nothing more than spy satellites, constantly circling the suburbs, listening for sounds of dissension.

Some people joked about Big Brother, and how what the classic book had preached had finally come to pass, but Thomas didn't think it was as bad as that. True, you had to watch what you said, the fear of being overheard a constant threat. True, you could lose your house and be thrown into prison for conspiracy under the Patriot Act, Homeland Security confiscating your home and everything you own without so much as an argument or a lawyer, but that only happened to people who deserved it, not common, hard working folk like himself. No, something like that would never happen to him or his wife. He was a good citizen, loyal to the state and therefore had nothing to worry about.

He chuckled at that, thinking about lawyers. He had been just a boy when lawyers had been abolished forever.

Now the state decided the fate of criminals, some never seeing the face of a judge, but spending the rest of their incarceration awaiting trial.

Checking the small clock on the wall, he realized he needed to leave soon, needing to stay on time. Shrugging into his jacket, he heard the floorboards creaking at the other end of the house. His wife was up.

He thought about calling up to her, to say goodbye, but in the end decided against it. He would see her in thirteen hours, when he returned from work, and they would talk then.

They had been married for almost twenty years and there wasn't always that much to talk about that was new and interesting anyway.

Stepping out into the light of the new morning, the sun just starting to peek its way on the horizon, he headed off for the bus stop.

He had once owned a car, but with a gallon of gas going for almost fifty Ameros, an Amero replacing the dollar as the official currency for the America's in 2019, he'd had to give it up. Just one more of life's small luxuries he had to do without, nowadays.

The walk to the bus stop was uneventful and before he knew it he was standing in the large crowd of commuters. Glancing at the faces of his fellow men and women, he barely noticed that with the exception of one or two, all were of Spanish or Mexican descent.

Thomas' own pale complexion was a stark contrast to their dark complexions. He didn't give it much thought, though. Being one of the minority citizens had been an everyday occurrence for more than half his life, and the people surrounding him were all hard working people just trying to survive, the same as him.

For more than fifty years the races had been mingling and with the influx of Mexican citizens it had cinched it forever. Thomas may be white with a heritage of Polish blood and a small amount of Italian, but he was one of the minorities, nowadays.

And the fact that he only spoke English as his native language only further complicated things. All around him people were talking amongst themselves, Thomas barely noticing what they were saying. True, he might pick up a word or two in passing, who wouldn't after hearing the language day after day, but he had never learned to speak Spanish fluently, which was why he had a dead end job, where talking to others wasn't a must.

The bus rumbled up to the bus stop, the side of its chassis splashed with posters for toothpaste and whatever movie was popular at the moment. Thomas could only look at the pictures, all the words in bold Spanish.

Climbing on board the bus, the rumbling diesel revved higher, the bus pulling back into the street. There weren't many other vehicles on the road at this time of the morning. Plus, in this part of town there weren't very many cars to begin with.

Though Thomas had a house to call his own, that was about all he did have. Both he and his wife struggled to get by and so far had managed to do just that, barely. But Thomas knew his home was hanging on by a shoe string. If he lost his job for any reason, his house would be the first thing to go and both he and his wife would be living on the street.

Looking out the dirty windows of the bus, he watched the houses drift by the windows. Most were nothing more than shacks, the owners not having enough Ameros to fix them up or maintain them properly.

Other people were on the streets, shuffling toward the city, going to their own places of work.

While Thomas watched the houses drift by, he barely noticed how the houses gradually became more well kept and before he knew it he was in a much nicer part of town, where perfect, manicured lawns stood out in front of quaint million-dollar homes.

The bus pulled onto the highway and headed off into the city. Already the smokestacks and the taller of the buildings could be seen through the large glass windshield of the bus. Thomas let out a sigh, moving his arm, which was being crushed by a neighboring commuter.

The bus smelled of spices and human sweat, nothing new to his olfactory senses. Tuning out the voices around him, he let his mind wander away, daydreaming of years before, when things had been better and a citizen still had at least a few rights to protect them from the government.

He continued to gaze out the bus' window, watching a squad of soldiers march by as the bus rolled to a stop. More than thirty years ago, the military had taken over the responsibility of policing the states. Police stations were closed, the men and women in blue discharged to find other positions. Some joined the military and continued what they knew best, others simply faded away, not agreeing with the establishment.

Thomas didn't care one way or the other. He did his best to keep his nose clean and had always figured if he stayed away from trouble, then the soldiers wouldn't bother him.

So far his plan had gone well, as he had always stayed under the radar of any brewing trouble. Politics had never been his strong suit. He'd always figured it didn't really matter who was in charge, because to the little guy, like Thomas, things always stayed the same.

He looked up to see the bus unloading its passengers. When it was finally his turn, he shuffled off the bus and stopped when he was on the sidewalk, out of the way of the pedestrians moving about, all with purpose.

Reaching into his pocket, he made sure his National ID card was safe. It wouldn't do well to not have it when he was asked by one of the roving patrols.

The sun had finally started to come up, though its rays found it hard to penetrate the smoke cloud that hung over the city night and day.

Alternative fuels had been retired back when Thomas had been a small boy; the oil company's squashing the environmentalist movement once and for all, until it was nearly nonexistent. Not that they were really needed nowadays.

Ever since the United States had taken control of Iraq and the surrounding provinces, oil had continued to flow steadily.

Once the continental pipeline had been built, the black gold became never ending, only the Men in power deciding how much each barrel would cost on any given day.

All Thomas knew was that a gallon of gas was far beyond his power to afford, nowadays, and so he left the politics of the world economy to men more qualified than himself.

Stepping into the flow of pedestrians, he walked the five blocks to work. He barely noticed the rubbish in the streets or the homeless spread out on almost every street corner. He had learned a long time ago it was best to watch the sidewalk and only look up enough to prevent from walking into the person in front of him. It was in this position that he was presently in when he thought he heard his name being called.

At first he ignored it, imagining it was all in his head. After all, who would he know out here in the middle of the street who would be foolish enough to call his name?

But the person calling his name continued to do so loudly and Thomas had no choice but to slow down and to look around himself.

He was pushed and nudged by other pedestrians until he managed to move to the side of the flowing bodies, coming up against an old brick building, its function unknown, when he heard his name yet again.

Looking over the heads of the pedestrians he finally saw a dirty face with big blue eyes. He squinted to try and see better, realizing the person was wearing what might have been clothing at one time, but now was no more than rags draped over his body.

The man was obviously homeless and Thomas waited against the building while the man ran up to him.

"Thomas, I knew that was you. Don't you remember me? It's Bugsy, Bugsy Malloy!" The man said happily.

Thomas gazed at the wretch of a man in front of him and then recognition dawned on him. Now the man looked familiar. Under the layers of dirt and filth, Thomas could make out the lines of his friend.

"Bugsy? Oh my God, it is you. Where have you been, I thought you were taken away," Thomas said with surprise.

Bugsy nodded, his greasy hair falling in front of his face. "I was. They took me to one of their interrogation centers, said I was in league with the terrorists. I had no idea what they were talking about, but they didn't care. They did things to me to make me talk, but I had nothing to say. A year later they let me go, having nothing to charge me with, but when I was released I was told they had confiscated my house and all my possessions. I was homeless, jobless, and had no money." He looked down at the dirty sidewalk for a moment and then looked back up into Thomas' Face. "They took my wife, too. I haven't seen Wilma since."

Thomas stared with a blank face, finding it hard to believe the tale he'd just heard, but looking at the proof in front of him.

"I don't know what to say, Bugsy. If they took you, there must have been a reason," Thomas stated.

"A reason?" Bugsy chuckled. "Are you daft, man? They don't need a reason. If they think you're a problem then they pick you up and do whatever the hell they want to you. Then, when they let you go they warn you not to say anything or face further charges!" His voice was escalating and Thomas became nervous. If one of the patrols saw him arguing with an assumed terrorist then, he too, could be charged.

"Look, Bugsy, I'm sorry for everything that's happened to you and your wife, but I have to go, I'll be late for work."

Thomas started walking away, not looking behind him in fear that Bugsy would be following him, but his worries were for naught.

"Go ahead; walk away, just like everyone else! As long as no one cares that it's not happening to them, it'll keep happening! You'll see, Thomas; you'll be next, just wait! Don't say I didn't warn you!"

Thomas turned a corner, at the next intersection and the man's taunting was lost in the din of the city. Thomas moved out of the mainstream of walkers and leaned against a wall, breathing heavily; thanking God no one had seen him. He looked up to the top of a ten foot black pole on the edge of the sidewalk. The poles were on every street corner and in front of every building. On the top of the poles were cameras. Each one watching everything you did.

If someone had been watching the camera that had been near Thomas, even now a patrol would be dispatched to investigate.

Looking left and right, he saw nothing amiss, just the same drawn faces as himself, all hurrying to reach their work stations before the allotted time was past.

He could feel his heart hammering in his chest and he closed his eyes for a moment, trying to calm himself. The only thing worse than doing something wrong was acting like you were doing something wrong.

When he was sure he was in control of himself, he moved back into the line of pedestrians and hurried along. Checking his watch, he saw he still had time to make it to work if he just picked his pace up a little more.

With one quick glance over his shoulder to make sure he wasn't being followed, he walked a little faster, blending into the cityscape until he was lost from sight, just another body moving to its destination.

Fifteen minutes later, he'd reached his place of employment. The drab building offered no insight to what its true purpose was, not that it would matter even if there had been a sign above the top floor, twenty feet high proclaiming: **WE BUILD PIECES OF BOMBS HERE!**

Not that Thomas was absolutely sure what the small devices he helped fabricate were for. But like any place of business, the rumor mill worked overtime. This one had heard what that one had told him, etc, etc.

If he was to believe everything he'd heard, then he would have to believe he was helping to build bombs. His department handled just one of a thousand different parts, that when once combined would build a weapon of death and destruction; which would then be used to slaughter the citizens of other countries.

Not that it bothered Thomas in the slightest. The company made sure to keep each department in the dark from the others so no one knew exactly how all the pieces would fit together to make the actual bomb.

Thomas got in line with his fellow workers as they shuffled into the doorway. A stone faced guard stood just inside the entrance of the door. In his hand was a scanner. The man was checking ID's as each person walked by him. Thomas slowly shuffled closer, his eyes glancing down to the side arm on the guard's hip, as well as the plastic ties the man would use for handcuffs, secured to his belt.

Thomas made sure not to make eye contact while he was scanned and let inside the dark, dreary building. A woman was off to the side of the entrance. She stood with head down, hands secured to her body by the plastic handcuffs. Thomas glanced at her face and realized he knew her, but as the woman's haggard eyes looked into his, he quickly looked away and continued into the building.

Whatever had happened to her, the reason why she was being detained wasn't his problem.

Moving along the dimly lit corridor, he followed the back of the man in front of him, knowing exactly where he was going.

At the end of the long hall was a set of double doors, Thomas filed through it along with countless others.

On the other side of the opening was a warehouse size room, each section made up into smaller sections.

Parts of the warehouse were an assembly line where dirty faced men and women worked twenty four hours a day on rotating shifts of two.

The average work day was twelve hours, overtime never an option.

The average work week was seventy hours, the government hoping that by working its populace so hard, the same populace would just be too damn tired to revolt at the end of a long work week.

Thomas slid into his corner of the room, patting a man on the back to relieve him. The man, who's name was Terrance, turned to look into Thomas' eyes and all Thomas could see was a spirit crushed and beaten.

Terrance smiled wanly and then shuffled away, to finally go home after a long overnight shift.

Thomas was one of the lucky ones, at least working the morning to evening shift.

Reaching out, he picked up the first piece of machinery he saw on the assembly line and got to work. The only break he would get, as well as the time he would use to eat, was nearly six hours away.

Trying to become comfortable, he tried to blank his mind, trying to be just another automaton in a world filled with nothing but.

Meanwhile the machinery cranked on.

A piercing whistle sounded across the factory, proclaiming it was time for his break, as well as the other three hundred workers.

Reaching into a small side drawer near his work station, he pulled out the small lunch bag that contained his lunch. All round him others were doing much the same thing. A few hushed voices could be heard, a few of the workers talking amongst one another, but with a limited time to eat, most just concentrated on eating.

Thomas did the same, trying to ignore the other workers around him, but just as he knew it would happen, as it happened everyday for the past three months, the man who had his station next to Thomas' called over to him.

"'Oy, mate, hey there, Thomas. What you got in that there sack? Did the Missus make you anything good?"

Thomas sighed; the man's accent always drove him crazy. If Thomas was correct, then he'd said he was from Australia, where he had told Thomas multiple times that things weren't much better there. That was the reason why the man had made the journey to America.

"Edgar, I really don't have time to talk with you. I tell you that everyday. Now please, just let me eat in peace."

Edgar would have none of it, and instead leaned closer so as not to let the entire section hear his voice.

"'Oy, did you hear about Johnston?"

Despite himself, Thomas grew curious. Phillip Johnston had been the floor foreman up to a few days ago until he had been mysteriously replaced.

Since then, idle rumors had circulated amongst the workers, but nothing substantial.

Thomas shook his head. "No, what've you heard? And it better not be the same old junk that's been floating around."

Edgar shook his head, fast and hard. "No way, mate. I've got a friend in the military and he said Johnston was protesting the war. The upper class got word and they arrested him. Took him right out of his bed in the middle of the night, they did. Those damn Black Boots will getcha every time. It's the stuff of nightmares, it is."

Thomas scoffed at Edgar, waving his hand in front of him, dismissing the man. He'd heard rumors of the legendary night guard, nicknamed the Black Boots, for their thigh high leather boots, similar to riding boots.

"That's ridiculous; he's probably just on a vacation or he took a leave of absence."

"You think so? Listen, brother, sometimes I think you've got your head buried so far in the sand that it's your arse that's doing the thinking for ya, Thomas."

Edgar moved a little closer, so he was practically leaning on Thomas' shoulder.

"Just where exactly do you think all those people go when they disappear?"

Thomas made a disapproving face, and took another bite from his cheese sandwich. "I try not to think about it. Besides, if Johnston was arrested, then he probably deserved it. Who knows what he could have been doing behind closed doors, not you and certainly not me."

Edgar shook his head, exasperated. "Fine, Thomas, I give up. You just go 'head and continue living in your happy little world, but mark my words, one day the real world is gonna sneak up and bite you in the ass!" Then he turned around and scuttled back to his station, muttering to himself about fools and idiots.

Thomas shook his head. If anyone was a fool, then it was Edgar. If he continued talking like that and the wrong person heard him, it would be he that the other workers would be starting rumors about soon enough.

Thomas casually glanced up at the camera slowly moving by overhead. It was mounted on a long steel rail and would move all around the warehouse. There was nowhere the camera couldn't go, the steel rails mounted in a crisscross pattern along the ceiling.

Though it only saw video, no sound attached, it was sometimes easy to have illicit conversations, but Thomas knew there were strategically placed listening devices scattered all across the factory. No one knew exactly where they were and so no location was safe.

Thomas never worried, though. If you just did your job and kept your thoughts to yourself, then how could there possibly ever be a problem?

The whistle sounded, informing him that his break was over.

Within moments the factory was filled with the sounds of machinery as the workers resumed their shift.

Letting out a slight sigh, Thomas placed the rest of his lunch in the drawer and then got back to work. Though he had many hours left to go before his shift was finished, he was already looking forward to going home, and seeing his wife.

When they were alone, together in their small home, the rest of the world seemed to melt away.

Reaching out to pick up a piece of tubing on the assembly line, he started working again, his mind wandering to his wife and her smiling face.

While Thomas worked, concentrating on keeping up his quota, he didn't notice the camera overhead had stopped and focused on him. The zoom lens extended and the camera began snapping pictures, the soft click from the camera being lost in the din of the factory.

After only a few a seconds, the camera stopped and resumed its circuit of the factory, the images being digitally sent to an unknown recipient.

Oblivious, Thomas continued working, never knowing he had become more than just another nameless worker.

The piercing whistle proclaimed his shift was over and as he stood up and gathered his belongings the same man he had relieved twelve hours earlier was standing behind him.

Terrance patted Thomas on the shoulder and took his place on the line. Thomas was too tired to do anything more than glance at the man, much in the same way

Terrance had looked twelve hours ago when Thomas had taken over for him.

The two men saw each other for a few minutes everyday and yet had never spoken more than a few words to each other the entire time they had been co-workers.

While Terrance took Thomas' seat and continued working, Thomas idly wondered if the man was married or if he had any children. Did he have any hobbies or interests that were similar to his own?

Deciding it could wait for another day, he stumbled into the procession of leaving workers and out into the night sky.

It was well past nine o' clock by the time Thomas was once again on the bus for the return trip out of the city.

The twinkling lights faded away to be replaced by the dingy houses that bordered his own section of town. With night having descended, all the homes were wreathed in darkness. Only a few had lights on, peeking around the tattered remains of old curtains and shades.

When the bus finally reached his stop, he climbed down the stairs and onto the sidewalk, others pushing past him on their way to their families.

The bus rumbled away and in less than a minute he was the only person standing on the sidewalk, the other commuters lost in the darkness.

He stood there for a moment, enjoying the night air and the almost silence of a small town.

A dog barked off to his right, telling its owner to let it back inside the house and a car backfired as it moved down a street, two over from where he stood.

With a silent sigh, Thomas started walking.

He'd be home in a few minutes and was looking forward to dinner and seeing his wife.

With dinner finished, Thomas leaned back on the beat-up couch in his living room and relaxed. His wife was in the kitchen, washing the few plates used from the meal.

Ten minutes later, she stepped into the living room, wiping her hands dry on a dishtowel.

"I'm going to bed, dear, will you be up soon?" She asked.

Thomas nodded. "Sure will, just give me five minutes to let dinner digest," he said, patting his stomach. He wanted to stay awake for just a few minutes longer, despite the fact his eyes were heavy with exhaustion; and a full stomach didn't help. They had eaten pasta. They had pasta almost every night, one of the few meals they could still afford on their tight budget.

"All right, but don't you fall asleep on the couch again, like the other night. I never get to see you as it is. At least we can sleep in the same bed," she said.

Thomas waved her away and with a wan smile, she went off to the bathroom to prepare for bed.

Thomas glanced at the small clock on the wall. It was already past eleven. He watched a few more minutes of television, some news show was on, explaining how the United States had done the correct thing by invading Iran years before and overthrowing their government. How they had weapons of mass destruction that would have surely been used on the American people.

Thomas barely listened and soon turned it off, and with the room bathed in darkness, walked to the bathroom to prepare for bed.

Outside a soft rumbling proclaimed he was being monitored, the Homeland Security van driving down his street, a subtle reminder of the new world he now lived in.

Thomas was fast asleep. He was lost in a whimsical dream.

Both he and his wife were on a beautiful beach, the crisp clear water crashing against the rocks. Seagulls cried in the sky, looking for food, their bodies gliding on the wind.

He turned to his wife and kissed her. She hadn't looked as lovely as she did right now since before they were married. The lines on her face were miraculously gone, her eyes looking bright and all seeing.

Her hair glistened in the sun's radiance and he felt the love he had for her begin to grow even larger.

Another wave crashed against the shoreline, seeming to sound like thunder.

He tossed in his bed, the noise distracting him from his dream, and it was only when he felt himself being pulled from his bed and thrown against the wall that he realized the thunder was real and his dream was gone.

A bag was pulled over his head and he felt his hands pulled tight behind his back. A second later, he felt the cutting bindings of plastic handcuffs around his wrists.

He tried to call out to his wife, his heart hammering so fast in his chest it was amazing it just didn't explode, when he felt a knee-weakening blow to his back.

Letting out all the air in his lungs, he sagged to the floor, just trying to take in air, the hood over his face making the simple act of breathing more difficult.

He heard his wife scream and though his voice was gone, he hoarsely cried out to her. He was rewarded with another kick to his back.

He dropped to the floor, face down and writhed in pain; flashes of light appearing in front of his eyes from the pain.

The sounds of scuffling filled his ears and he heard different voices, terse and low.

In a daze of blackness and pain, he felt himself being picked up and carried. With the hood over his face he was lost, the movement of his body while he was carried feeling like he was on a boat in rough waters.

His head struck the doorframe of his front door-by one of his careless captors- when he was carried through it, and an explosion of light filled his head, followed by a dull thumping that filled his skull.

The parts of his skin that were uncovered felt the cool night air and he realized he was outside. Before he could so much as ask where he was being taken he was thrown into the back of a vehicle and a second later he heard the distinctive sound of the rear doors of his rolling prison slamming shut.

He lay on his back, his face covered by the hood, head and back pounding a staccato of agony. With every exhale his face grew hot, his breath bouncing back to hit his face, the heavy material of the hood keeping his breath inside it.

He idly wondered if he would suffocate, but realized if his captors had wanted him dead, there would have been easier ways than to suffocate him while in a moving vehicle.

Swallowing hard, he called out to his wife, but there was no answer. The floor of the vehicle bounced, the tires hitting a bump in the road.

His mind was going wild with fright, visceral scenarios flooding through his mind. All the rumors he'd heard were now coming back to him, of men and women being taken in the middle of the night. The faces of Edgar and Bugsy flashed across his open eyes, seeing only darkness, thanks to the hood.

Now their stories didn't sound so far fetched. But why would he be taken for interrogation? He knew nothing, he was harmless. All he did was work and mind his own business; the same went for his wife.

While the vehicle bounced and swerved around unseen obstacles, Thomas tried to regain some of his composure.

Surely this was all a mistake and once he arrived at his destination, he was sure he could make his captors understand that.

With his newfound reasoning calming him down, somewhat, he could only wait as the vehicle drove on.

The vehicle stopped and the rear doors were thrown open. He felt rough hands grab his arms and legs and then he felt himself being carried between two people. The sounds of doors opening and closing and the echo of footsteps came to his ears, but with the blasted hood on he couldn't see anything.

After more than ten minutes of being carried, his captors stopped and he heard the distinctive sound of a lock being opened and a door swinging open; the heavy metal hinges squeaking and the sound of a door clanging when it hit the wall.

Before he was prepared, he was thrown into the room, the hood coming off as he fell.

Before he could so much as turn around to see his captor's identities, the door had closed and he was alone.

He looked around his small prison and frowned.

A monitor was built into the far wall, a heavy mesh grating covering it to protect it from violent prisoners. The only two objects in the room, besides the monitor, was a small bed with the padding connected to the metal frame and a small steel toilet in the corner. Both items were bolted to the wall and floor.

Coming to a sitting position, he was about to cry out to be released when the ceiling lights began to strobe like a light show at a music concert. Closing his eyes to try and block out the light, hidden speakers began blasting loud music, the volume so loud the actual music wasn't discernable.

With his hands on his ears, he screamed and huddled into a ball, the music overwhelming. Thinking was next to impossible and he lay there in the corner, eyes shut, hands on ears for an undeterminable amount of time.

He zoned out after the first hour, the music blocking out all other noise in the small room.

He couldn't think, he couldn't see, the light so bright, and when he tried to open them, even a little; he became dizzy and so closed them once more.

Unbelievably, as the hours passed he thought he might have actually dozed off, his mind becoming accustomed to the blasting light and sound.

When the noise and lights stopped, and the light in the room became similar to an average sunlit day, it took him a full five minutes to realize that the bombardment had stopped.

With ears still ringing, he sat up and opened his eyes.

The monitor was on and a woman's face glared back at him. The face reminded him of a school teacher or a librarian, a stern task master, either way. Her hair was tied in a bun on top of her head and was almost gray, only a few streaks of black still present. Age lines creased the sides of her eyes and on both sides of her mouth and Thomas truly believed she was a woman who didn't smile often, if ever.

At first he did nothing, simply stared at the face, but soon the face nodded to the bed and spoke.

"Mr. Jones, why don't you make yourself more comfortable? Sit on the bed, there, will you please?" Though polite, the face showed no warmth.

Doing as he was asked, he stood up and shambled to the bed, sitting down with a sigh of pain.

"Do you know why you are here, Mr. Jones?" The face asked.

He shook his head and said: "I don't even know where here is. Where's my wife, I want to see her. This is all some kind of mistake. I haven't done anything."

"All in good time, Mr. Jones." The woman's eyes seemed to almost glow as she stared down at Thomas from the screen.

"You're here because you have been seen talking to known seditionists and were overheard at your work station. We don't enjoy being undermined by the very citizens we are seeking to protect, Mr. Jones."

Thomas shook his head from side to side. "But it's not true, I'm innocent, I swear. This is all a misunderstanding!"

The woman cocked her head to the side, as if she was weighing his protest.

"Perhaps, Mr. Jones, perhaps. But what is far more likely, is that you are an excellent liar." She pursed her lips and turned her head, talking to someone off screen. Then she looked back to Thomas. Now her eyes were wide with anger. "We have searched your house and work station and have found some things of interest to us. Get comfortable, Mr. Jones. Because I assure you, you will be spending quite a lot of time in there."

"But I didn't do anything!" He pleaded. "This is all a big mistake! Where's my wife, dammit! I'll tell you what you want, I swear, but I don't know anything!"

The woman frowned, a gesture she used often, the frown lines on her face evident.

"I have no doubt you will tell us everything we want to know, Mr. Jones. Everyone does eventually. As for your wife, you won't be seeing her anytime soon and your house has been confiscated by Homeland Security, as well as any and all finances you might have. You are now the property of the state, Mr. Jones and if you would ever like to leave this place, I suggest you cooperate."

The screen went black, Thomas staring at the blank monitor with mouth hanging open. It was like all the worst dreams he had ever had all rolled up into one giant nightmare.

He was about to start yelling at the monitor, knowing they could hear him when the lights began flashing once more and the loud music started up once again.

Screaming his frustration, he closed his eyes and lay on the bed.

"I don't know anything, dammit, I'm innocent!" He screamed to the walls of the room, his voice washed out by the music.

With his head on the mattress, his eyes squeezed tight, a single tear escaped his left eyelid and rolled down his face to land on the mattress.

SIX MONTHS LATER

Edgar was in a rush. He had less than fifteen minutes before he was late for his shift at the factory. Weaving in and out of the pedestrians on the sidewalk, he made his way through the crowd.

He ignored the other people walking next to him, not wanting to make eye contact. He glanced at the cameras perched on the metal poles that lined the street and then tried to ignore them, concentrating on walking without bumping into anyone.

Just before he reached the last intersection that would take him to the factory, he slowed and looked down at the man sitting against the wall of the nearest building. Homeless men and women were nothing new to the city, but for some reason this particular man looked familiar.

The man was in rags, a pack of clothes lying next to him. The man had a battered coffee cup held out in front of him, hoping someone would show pity on him and give him some spare change. Despite the dirt and grime covering the man's face, Edgar recognized him immediately.

"Thomas, is that really you? Oh my Lord, I thought you were dead," Edgar said, stepping closer to the man.

Thomas looked up into Edgar's face. "Do I know you? Spare some change?" He said, shaking the cup in front of him.

Though money was tight, Edgar pulled out five Ameros and dropped them into the cup.

"Thank you, sir, and God bless you," Thomas said, taking the money and making it disappear into his rags.

"What happened to you? One day you didn't show up for work and then that was that; no more Thomas."

Thomas shrugged. "I was a seditionist. The State had to punish me. Took my house and all my money. They said my wife died of a heart attack while being questioned. Don't know if it's true or not, guess it doesn't really matter." Thomas looked up into Edgar's face. "Who are you again?

"It's me. Edgar, from the factory. Look, if you need a place to stay, I've got room, it's not much, but you can sleep on the floor."

Thomas stared at Edgar, not fully understanding what he was saying.

Then Edgar looked behind him and saw three soldiers walking down the sidewalk, coming directly for them. "Look, mate, I've got to go. If I'm seen talking to you, well, you know what'll happen. I'll try to come back and see you after work."

Then he was off, quickly disappearing into the crowd. The soldiers reached Thomas and looked down at him, then at the crowd on the sidewalk. Thomas shook his cup in front of them. "Spare some change?" He asked.

One of the soldiers made a disgusted face and then all three moved on.

That night after work, Edgar returned to the spot he had found Thomas, but there was no sign of him.

Every day for almost a month following his first encounter with Thomas, Edgar tried to find his co-worker, but he never found him again.

It was like the man had vanished once more, like he had more than six months ago.

Like so many others before him.

Bad Memories

George Tompkins opened his eyes, but there was nothing there but blackness. It was as if a shroud of darkness had enveloped him. He tried to remember where he was, but no matter how hard he tried, nothing would come.

He lay perfectly still. He could feel the softness of a mattress underneath him and when he shifted position, he could hear the squeaking springs.

He heard a scream sounding from far away and his head turned to the left, despite the fact he could see nothing. He felt his heart pounding in his chest and the fear he felt was slowly turning into terror. His head was pounding; a sharp pain that he thought would rip his head clear off his shoulders.

He blinked his eyes again, trying to clear his vision and was rewarded with a splash of light.

Nothing exceptional, but progress all the same.

His breathing grew louder and he realized quickly if he didn't get control of himself, he'd end up hyperventilating.

Closing his eyes, he tried to picture an ocean sunrise, his feet curling in the cool sand, the water pounding the surf.

It was working, he was slowly growing calmer. At least until a gun shot sounded from somewhere and his attention was shattered. The gun shot had sounded from far away, only the tail end of the blast reaching his ears.

He raised his arms to his eyes, rubbing them, trying to will himself to see. His arms felt heavy and were difficult to manage.

He had a brief idea that maybe he had been drugged. That would explain the lack of sight and loss of muscle control.

There was a smell in the room, as well. It was bitter with a touch of cinnamon. For the life of him he had no idea what it could be. Another scream rent the air and he realized whatever was happening around him, it would probably be prudent not to be in the immediate area.

Sliding off the bed, his feet dangled for a moment and he debated if he should slide off the edge. For all he knew, he was a thousand feet up on the ledge of a building and the moment he stepped off the bed, he would plummet to his death, his head shattering on the hard concrete below.

He shook off the morbid image and tried to think of sunsets again.

It didn't work.

An explosion rocked the building he was in, and he felt the vibration through his body, the smell of burning gas filling his nose. He decided he really had nothing to lose. With a tensing of uncooperative muscles, he pushed himself off the bed. His feet were bare and he felt the coldness of the floor shoot through his body.

His legs wobbled and he felt himself tumbling to the floor. His head hit the cold tile with a resounding whack and his vision filled with white light, then blackness again.

He groaned from the pain and rolled onto his back. His ears had heard his groan and it didn't sound like him at all. He tried to say something else, but the only things coming to mind were curses. He said a few while he listened to his voice.

He frowned.

It was his voice and yet somehow it was different, hoarser. Perhaps a side effect of the drugs he must have been pumped full of.

He reached out with his hands, trying to find something to grab onto and his wrist smacked the leg of the bedside table.

He let out another curse, now his wrist hurting, as well. His vision was still muddled, but did he detect a hint of light where there was none before?

He couldn't be sure and disregarded it as irrelevant.

Panic seized him again as he realized he might be blind forever. He didn't believe he had the strength to live the rest of his life in darkness, but as the fear grew, he pushed it down. It was far too early to worry about that yet.

He called out then, his hoarse voice bouncing off the walls of his prison, but if there was someone within the sound of his voice, they did not answer.

He started to crawl around the room, his outstretched hands more wary after hitting the table leg. He felt the linen on the bed brush his face and he continued along its contour until he was at its end. His hands hit something light and he reached out to it. It was a shoe and next to it was a sock. So whatever had happened here, he had taken the time to take off his shoes and socks. That seemed odd, given his current situation, but then he still didn't have all the facts.

He tried to remember again how he could have gotten to where he was now, so he decided to start at the beginning.

His name was George Tompkins and he lived in New York City. He was a student at the community college and he worked in a small deli just down the street from his apartment. He had a girlfriend, Mindy. He had been seeing her for a little over three weeks now and things were going great.

Mindy was going to school in Boston, at Northeastern University, but she lived in New York, so would come home every weekend. They had met one day when she had come into the deli to get a sandwich. George had waited on her and the second their eyes had met, he knew he loved her.

He had never believed in love at first sight, but after that day, he was a full believer. Before she had left the deli, he had taken a chance and asked her if she would like to go out for coffee one day.

She had hesitated at first, the friend she was with not wanting to stay in the deli any longer than possible, and George had figured he was going down in flames. But then to his surprise, she had nodded yes and had written her number down on an errant napkin.

He had waited the standard three days before calling her, every hour a torture in the art of patience. When he had finally called, he had received nothing more than her answering machine. Cursing his luck, he'd still taken a chance and left his name and number with a brief explanation of why he'd called.

He figured that would have been it. He could imagine her coming home and listening to her messages, hearing George's voice and laughing at the idiot who thought he had a chance with her. Then she would erase his voice, casting it into the void to join the millions of other dead messages.

So to say he was shocked when he had received a phone call that night and it was Mindy's voice, nearly had him collapsing onto the floor.

She had apologized for missing his call and wanted to set up a time to get together. George had eagerly agreed and after setting up a date, they had talked for more than an hour on the phone. Mindy finally had to go, though, when her roommate was complaining that she needed the phone. He had said his goodbyes and had hung up.

He looked at the calendar. It was Wednesday. Their date was for Saturday when she returned home from school. That was the longest three days of his life, even longer than when he had to wait to call her after receiving her number.

When Saturday finally came, he had met her in Central Park and the two had walked and talked together, getting along splendidly, and for dinner had gotten a couple of hot dogs from a local street vendor.

It had been a wonderful date.

Almost perfect in fact, but for one thing.

It would have been a perfect date with the exception that they had witnessed a horrible crime. It appeared that a homeless man had attacked a jogger while the woman was running through the park. The odd thing was the homeless man had actually taken a bite out of the woman. His teeth had ripped into her flesh and had torn a two-inch chunk from her arm like he had been eating a turkey leg.

George and Mindy had arrived at the end of all the commotion. The police had the homeless man in handcuffs and paramedics were helping the woman. Mindy had pressed herself against him when she saw the homeless man's face. His eyes were wide with rage and his mouth and chin were stained a dark red from his attack. George watched as a paramedic checked over the homeless man, being extra wary of the violent man.

Every time the paramedic would try to check him, the man would snap his teeth at the paramedic. After the second time the man had tried to bite him, the paramedic stepped away and after a brief conversation with a police officer, they agreed the examination was finished.

The homeless man was thrown into the back of a squad car and the woman went into an ambulance. With flashing lights and sirens that were synonymous with New York City, the two vehicles sped up the bike path and out of the park.

Mindy was still curled up tight against him and George realized the commotion might have been the best thing that could have happened to him. Much better than seeing a scary movie and hoping your date will grab your hand in a fit of terror. They had left the park then, deciding to call it a night. He had played it cool and had just given her a kiss on the cheek.

Besides, that was all he wanted. He really liked her and wanted it to work, not just a quick couple of times under the sheets, so he was happy to take it slow.

He saw in her eyes that she was surprised he wasn't trying to get anything from her and she smiled, her cheeks curling up in a way that made his heart skip a beat. He told himself at that moment that he would marry this girl someday.

He had left then and headed home.

He was more than halfway there when he had slowed to watch an argument between a man and a woman. They were inside their apartment on the first floor and the windows were all open to let in the cool summer breeze.

The odd thing about the situation was that it was the man who was running away from the woman. She kept trying to jump on him and he would push her off. One time it looked like she had tried to bite him, but that could have just been a trick of the fading light as the sun started its descent in the sky.

He had watched for another minute or so, watching the woman continually try to attack the man. The man had to pick up a wooden chair and was desperately trying to fend her off without hurting her. Just when George thought things were getting interesting, a police squad car rolled up onto the sidewalk and two cops jumped out, charging up the stairs to answer yet another domestic disturbance. He watched as the cops wrestled the woman to the ground and handcuffed her. George watched through the windows as they proceeded to bring her outside. He wasn't alone now, a large crowd had gathered around him, all eager to get some dirt on their fellow neighbors.

The police placed her in the back of the cruiser and she bounced off the glass the entire time. George figured she must be high on something, maybe Meth or LSD.

The husband came out next, yelling at the cops. Telling them he wanted to press charges and that they better lock the bitch up forever.

The cruiser pulled away and George continued home. What he had seen in the park and on the street with the man and woman was nothing new, just another day in New York.

He tried to sit up in a chair he had found with his searching hands, but he didn't believe he had the strength; at least not yet. His vision was getting better though. Instead of nothing but darkness, he could now definitely see light on the edges of the blackness. His head was still killing him, though, a pounding like a bongo drum.

More sounds of chaos drifted to his ears. The sound of metal crunching as two vehicles collided followed by more screams and gunshots, as well.

Whatever was happening, it sounded like a full-scale riot. He tried to remember what possibly could have happened to him to leave him in his present state, but nothing was there. His short-term memory was gone. He felt hungry as well, but for the moment ignored it.

He decided to think of Mindy some more; that made him feel warm inside.

After their first date he had talked to her on and off, always on the phone until the weekend had finally arrived. Then she came back from Boston and they got together again.

This time they had decided to go to the movies. There was a new Al Pacino movie playing that they both wanted to see. He had picked her up at precisely seven o' clock and was rewarded with a kiss on the cheek. That made him feel all warm inside and he had wrapped his arm around her and they had walked to the subway together. Inside the tunnel that led down from the main terminal to the platform, a man was lying against the wall. George glanced at him, used to seeing bums sleeping wherever they wanted, but this one struck him as odd.

He slowed as they passed by him and George looked a little harder at his face. Only one eye could be seen, the other hidden in the folds of the bum's coat and George could have sworn the one eye was open and staring blankly at nothing, as if he was dead, and a small trickle of what must have been blood leaked out of his mouth. He was about to bring it up to Mindy when the tunnel became much more crowded, the nearby train disgorging it passengers.

In seconds the tunnel was filled with bodies and George decided to forget about it. Besides, it really wasn't his problem anyway. The transit police would take care of the bum.

They had run to the train then, and had just made it as the doors closed. The trip was uneventful from there and they made it to the movie theatre with time to spare. They spent the extra minutes playing video games in the lobby, then had gone into the theatre.

With popcorn and soda in hand, they had settled down to watch the movie.

Mindy had placed her head on his shoulder and he had reciprocated by placing his arm around her.

The date was going absolutely perfect.

Until someone started to go crazy somewhere in the back row. From where he sat, George wasn't able to see and hear everything, but apparently a crazy man wearing an Armani suit had charged into the theater and had attacked the first person he had encountered.

A couple of teenagers had been the unfortunates and one of the teens had been bitten by the lunatic. The young man's ear had been ripped completely off and there was no hope to sew it back on because the lunatic had devoured it as he stood over the screaming teen.

Finally the movie was turned off and the houselights had come on. George stood up with Mindy at his side and they were able to see the man on the ground, a few movie patrons holding him down. George heard one of the ushers say he had just called the police and the teenage boy was sitting in his seat with a handkerchief over his torn ear. An older man hovered nearby, the donor of the handkerchief.

Everyone was mumbling to themselves, surprised to see such unnecessary violence for no reason. Even hardened New Yorkers were taken aback.

George decided they should just get out of there and they had left through one of the exits at the bottom of the theatre. Neither wanted to have to spend the next hour or more answering police questions about something they knew nothing about.

Both of them being pretty shaken up, they decided to call it a night. They had taken a cab then, not wanting to deal with the subway. George cringed when he had to pay the forty dollar fare.

Once the cab had pulled away, they stood on her stoop and talked about what they had seen, saying how weird it was. After some more small talk, Mindy had said she wanted to go inside. George was prepared for that awkward moment when he didn't know if he should kiss her or not, but Mindy solved that question easily. She had leaned forward with her eyes closed and George had kissed her. Tongues met gently and his entire body felt alive as it tingled with the sensation.

She pulled away and looked up into his eyes and smiled. She told him the kiss was nice and he agreed.

Then she leaned closer again and they kissed for the second time. This time was better than the first and he reveled in it. When she pulled away, he wanted to scream to her, no, just a few more minutes, but he was smart enough to stay quiet.

She backed away from him then, moved further up the stoop and waved goodnight. He said he'd call her and she nodded, then slipped through the door and was gone.

George backed down the stairs, almost falling on his ass, he was so disoriented. His head was flying in the clouds and he couldn't remember feeling as happy as he did right now.

He had decided to walk home, cab fare totally out of the question. Between school and the apartment, the money he earned at the deli didn't go too far.

He walked along the sidewalk, the cars lined up on his left, and the buildings with their quaint front stoops on his right. He was so preoccupied with thinking of Mindy and the future possibilities that he never noticed the man who was hiding in the alley to his right.

Before George realized he was in trouble, the man jumped out of the shadows and attacked him. George screamed in surprise and was roughly forced to the cement of the sidewalk. His hands went up in front of himself instinctually, trying to fend off the madman, but he was too strong. The man was drooling salvia, the spittle dripping onto George's face. His attacker's teeth were gnashing back and forth and his head continued to dive at George's exposed throat.

George fought and screamed, hoping someone might come to his aid, but soon realized in the seconds that had passed that it might be too late by the time someone arrived.

George kicked up with his leg, trying to crush the man's testicles with his knee. If the madman noticed, he didn't let on. George struggled with the man, finally managing to shift his weight and push the man off of himself, but not before the man managed to take a small bite out of his shoulder.

George shrieked from the pain and managed to punch his attacker in the face. His hand vibrated from the blow and he wondered if he had broken a finger or two. He was no fighter and had no idea how to properly make a fist. If his fingers had been in the wrong position?

Then there was no time for such idle thoughts, because the madman was coming back for more, having recovered from the punch to the face.

George started backing up the sidewalk, his legs and arms pushing him along, like a crab, the man right behind him. He felt a hand on his ankle stop his motion and he kicked out, hitting the deranged psychopath in the face. Cartilage collapsed under the impact of the leather sole of his shoe and blood gushed from the man's wounded nose.

The attacker never even slowed, but just growled in his throat and lunged at him again.

With another call for help to anyone within earshot, George climbed to his feet and ran off down the sidewalk. At the same time he started to run away a burly man with a chest full of hair stepped out of his ground floor apartment. He was wearing a V-neck T-shirt with the sleeves cut off and his head was swiveling back and forth to see what all the yelling was about outside his windows.

That was what saved George. The madman took one look at the new person in front of him and jumped at him instead, knocking him to the sidewalk and tearing a three inch piece of flesh from his throat. The man yelled loud enough to wake the dead and lights began coming on in the nearby windows of adjacent houses.

George never slowed, too terrified to help the beleaguered man. Instead, he turned and ran; his legs pumping like the demons of Hell were chasing him. What he didn't realize at the time was that he wasn't that far off from the truth.

George lay on the floor of his room, still squinting up at the darkness. He remembered now, he had been attacked by some nut similar to the other attacks that had been happening all over the city. He remembered just the day before a woman had been found in an alley off Time's Square. She had been mutilated to the point that she had to be identified by her dental records. The authorities were assuming it was some kind of pack of wild dogs roaming the streets. Others were starting rumors on the internet that it was the giant crocodiles that lived in the sewers that would come out at night to feed.

George thought they were all crazy. It was probably some nut who had escaped from a mental institution or something like that. If New York had one thing, it was its fair share of nutjobs.

His hands reached out around him, trying to find the phone. Maybe if he called the police for help, they could send an ambulance or something.

His hands felt along the floor some more and they stopped when he felt another shoe, except this one was a woman's shoe. His hand felt the contours of the leather and he realized it belonged to

Mindy. She had been wearing a pair similar to what he had in his hand the night before when he had left her at her apartment.

That brought more of his memory to the surface. He recalled stumbling home after the lunatic had attacked him. He had managed to make it the rest of the way without incident, although he saw a distressing amount of people on the street with him, each doing odd things, such as one couple that was fornicating on top of a parked car, the metal hood below them dented from their writhing bodies. Another man seemed to be tearing a black cat to pieces with his teeth and hands, the animal long dead. Pieces of fur stuck to the sides of his mouth as he dove into the bloody mess for more.

Whatever was happening was spreading.

He had stumbled into his front door with a heavy sigh of relief. He heard raised voices coming from his downstairs neighbor's apartment and then the sound of screams and broken glass.

He ignored it, having his own problems to deal with and had then walked up the two flights of stairs until he had made it to his front door, then with shaking hands, had let himself into his small apartment.

Sounds of more trouble floated to him from the street outside so he went over to the window that overlooked it. Outside he saw a man running naked in the middle of the street while another appeared to be chasing him.

George backed away from the window and had lain down in his bed. His wound hurt him, but he was too exhausted to deal with it at the moment. He looked at it and gingerly touched it with the tip of his finger, wincing as fresh pain filled his head, creating a powerful migraine. Then the phone had rung and he had reached over and answered it. It was Mindy. She was telling him about all the crazy things that were happening in her building, about all the other tenants screaming and running around like animals. She told him that her parents had gone away for the weekend and that she was alone and scared. She asked if she could come over to his apartment. George had quickly agreed and she had said she would be right over, just as soon as she called for a cab.

George had hung up then and had laid his head on his pillow, looking forward to seeing her again, to hold her in his arms. He was exhausted, though, and his wound throbbed like it was on fire, matching his headache. He had taken a few aspirin then and without realizing it, had passed out, falling into a deep sleep.

And that was his most recent memory; everything after that was a blank slate, and no matter how hard he tried, nothing would surface from the depths of his fractured mind.

His vision was starting to clear, though. Instead of everything being black, now everything was grey mixed in with shapes of light. His hands dropped the shoe and continued searching for the phone. In the blackness that was his world, he realized he was at the entrance to another room. He crawled inside, but stopped when he hit something heavy and soft in his path. His hands went out to feel what it was and his breath lodged in his chest when he realized it was a body.

Hands traveled up the prone figure until he reached the face. With a gentle touch to the left side of her face, he realized it was Mindy. If he wasn't positive, then once his hand found the heart necklace she had worn around her neck, he knew for sure. He pulled his hand away in shock and realized it was covered in something sticky. Without his eyes he could only guess and he prayed it wasn't what he thought.

He shook her body to try and revive her, but nothing would work. Finding her wrist, he held it in his hand, trying to find a pulse, but in his panic felt nothing.

His vision was clearing a little more and he blinked his eyes to see better.

The blurry shape of Mindy was in front of him now, but nothing was in focus. He had no idea what to do. His girlfriend appeared to be dead in front of him and he was too incapacitated himself to do anything about it.

And to top it all off, his head was killing him. It felt like a dozen little jackhammers were going at the same time, trying to dig his brain from his skull.

He rolled onto his side and stared up at the blurry ceiling. Another explosion rocked the apartment and his heart jumped in his chest. His head continued pounding and for a moment he had thought he'd lost consciousness.

He was becoming more afraid with each passing second.

What was happening to him and the world outside?

He wiped his hands on his shirt, but stopped when he realized his shirt was already wet. He moved back to the bed and used the linen as a makeshift towel.

Then his eyes seemed to come into focus and he was looking down at the bed sheet still clutched in his hand.

He blinked again, trying to will his eyes to clear and after a few more seconds his surroundings came into focus. His headache was still there and his shoulder hurt more than before, but at least he could see now.

Relief flooded through him and he turned to look around the room. He was happy to see it was his own apartment. The entire place was trashed. Lamps were knocked over and books and pictures had fallen on the floor or were knocked askew. He looked down at himself and saw his clothes were covered in blood. He wondered if it could be his, but then remembered Mindy lying dead in the bathroom.

Everything else was forgotten as he stumbled to his feet and charged into the bathroom to see to his girlfriend. What he saw made him turn and vomit into the bathtub. When he had control of himself again, he turned to look at what was left of his girlfriend. Her throat was torn out and one side of her face was missing. In his blindness he had only touched the undamaged side of her face.

Her eyes were open, vacant, staring at nothing and he quickly realized she was most definitely dead.

His head started to pound some more and he put both of his bloody hands to his ears to try and stop it. He thought he was going to vomit again and turned toward the bathtub again.

And that's when he saw what had been the contents of his stomach.

Bits of flesh and blood were covering the bottom of the tub, as well as undigested popcorn. The realization of what had happened hit him like a runaway freight train. It was then that it all came back to him, making him cry out in shame and horror.

He remembered Mindy knocking on the door and himself opening it and letting her in. Her face was a mask of terror as she told him of her cab ride over to his apartment. She had seen people going absolutely crazy and police trying to stop them. One police-man had been attacked and had shot a woman at point blank range in the face. Mindy was sitting in the cab, the vehicle idling in the street, waiting for the light to change to green and the woman had been on the sidewalk, and Mindy had watched as the back of her head had exploded outward in a spray of skull and brain matter. Then the cab driver had hit the gas and they had gotten out of there.

George held her to him while she cried. He remembered the smell of her perfume, like cinnamon, and felt her heart necklace against his chest, the edge poking his skin. He hadn't minded at all.

The two of them had gone to his couch and had sat down. He had put the television on while she examined his wound. He had enjoyed the way she fussed over him. His headache had been bad even then, a white hot flash of pain that made his shoulder feel like a pinprick. The news was on and the reporter was talking about a city wide outbreak of mass paranoia and lunacy. People were running amok, attacking perfect strangers and practicing cannibalism. Their bites were infectious, and if someone was bitten by another raving lunatic, said person should seek immediate medical help.

George had ignored the bulletin, thinking it was ridiculous. Mindy had come back from the bathroom with a towel and some peroxide to clean his wound. She had sat next to him and he had smelled her again. But this time it wasn't her perfume he smelled. This time he smelled her body, her sweat. His eyes watched the blood pulsing in her veins on the side of her neck and he felt himself becoming hungry.

But not just hungry, ravenous.

She looked up at him then, as if she sensed something was wrong. She asked him if he was okay, but all he did was grin malevolently.

She backed away from him, her eyes showing the fear she felt, though she tried to hide it from him.

It didn't matter though; he could smell the fear coming off her from a mile away. His head was pounding, not letting him think and his stomach screamed for food. Then he understood what was happening to him. He was becoming better than he was before, stronger, faster. When he looked at her now she wasn't his girlfriend, she was a piece of meat, there only for him to quench his hunger.

He tossed the small coffee table in front of him across the room and lunged at her. Mindy had screamed and had made a run for the bathroom, but he was faster. His foot jammed in the door frame as she tried to close the door and with one good push, he was inside the small room with her.

She pleaded then, somehow knowing something bad was going to happen. He ignored her and jumped at her, knocking her up-raised arms aside like they were fragile twigs. His teeth sank into her throat and he heard her scream as the warm blood flooded his mouth and he swallowed gleefully.

Her body convulsed in his arms and he held her tight, then when she went limp, he set her on the floor and continued feeding.

George remembered this and believed that was when he finally blacked out, not coming back from the abyss until he had woken up in his bed.

His head felt like a giant hammer was pounding a nail repeatedly and his hunger was starting to become overwhelming. Something inside him filled with grief as he looked down at his girlfriend, but then something stronger, more primal pushed it away.

Shrieks for help and screaming drew him to the window again and he looked out to see chaos and carnage. And he realized he wanted to be out there, too, satisfying his hunger. He turned to look at Mindy, wondering if he could feed on her again and then his stomach rolled in distaste.

No, he wanted live prey. He wanted to feel their life's blood filling him while he sucked the very essence from their bodies.

Then the headache disappeared as if a switch had been flicked off. For the first time since he had awakened his mind was clear. He knew who he was and what he wanted to do. And what he wanted to do was go hunt and kill and fuck. No inhibitions, whatever he wanted, he'd take.

He opened the front door of his apartment and without a backward glance at Mindy's corpse, ran down the stairs two at a time.

He threw the door open that led out to the street and stepped outside. From his vantage point, the New York skyline was spread out in front of him.

But it wasn't the same as before.

Now the skyline was marred by burning buildings, the smoke mixing with the dusk of night to give the street in front of him an eerie glow. Burning cars were everywhere, the occupants long gone. Unmoving bodies littered the streets and sidewalks while running figures darted back and forth. The building next to him was on fire and the sounds of gunshots could be heard coming from the next street over. Sirens pierced the night, adding to the screams and yells for help.

He stood on his front stoop and raised his hands into the air in front of him as if he could take the entire city and crush it to his breast.

A new world was about to be born and he was one of the chosen. The city was now his, as well as others like him.

A screaming woman ran by him, her partially clothed body causing him to turn and look. Her pale skin reflected the light from the streetlamps and he licked his lips. He grinned malevolently, his stomach rumbling. The man who was once George Tompkins was still inside his mind, but he was changed now.

Now a more animalistic personality had risen to take control, one that would act first and be damned the consequences. There was a rage inside him now that could only be quenched with blood. With the city burning in flames, he leapt down onto the sidewalk and charged after the frightened woman.

He was hungry and she would do nicely.

DEAD RECKONING: DAWNING OF THE DEAD
By Anthony Giangregorio

THE DEAD HAVE RISEN!

In the dead city of Pittsburgh, two small enclaves struggle to survive, eking out an existence of hand to mouth.
But instead of working together, both groups battle for the last remaining fuel and supplies of a city filled with the living dead.
Six months after the initial outbreak, a lone helicopter arrives bearing two more survivors and a newborn baby. One enclave welcomes them, while the other schemes to steal their helicopter and escape the decaying city.
With no police, fire, or social services existing, the two will battle for dominance in the steel city of the walking dead.
But when the dust settles, the question is: will the remaining humans be the winners, or the losers?
When the dead walk, the line between Heaven and Hell is so twisted and bent there is no line at all.

RISE OF THE DEAD
By Anthony Giangregorio

DEATH IS ONLY THE BEGINNING

In less than forty-eight hours, more than half the globe was infected.
In another forty-eight, the rest would be enveloped.
The reason?
A science experiment gone horribly wrong which enabled the dead to walk, their flesh rotting on their bones even as they seek human prey.

Jeremy was an ordinary nineteen year old slacker. He partied too much and had done poorly in high school. After a night of drinking and drugs, he awoke to find the world a very different place from the one he'd left the night before.
The dead were walking and feeding on the living, and as Jeremy stepped out into a world gone mad, the dead spotting him alone and unarmed in the middle of the street, he had to wonder if he would live long enough to see his twentieth birthday.

BOOK 6

DEAD UNION
By Anthony Giangregorio

BRAVE NEW WORLD

More than a year has passed since the world died not with a bang, but with a moan.
Where sprawling cities once stood, now only the dead inhabit the hollow walls of a shattered civilization; a mockery of lives once led.
But there are still survivors in this barren world, all slowly struggling to take back what was stripped from their birthright; the promise of a world free of the undead.
Fortified towns have shunned the outside world, becoming massive fortresses in their own right. These refugees of a world torn asunder are once again trying to carve out a new piece of the earth, or hold onto what little they already possess.

HOSTAGES

Henry Watson and his warrior survivalists are conscripted by a mad colonel, one of the last military leaders still functioning in the decimated United States. The colonel has settled in Fort Knox, and from there plans to rule the world with his slave army of lost souls and the last remaining soldiers of a defunct army.
But first he must take back America and mold it in his own image; and he will crush all who oppose him, including the new recruits of Henry and crew.
The battle lines are drawn with the fate of America at stake, and this time, the outcome may be unsure.
In a world where the dead walk, even the grave isn't safe.

THE DARK
By Anthony Giangregorio

DARKNESS FALLS

The darkness came without warning.

First New York, then the rest of United States, and then the world became enveloped in a perpetual night without end.

With no sunlight, eventually the planet will wither and die, bringing on a new Ice Age. But that isn't problem for the human race, for humanity will be dead long before that happens.

There is something in the dark, creatures only seen in nightmares, and they are on the prowl.

Evolution has changed and man is no longer the dominant species.

When we are children, we are told not to fear the dark, that what we believe to exist in the shadows is false.

Unfortunately, that is no longer true.

ANOTHER EXCITING CHAPTER IN THE DEADWATER SERIES!

DEADRAIN
By Anthony Giangregorio

Welcome to the New America, population: 0

When a bacterial outbreak contaminates America's lower atmosphere, the resulting rain mutates into a deadly conduit for death.

Human's all over America are exposed and within a matter of days society has crumbled and the walking dead rule the land.

The America we know is gone, replaced by a new order; where the dead walk and humans are the prey.

Henry Watson and his small group of companions travel the country, searching for someplace better, someplace where the rain is safe.

In the New America the rules have changed; survive or perish.

DARK PLACES
By Anthony Giangregorio

A cave-in inside the Boston subway unleashes something that should have stayed buried forever

Three boys sneak out to a haunted junkyard after dark and find more than they gambled on.

In a world where everyone over twelve has died from a mysterious illness, one young boy tries to carry on.

A mysterious man in black tries his hand at a game of chance at a local carnival, to interesting results.

God, Allah, and Buddha play a friendly game of poker with the fate of the Earth resting in the balance.

Ever have one of those days where everything that can go wrong, does? Well, so did Byron, and no one should have a day like this!

Thad had an imaginary friend named Charlie when he was a child. Charlie would make him do bad things. Now Thad is all grown up and guess who's coming for a visit?

These and other short stories, all filled with frozen moments of dread and wonder, will keep you captivated long into the night.

Just be sure to watch out when you turn off the light!

SEE HOW IT ALL BEGAN IN THE NEW DOUBLE-SIZED EDITION!

DEADWATER: EXPANDED EDITION
By Anthony Giangregorio

Through a series of tragic mishaps, a small town's water supply is contaminated with a deadly bacterium that transforms the town's population into flesh eating ghouls.

Without warning, Henry Watson finds himself thrown into a living hell where the living dead walk and want nothing more than to feed on the living.

Now Henry's trying to escape the undead town before he becomes the next victim.

With the military on one side, shooting civilians on sight, and a horde of bloodthirsty zombies on the other, Henry must try to battle his way to freedom.

With a small group of survivors, including a beautiful secretary and a wise-cracking janitor to aid him, the ragtag group will do their best to stay alive and escape the city codenamed: **Deadwater**.

THE MONSTER UNDER THE BED
By Anthony Giangregorio

Rupert was just one of many monsters that inhabit the human world, scaring children before bed. Only Rupert wanted to play with the children he was forced to scare.

When Rupert meets Timmy, an instant friendship is born. Running away from his abusive step-father, Timmy leaves home, embarking on a journey that leads him to New York City.

On his way, Timmy will realize that the true monsters are other adults who are just waiting to take advantage of a small boy, all alone in the big city.

Can Rupert save him?

Or will Timmy just become another statistic.

SOULEATER
By Anthony Giangregorio

Twenty years ago, Jason Lawson witnessed the brutal death of his father by something only seen in nightmares, something so horrible he'd blocked it from his mind.

Now twenty years later the creature is back, this time for his son.

Jason won't let that happen.

He'll travel to the demon's world, struggling every second to rescue his son from its clutches.

But what he doesn't know is that the portal will only be open for a finite time and if he doesn't return with his son before it closes, then he'll be trapped in the demon's dimension forever.

DEADFREEZE
By Anthony Giangregorio

THIS IS WHAT HELL WOULD BE LIKE IF IT FROZE OVER.

When an experimental serum for hypothermia goes horribly wrong, a small research station in the middle of Antarctica becomes overrun with an army of the frozen dead.

Now a small group of survivors must battle the arctic weather and a horde of frozen zombies as they make their way across the frozen plains of Antarctica to a neighboring research station.

What they don't realize is that they are being hunted by an entity whose sole reason for existing is vengeance; and it will find them wherever they run.

DEADFALL
By Anthony Giangregorio

It's Halloween in the small suburban town of Wakefield, Mass.

While parents take their children trick or treating and others throw costume parties, a swarm of meteorites enter the earth's atmosphere and crash to earth.

Inside are small parasitic worms, no larger than maggots.

The worms quickly infect the corpses at a local cemetery and so begins the rise of the undead.

The walking dead soon get the upper hand, with no one believing the truth.

That the dead now walk.

Will a small group of survivors live through the zombie apocalypse?

Or will they, too, succumb to the Deadfall.

ANOTHER EXCITING CHAPTER IN THE DEADWATER SERIES!

DEAD CITY
By Anthony Giangregorio

NEW PERILS IN AN UNDEAD WORLD

After narrowly surviving an attack by a large pack of blood thirsty, wild dogs, Henry and his companions stumble upon an enclave that has made its home in an abandoned shopping mall.

Hoping for a respite from the perils of the walking dead, Henry and the others plan to settle down for the winter, safe in the company of fellow survivors of the zombie apocalypse.

But unknown to the group is the dark secret the enclave keeps, a secret that could threaten to destroy the companions and anyone else unfortunate enough to be caught in the trap.

In a dead world the only thing still living... is hope.

BOOK 5

DEAD HARVEST
By Anthony Giangregorio

Lost at sea and fearing for their lives, a miracle arrives on the horizon, in the shape of a cruise ship, saving Henry Watson and his friends from a watery grave.

Enjoying the safety of the commandeered ship, Henry and his companions take a much needed rest and settle down for a life at sea, but after a devastating storm sends the companions adrift once again, they find themselves separated, exhausted, and washed ashore on the coast of California.

With each person believing the others in the group are dead; they fall into the middle of a feud between two neighboring towns, the companions now unknowingly battling against one another.

Needing to escape their newfound prisons, each one struggles to adapt to their new life, while the tableau of life continues around them.

But one sadistic ruler will seek to unleash the awesome power of the living dead on his unsuspecting adversaries, wiping the populace from the face of the earth, and in doing so, take Henry and his friends with them.

Though death looms around every corner, man's journey is far from over.

DEAD END: A ZOMBIE NOVEL
By Anthony Giangregorio

THE DEAD WALK!

Newspapers everywhere proclaim the dead have returned to feast on the living!

A small group of survivors hole up in a cellar, afraid to brave the masses of animated corpses, but when food runs out, they have no choice but to venture out into a world gone mad.

What they will discover, however, is that the fall of civilization has brought out the worst in their fellow man.

Cannibals, psychotic preachers and rapists are just some of the atrocities they must face.

In a world turned upside down, it is life that has hit a Dead End.

LIVING DEAD PRESS

Where the Dead Walk

www.livingdeadpress.com